SAUDI CHAMPAGNE

NADIA SAKKAL

Author: Nadia Sakkal

Development editor: Rebecca Robinson

Technical editor: Robert Harrison

Book cover: Ryan Altounji

First edition 2023

To my daughter and my son, I hope you chase your wildest dreams, especially if they scare you. To my husband, I hope you read this book one day. If not, it's okay, I'll still love you until we're standing in front of the twelve elders.

FOREWORD

I have only known Nadia for a short period of time, but I was excited from the moment she first told me about her project, *Saudi Champagne*. When I think of Saudi, I think of the territory of the Harb tribe in Mecca, a place that played such a big role in who I am today.

Nadia also grew up in Saudi Arabia, and she understands the struggle of having to hide parts of her identity that urgently want to bloom. Unlike Nadia, I stood out, as I was a "light-skinned Sudanese," in a place that had a tight preexisting box for my people. Just like her main character, John, I was forced into a state of constant defensive adaptation, like a helpless animal in the wild, mimicking other boys instead of playing with dolls and camouflaging whenever an attractive boy shook my hand.

I find my memories unravelling as I follow John on his journey of self-discovery. Nadia's writing is reminiscent of Arabic culture, as she dives head first into the differences between gender roles, religions and lifestyle through the lens of an American expat with little knowledge of Islam.

I understood John's apprehension when his partner, Patrick,

first expressed his interest in moving to Saudi Arabia. I remember a time in which every mosque warned men of the danger of AIDs, although this society has changed exponentially since I was a child. Regardless, as we see through John, there is still a cultural barrier that he has to tackle as he gains control of his anxiety and begins to blur the boundaries between the West and the East that he had so clearly drawn and explained to Patrick. As their family adapts to their new environment, we see John learn the true value of what it means to be accepted by another culture.

While Nadia presents a Saudi that has rapidly progressed from the stereotype the West has adopted, there is still a lot of work to be done. As long as death is lurking on the edge of a kiss between same-sex lovers, stories like Nadia's will play a vital role in representing Arab queers.

I hope that, through her novel, the boy struggling to understand his sexuality knows he isn't alone, and the girl who's afraid of Allah's punishment for standing against his natural order will know that there is nothing unnatural about her.

So, if there is ever a good time to open up a discussion, it's now, and I hope that whatever your opinion is on the events that unfold in this novel, John inspires you to look deeper into the LGBTQIA+ community and their representation in Arabic culture.

I hope that the journey John takes you on helps you envision and understand the world I grew up in. By being able to step into the culture of Saudi Arabia, I am sure you will be better able to understand the landscape that people like me lived, and still live, within.

—*Ahmed Umar, Sudanese-Norwegian visual artist and LGBTQ+ activist.*

ACKNOWLEDGMENTS

I always loved reading the acknowledgement at the start of the book, never thinking I'd be writing one myself. Whenever the author thanked their editor, claiming they'd be lost without them, I thought they were exaggerating. Turns out they weren't! Becky, what would I have done without you? That's one of the many things I'm thankful to Robert for, as he introduced me to you. Robert, thank you a million times for your patience, for believing in me, and for making a girl blush.

To my parents, thank you for moving to Saudi Arabia. Without that big sacrifice, this book wouldn't be. That, and it's given us countless opportunities in life.

To my brother and sister, thank you for never questioning my abilities.

To my fans on social media (that's how I like to think of you, whether you actually are fans or not), thank you for the continued support. The book is finally here! Can you believe it? I hope it's everything you've hoped it would be and more. Take your time reading it, because if you ask me for the next one in the series, chances are that it won't be ready. Sorry not sorry.

To Saudi Arabia, thank you for everything you gave me that my own countries couldn't. Thank you for the friendships, the memories, the education, the growth.

A NOTE TO READERS

One last thing before you dive in: John's opinions are not my own. Some parts of the book might shock you. Remember to hate him, not me.

CHAPTER ONE

"Why would I want to move to a country where people like us are treated like criminals and pay the price with their own lives?"

Even though my voice was calm and my body stiff, I was raging on the inside, not knowing that, in less than twenty-four hours, I'd come up with my own answer, a rather convincing one, too.

Patrick, my partner, danced proudly, dad bod on full display, carrying the ingredients for his famous lasagne from one countertop to another. He then mixed them altogether in the pot, similar to the tornado that had taken over my mind for the past two weeks.

During the break between songs, he repeated the reasons for moving to Saudi Arabia:

1. It's not really that bad, the media like to exaggerate.
2. It'll take us two years to make what would take us ten years if we don't go.

3. Life has become so dull here, don't you long for a new challenge?

That last one particularly ticked me off, because if Patrick wanted to move every time life got dull, we'd quickly run out of places to go.

As Patrick covered the pot with a lid, the sound of sizzles was taken over by my quick breaths. Careful not to bump into Patrick, I made my way around the island and stood close to the stove, which was when the lid started to jiggle, accepting defeat against the steam, saving us from an explosion. I, too, had steam coming out of my ears, of which Patrick was oblivious to, so unlike our lasagne, I was going to blow up.

Patrick's lips moved, but I zoned out. How could a man wearing an "'LGBTQ' is the only 'ABC' I need to know" shirt possibly survive in Saudi Arabia? Maybe it was my fault for thinking he would lose interest the same way he did when he said he wanted to buy a treadmill or start vlogging. Sure, it was a venture he was curious to try, but even *he* knew lack of commitment was a foregone conclusion.

My breath quickened once again, so I closed my eyes, took a deep breath in, and our life together flashed before me.

Patrick and I had known each other our entire lives, but it was only in high school that we became a thing, the day I kissed him in front of the whole class because he'd helped me pass English. Try as I did, there was no force in the universe that could get him to pass chemistry. Patrick swears to this day that, before our kiss, he genuinely believed he was straight, but I beg to differ —he used homophobia as a disguise to protect himself from being uncovered and rejected.

We were suspended for our public display of affection, and by some celestial miracle, our parents didn't prohibit us from hanging out. While our friends were stuck in school, we were wandering aimlessly at the mall, our community playground, or wherever else our bikes took us. Those were the days when Patrick was no longer a crush; I knew I wanted to spend the rest of my life with him.

We weren't those people anymore; we had responsibilities, friendships, and careers.

Snap back to reality, John. It's time to have this discussion with the man who wants to move to an Asian country he thought was in Africa. You better sit down.

"Anyway," said Patrick, as he handed Koala, our Pomeranian, a piece of meat, "I've been thinking—"

When Timothy interrupted Patrick, something triggered in my mind, like a switch, and even though I tried to stop myself, I shouted, "Timothy! You know better than to interrupt adults when we're talking. Go to your room right now!"

It wasn't the first time I felt like the world's worst dad, damaging my son and causing him to face years of healing from a traumatic parent. And all that for what? For being an eleven-year-old?

"Timothy, I—" I paused, searching for words that could wash away the fear on his face. "I'm such a monster. I'm sorry, I don't know why I said that."

Fear turned to sadness, and with tears racing down his face, he ran to Patrick and pressed his tiny body against his. I had lost track of the number of times I'd promised to be a better father. It was unfair, but I didn't know how to tame myself.

"I just wanted to know if I could have ice cream after dinner," he said, his voice breaking between syllables, as if he had been attacked by that villain from that movie that had him wetting his bed for a week straight when he was younger. *Was it Ursula? Maybe it was Cruella. Ugh, this is just too much for me to handle.*

That was the first sign that change was exactly what I needed, radical change, like moving to Saudi Arabia.

Patrick patiently waited for Timothy to stop crying before graciously finding the right words that made my broken-hearted son want to hug me again. Those were words I'd heard Patrick repeat countless times to Timothy, and although I'd practiced them regularly in front of the bathroom mirror, my mind froze when the chance arose. How hard was it to say, "I'm sorry I yelled at you. I lost control of my emotions. You don't deserve to be spoken to like that. If you'll forgive me, I'd like to try again."

Following Julio, my psychologist's advice, I pushed my mind to back when I was a grad holding a not-so-credible degree in hand. I was prepared to do the impossible in order to find a decent job and share a fun life with the love of my life. I sent my resume to all my friends and practically forced them to share it with their peers. I looked up all the addresses of engineering companies up to an hour from where Patrick lived at the time and knocked on their doors, asking if they were hiring. That was when I found Brackenridge Engineering Inc., which hired me for the exact same reason those universities had rejected me. The owner, Wade Brackenridge, was gay, and, well, for once, I used discrimination to my advantage and landed myself my very first job.

Patrick and I moved in together, and a couple of years down the line, we were ready for a child. He and my sister technically slept together (not really, though), and our greatest blessing, Timothy, was born. Becoming a father changed me in ways I never knew needed changing. After Timothy said, "Stupid" for the first time, I memorized the NATO phonetic alphabet and "stupid" became "sierra."

Sadly, bad words had become the least of my concerns as a father. In the professional world, though, I was crushing it. Over the years, I stayed with the same company and made a big bunch of mistakes, which made me a better engineer.

Patrick, however, desperate to somehow become a famous

dancer, took different jobs that always led him back to square one. It was like Patrick and I completed each other.

The professional world didn't mean much to me. What did matter to me were the friends we made, and those we lost. The moments of laughter we wanted to remember forever, and the tearful moments we wished we could erase from our life's story. Life was supposed to include the good and the bad, the exciting and the dull, and looking at the bigger picture, we had it all. And even if we didn't, it was never so bad that we would have to move to a country where we would be decapitated if the wrong person found out about our sexuality. So even though I had one good reason to move there, it didn't outweigh the risk of losing our lives.

"Would you like to make the salad tonight?" asked Patrick as he extended a lettuce and other vegetables toward me. My guess was this was an attempt to deviate from the tension, because Patrick didn't need help in the kitchen. That was his own rule.

As we waited for the oven timer to go off, we needed a distraction from the smell of tomato and mozzarella that worked our stomachs up into a symphony of growls and gurgles.

"Do you remember the first time I made you a salad?" I asked Patrick as I put the bowl on the kitchen table, where I seated myself.

Patrick shook his head. "It was the last time, really. I'd invited you over for lunch after school, but my mom hadn't made anything that day. I pretended that I made salads on a regular basis. I was really just trying to impress you. Gosh, it feels like ages ago. What happened to those two kids?"

Patrick sat next to me, his eyes met mine, a gentle smile appeared on his face just like that day when we were innocent teenagers. "I had no idea you were trying to impress me. Heck, I didn't even know you were into boys. You hid it so well."

He paused, as if evaluating whether he should express what

was on his mind. "And that's why," he said, "I think no one will know you're gay if we move to Saudi Arabia."

Up until that last sentence, we'd shared a brief romantic moment, and I wished he hadn't ruined it with this cancerous topic that had sucked the energy out of us for a couple of weeks.

My knees hit Patrick's (a little bit intentionally) as I changed my position, so I wasn't looking at him anymore. I grabbed a fork off the table and dived right into the salad bowl. It was a horrible salad, but I didn't care.

Growing up, I never hid my identity from anyone, but people thought every gay man wore tight pants, waved his arms while he talked, and wore makeup and jewelry (which I didn't). So, yes, I did have to break a couple of girls' hearts, and yes, I did have to come out a thousand times, but just because I didn't scream about my sexuality from the rooftops didn't mean that I'd be willing to live a life led by a lie.

As I put my fork down, happy that I wouldn't have to take another bite of that horrendous appetizer, but angry that the conversation would have to continue, Patrick forced his head onto my right shoulder, and when I turned to face him, the black heads on his nose were louder than the words coming out of his mouth.

"It's not like someone is going to see us at a restaurant and call the cops on us. After all, this is a country where opposite-gender friendships aren't allowed, so guys hang out together all the time. What's punishable by death is the public display of affection between two men or two women. Heck, even between *men* and *women*. And I think we're smarter than to mess up that bad again."

Patrick's wink was met with a smirk from my side, not because of the things he said—he was starting to make sense— but because I disliked the person I'd become. Where was the guy who'd go far and beyond for the people who made him happy? I had so much to be thankful for, yet I always found something to complain about. Instead of coming to my loving, supportive partner about the heavy weight on my shoulders, I pushed my emotions down into my stomach, because I shouldn't be feeling them in the first place.

I would have liked for a move to Saudi Arabia to fix all my problems, especially the mental ones, but what if it didn't? Was I doomed?

As Timothy headed to the bathroom, I raced to the wine rack and grabbed the untouched bottle of Tequila, gulping down four mouthfuls in a desperate attempt to numb the pain of being an adult who'd lost their passion for life, who'd lost touch with his romantic side.

"Scott was right," I said as Patrick casually washed the salad bowl, "this is Mexico's best." Under my breath, I added, "I wish we still went on vacations like Scott and Shay. I wish you'd touch me like you used to."

Buzzed, I carried Timothy as he walked back into the kitchen, as if, for a brief moment, he was a toddler again and life was simpler. "What do you say, buddy, you want to move to Saudi Arabia?" I held his right hand and pretended to nibble on it, but before he could answer, Patrick gave us a monologue about how short life was and how crucial it was that we took risks and jumped at opportunities that came our way. Discouraged, I remained silent and put Timothy down, praying he'd tell Patrick he wanted to stay, but toddler or not, he didn't speak a single word.

Toward the end of Patrick's speech, I caught a sparkle in my partner's eyes that took me back to 2015, when same-sex marriage became legal. And for a second, I truly believed Patrick was as excited about us potentially moving to Saudi Arabia as he was when this law was first passed.

"Son," Patrick said, holding Timothy's hands in his, the three of us standing in the middle of our kitchen, "you know how you've been telling us that your summer break is boring?"

Timothy nodded, keeping his head down, as if he felt like we were dragging him into a conversation he wanted to be no part of. *Or he wants to tell us about our failures as parents. My failures as a parent.*

"Well," said Patrick, choking up, as if he was holding back tears, "I've been feeling the same, and not just in the summer. It's been a long time since I felt excited about my job, and when I started looking for a new one, I realized that maybe the problem isn't with my job, maybe it's the city. I've been here my whole life, so I did something naughty and checked out jobs in Austin."

But when I ask you to fold the laundry you say you don't have the time...

"But we've been to Austin a million times, we've practically lived there. Anyway, I'll spare you the details. Let's just say I was offered a job, teaching English literature at the American Diplomatic School of Jeddah."

Patrick paused, looking for a reaction from Timothy.

"That's in Saudi Arabia," I told Timothy, but he ignored me, which either meant he already knew that, or he didn't care where it was because something else was more important. Or both.

"What about my friends?" he whispered, barely audible. "What about Koala?"

"Yeah," I said. "What about his friends? And what about our friends?" I crossed my arms and stomped my feet as if I were Timothy's age.

It got pretty ugly pretty quick, and once again, we'd forced Timothy to play referee, although I'd sworn to never involve Timothy in a debate between his father and I after we fought over the color of our couch at the store.

Patrick gave me a disgusted look. "Don't put words in my mouth. I'm teaching our son about sacrifice and hard work."

"Here's what your father's not telling you, Timothy. Gay people aren't allowed in Saudi Arabia and going there would be a huge risk." Looking at Patrick, I said, "What are you going to do? Become straight?"

Apparently, I was telling a joke, because Patrick laughed hysterically. As his lips widened and his shoulders shook up and down, my body heated up and my teeth clenched.

"No, silly, I know I said that gay people weren't allowed in Saudi Arabia but I've got the solution."

Oh, yeah, Einstein, and what's that?

The room spinning, he said, "We'll get a job at the same school. And before you tell me you don't have a teaching certificate, let me tell you this, you don't need one. You can teach math. That way, we will have two separate residence permits, which means there will be no proof we are related. Actually, there's a job opening right now. I have your application ready. It's one click away!"

When Patrick mentioned residence permits, I realized he was in too deep, and he wasn't going to back out.

"Cool," I said, regretting the next words as they left my lips, "so does that mean we get to live in separate houses? Because that's actually tempting right now."

No need to say hurtful things, John, even if you're tipsy.

"I don't have it all figured out yet, but don't worry, you won't get away from me that easily." He winked at me, a sign for me to calm down in the presence of our son. The oven timer went off at the perfect moment because:

1. The tequila was about to make me puke.
2. We needed something to keep us from talking to each other.

CHAPTER TWO

Part of being depressed, Julio explained to me, was waking up to negative thoughts. "Normal people," whatever that meant, started their day by looking forward to things. I, on the other hand, dreaded the humiliation and guilt that haunted me from the day before. A new day meant new opportunities to mess up. Mess up as a dad, as a partner, and as an employee.

On top of that, I had a bad hangover, which I'd used as an excuse to stall for another day that should've been productive. Two months into my sabbatical, it became clear I was deviating from my goals. After a week of attending online classes to earn an Electrical Engineering Project Management (EEPM) certificate, my commitment level dropped, and I was behind schedule. There was no way I was going to complete the course, and without it, I wasn't returning to the office. I'd rather fake my death than face humiliation. *Why do I use the term humiliation so commonly to describe my situation?*

That had a domino effect on my other goals, pushing me further into my depression, the very thing I'd gone on a sabbatical for. Gone was my motivation to spend more time with Timothy (worst yet, it felt like a chore) and to renovate our home.

The more I dragged, the more lies I told myself, and it wasn't any different that morning.

Ugh, another day. Another day of having to look at myself in the mirror and face the truth. I'm a fraud. I'm the worst example to my son. Now I have to play with him when it's the last thing I want to do. I should've let Johanna take the promotion and accept that I'm a failure.

The banging inside my head worsened, forcing me to open my eyes. The summer sun shone bright through the windows, but I refused to fall for the false hope that it was going to be a good day. In fact, I wasn't ready for a new day, all I wanted was to keep dreaming, or even keep having nightmares. Anything but reality.

I flipped to the other side, my legs stretching across to Patrick's side because cuddles in bed were the only medicine my body seemed to accept, but Patrick wasn't there, which confirmed that it was going to be another miserable day.

As I tried to recollect my memories of hurtful things I may have said to Patrick or Timothy, there wasn't anything in particular that was worth stripping me of my partner's support. More than anything, I yearned for snuggles, his calves rubbing against my legs, and for quality time in his arms. Even if it was just a means to bribe me, so I would agree to move to Saudi Arabia.

Instead, he found it more motivating to be at the dance studio at 8 o'clock, two hours before his first class. The love of my life, the person I shared my bed with every night, was a distant roommate, and I was once again left to rot in my loneliness.

Checking my phone for a message from him, the disappointment that came with the empty notification list weighed heavily on my heart. I threw my phone somewhere on the bed. *Out of sight, out of mind.*

I was going to be lazy and stay in bed until Timothy woke up, but when I stretched my arms up like an infant who had been released from a swaddle, I choked on body odor, so I slowly got out of bed and dragged myself into the bathroom, taking my phone with me, *just in case.* Looking down at the toilet bowl, a wave of vertigo caught me by surprise, the vibrating device in my hand helping me stand straight.

"It's a text from Patrick," I said to myself, my whole body reacting in excitement, accidentally peeing on the toilet seat.

It was a link that led me to YouTube. I took off my boxers and listened closely to the lyrics of the song he had sent me, which was "Colour" by MNEK. I jumped in the shower and my headache drained away with every drop of water that ran down my body. Or maybe it was the song that soothed me.

The way Patrick's eyes shone brightly the night before made me want to give in to his request and go on this crazy adventure, but Timothy's tear-soaked face tore my heart into a million pieces. The day he was born, I'd promised myself that Timothy's interests would come before my own, so I was going to tell Patrick once and for all that moving to Saudi Arabia was out of the question, and we were never going to talk about it again.

The next song started, so I stuck my hand out and replayed "Colour," thinking I could push the Saudi charade to the side and listen to the lyrics. I giggled like a teenage girl who had received a text from her crush. I danced and almost slipped in the bathtub, but I did not care that I had almost broken a rib. I wanted to give the day a second chance, I really did, but unless I was occupied with important tasks, my mind would wander, and I would create a problem where there was none.

What if it's not as bad as I'm making it out to be in my head? What if we don't go and we're missing out on a better life? What if it turns out to be a great idea and Timothy likes it there? Together, we can make 240,000 dollars a year. All I have to do in return is keep my identity a secret, is that really a big deal? We can go for a couple of years and come back, our families and friends will still be here.

I held my breath under the water, appreciating a short moment of stagnation in a world that did not stop.

Alright, John, you're obviously not able to put this aside. You need to make up your mind. Are you in or are you out?

Dressed in all black clothes, I sat on the living room couch, a cup of coffee in one hand and a book I'd started (and stopped) reading over a month ago in the other. I couldn't even remember what the book was about. It just stared at me, every single day, as it collected dust. "The Rosie Project" by Graeme Simsion. I memorized the cover; a bright yellow background with a silhouette of a man standing next to a bike. Facing him was the silhouette of a woman. Neat arrows connected them together. Quotes about how great the book was. Why couldn't my life be so neat? Why couldn't the arrows of my life be so simple? Why was I feeling so lost?

"Dad?" Timothy called out to me from his bedroom. I loved being a father, I did, but I missed the freedom to be selfish, and well, unproductive. I wanted the space to be depressed.

The first weeks of summer, Timothy and I painted our kitchen cabinets and fixed minor things in the house, but we both got bored, and my plan to spend more time with him fell apart. Spending the day together, every day, required more creativity and effort than I'd realized, so I was tempted to do what I did every summer: drop him off at his grandmother's house, but with what excuse?

Sometimes, we played board games, which I loved, but only for a short while. When I had to find ways to rephrase myself so he understood certain rules, I lost my patience and my appetite to play. It was the same with our pretend fights; we giggled and laughed, but after he hurt me more than once, it was, "Go to your room and find something to play while I do the dishes."

When Timothy was younger, he was the highlight of my day. Time spent with him flowed naturally and came without the pressure I imposed on myself to make sure I built the best version of him possible. Over the years, however, a new day meant a new countdown until his bedtime, and I forced myself to play with him and enter his world because our hobbies were so far apart.

All he wanted to do was learn a new instrument and solve complex puzzles, whereas all *I* wanted to do was absolutely nothing, and because I couldn't not do anything, it made me want it even more. On the few occasions that I kept him distracted with a movie or video games while I lay in bed, the guilt took away my peace, because my sabbatical was supposed to be about me and him.

I loved my son with every inch of my body, but I was in no place to show him a healthy version of me, and I was afraid that if he saw how broken I was, he'd set that standard for himself.

Standing on his bed, his head held low, he said, "I'm sorry."

It took me a second to realize what he was sorry for. I sighed (knowing that was the reaction of a bad father), disappointed that Timothy had wet his bed again, but I didn't say anything.

In the past, before he was diagnosed with enuresis, I interpreted his bedwetting as an act of spite, a cry for attention, and I reacted accordingly. I'd said mean things like, "You're not a baby anymore," and "If you wet your bed one more time," and I followed up with unrealistic consequences, such as "you'll never see your friends again."

I wasn't the only one pointing fingers—the urologist speculated that Timothy's condition was a result of stress, caused by being the only kid in his class with two dads. I'll never forget that day, Timothy had told him, "My friend Alissa has two dads, but she doesn't wet the bed." After that incident, we decided to deal with it by ourselves, as a family, until we found a gay-friendly urologist.

I can guarantee, Patrick, we won't find one in Saudi Arabia.

Vowing to never blame Timothy for his accidents, I apologized a million times, but that wasn't enough, because he still thought it was his fault.

As he got older, the number of accidents decreased, and usually happened after I'd dressed the bed in freshly cleaned sheets, an epitome of my bad luck.

Though some days I would let the sheets dry off and hope the smell would evaporate, today, I pitied the little guy, more so than I did myself. He deserved more dignity than having to sleep in pee. Sheets washed and replaced, breakfast eaten, we were dressed and ready to meet the gang. That was what we called ourselves, but really, we were just a group of stay-at-home-dads with their kids.

It was Patrick's idea to get me out of the house more often, claiming that if I interacted with other people, my depression would take second place, and my "happy hormones" would take over. He agreed that it wouldn't solve the problem, but it was a step forward.

"Dad?" said Timothy in a low voice, once he was buckled in safely, "Are you and Daddy getting separated?"

"What?" I looked at him in the rear mirror. "What makes you think that?"

"He wants to move to Saudi Arabia, and you don't."

"Oh, baby, that doesn't mean we're getting separated. Your dad and I love each other very much."

"Good, because I think I like the idea of moving to Saudi Arabia. I think you should too."

"Yeah? What makes you think so?"

"You always complain about the price of oil being too high, and in Saudi Arabia, oil is cheaper than water."

I couldn't help but laugh.

"What about your friends?" I asked.

"Ayden is moving to Virginia. I bet I can make more friends than him."

Great, now I can't use Timothy as leverage to stay here.

Timothy, a tweenager whose universe revolved around himself and his friends, readily gave his world up to live in the unknown. Contrary to my worries, there wasn't a rod in his hand that awaited my first mistake and evaluated every decision I made as a parent. Although I'd been a father for over a decade, I still needed to remind myself that my parenting wasn't so much about what I did, or how much I did with and for Timothy, as much as it was about being there.

You are enough, I told myself to stop the lies that raced through my mind.

"Where did you learn all these facts about Saudi Arabia, anyway?" I asked, concluding the discussion.

"Kiddle."

We arrived at Woodlawn Lake Park. It was the perfect spot, considering the various ages of the gang's kids. We sat at a shaded picnic table in the middle of the park, so we could see our toddlers who ran to the playground and Timothy who'd made friends with teenagers shooting hoops.

When did we become so negligent about our appearance? Joshua, who was always a lady's man, no longer cared that one sock was checkered and the other decorated with every circus animal out there. Martin, the veteran, hadn't shaved (or brushed) his beard in weeks. Michael, consistently dressed in shirts with at least three holes, mocked me for wearing a broken pair of glasses.

Nobody warned us about the realities of parenthood before we got married, and our appearance was a reflection of our struggle, but whatever, among them, I blended. Together, we were the "Good And Not Great" (my own acronym for GANG).

Joshua dug right into the typical topics of discussion: shit. No, literally, two of the guys had toddlers, and apparently, they had no better topics to discuss. Poop-staining clothes. Broccoli pieces in excrement. Or kiwi seeds. The different poop colors and their meanings. And my personal favorite, having to change diapers in the middle of the night, with one testicle hanging out of their boxers.

Can we please discuss deeper, more meaningful issues for once, like, I don't know, the fact that Patrick wants to move to Saudi Arabia? Or that Timothy asked me if we were getting divorced today?

I'd only known these guys for a few weeks, so talking about my private life would make me too vulnerable, and I hadn't yet built that kind of trust with them. But, oh, I needed someone to talk to, and even though I was surrounded by people, a wave of loneliness washed over me, as if I was the only person at that park.

My thoughts spiraled. I'd never been one to dream of becoming a big career man or entrepreneur, but I discovered early on that I was good at something. When Timothy came into our lives, I took my job more seriously and pledged to work as hard as I could, with the goal of providing the most qualitative life I could. That meant working extra hours, being yelled at by clients, and losing lots of hair. How unfair of Patrick to ask me to throw that all away and do something totally unrelated, as if my sacrifices didn't matter.

John, why don't you look for engineering jobs in Jeddah? Yeah, genius, because companies love paying more money to bring in someone from overseas. Just accept it, you're going to Saudi Arabia to teach a bunch of six-year-olds one plus one equals two. Joke's on you, sucker, because you are living in the modern version of Romeo and Juliet.

The thought of our freedom being taken away gave me goosebumps. Tears welled in my throat, and I had an anxiety attack, not like the ones they showed on TV. In fact, no one could tell that I was having an attack, but that didn't make it any less real.

What if they don't have parks there? What if I don't meet a gang who'll encourage me to leave the house? What if Patrick and I get into a car accident one day? Who'll take care of Timothy? What if—

"Dad," said Timothy, "can I have some water, please?"

After handing him a bottle, I snuck my phone out of my pocket and googled "gay life in saudi arabia." I randomly clicked on one of the links and browsed through the article.

"Under the local Sharia law, same-sex sexual behavior is punishable by death or flogging. The precise sentence would depend on the perceived seriousness of the case. One of our respondents has been punished with up to 450 lashes and three years in jail for using social media to connect with other men."

Selected. Copied. Pasted. Sent to Patrick. I did not expect him to reply, but he did, referencing another website, "Compounds are where expats living in Jeddah go for the local nightlife. Every weekend, there is usually a party in at least one compound. You will be surprised to find that alcohol flows freely among non-Muslim communities. Compounds are off limits to Saudi's religious police. Moreover, vibrant communities of the LGBT exist in major cities like Jeddah. One respondent even titled the Saudi capital 'gay heaven.'"

What are the religious police? A Muslim version of the KKK? That can't be nice. Is "compound" the term they use for prison? And what kind of journalist uses the term "exist" to describe a community? Like, we don't know anything about them, we can't even prove it, but they exist. They must!

I put my phone back in my pocket and caught up on the conversation.

"I don't understand," said Joshua as he ate his daughter's Goldfish, "why is parenting so draining?"

Everyone looked at me when I suddenly interrupted. I didn't recognize myself as I uttered the words, "Guys, speed bumps are a part of life, and they're temporary. It's up to the couple to decide how much they're willing to sacrifice to make their relationship work. After all, what is love if not a bunch of sacrifices?"

My question drowned in the silence, probably because it had nothing to do with parenting. I awarded myself "Hypocrite of the Day," the one who preached about sacrifice but wasn't willing in the slightest bit to sacrifice, especially because I knew without a doubt that Patrick would have moved to Saudi for me, not only because he's crazy, but because he loves me more than anything.

I pulled my phone out again. I hated that I was so addicted to my phone, to grabbing it from my pocket, flipping it in my hand, clicking on the side button, and using my fingertips to unlock it. It was my cigarette, and I reached out to it multiple times a day, even though there was no escaping reality.

Oh, I received a text from Mariana, I wonder what it could be.

MARIANA

John, call me when you can. Alexander is making major changes at work.

Maybe this is a good time for a confession; I hadn't applied for a sabbatical, but Julio forced me to take time off, under the pretext that "my mental health was deteriorating." Following his lousy advice of looking on the bright side, I framed it as a sabbatical.

Less than five minutes after I'd received Mariana's text, Alexander (my boss) called me, but I ignored it for two reasons:

1. There was no way in hell I was going to be yelled at in front of the gang.

2. I had to speak with Mariana first and plan my
   reaction.

MARIANA

Seriously, call me. Alexander looks
pissed!

CHAPTER THREE

"John, what are you doing here?" asked Patrick, surprised that I was visiting him at the studio.

I walked up closer to him so that only he could hear me and whispered, "I just wanted to let you know that I called Alexander and told him I was leaving."

Patrick jumped up and down in excitement, and when he hugged me, I lost balance, stepping over one of his students.

"I knew you'd come around," he said, raising his head high, as if to show he was proud of me. "In fact, there's something I want to show you. I've been working all morning on this choreography for you."

As "Hurts 2B Human" by P!nk and Khalid played in the background, guilt ran through my veins, but the courage to speak the truth escaped me.

Once the gang had left the park, and while Timothy was still occupied with the friends he'd made, I had called Mariana. Johanna, aka, my biggest competitor at the company, had made an offer to Alexander that he couldn't turn down:

1. She enrolled in the same EEPM course I was attending at her own expense. (Did I mention that she was paying for it, which meant that, unlike me, she was costing the company nothing?)

2. She had received a job offer at another company and threatened to leave if she didn't get the promotion we were competing for. (Knowing her, she must have convinced Alexander that my depression would always interrupt my productivity and that he'd be losing his only two electrical engineers if she left.)

3. She had caught a big fish that we'd been hunting for years, so if she left, the fish left too.

I was about to become the scapegoat unless I called and quit first. Ten years of commitment and dedication fell apart in a five-minute phone call, which sounded more like a marriage ending in a bad divorce. Alexander and I said hurtful things to each other, we brought up conflicts from years past, and blamed one another for honest mistakes we'd both made.

There was a time when my job was my source of income, not my source of self-approval, but as the profession became more competitive, things changed. How well I performed my job was a sign of who I was, another lie I'd internalized.

Because it ended unkindly, I knew that Alexander would give me a bad reference to any interviewer if I tried to get an engineering job in our city. In other words, my career in that industry was over, but thankfully, my partner wanted us to get a job halfway across the world. If my future boss asks, I'd tell him I quit because I wanted a career change, and I'd cross my fingers on both hands that he wouldn't call Alexander.

So I didn't lie to Patrick; I simply withheld specific information. They're two different things, which is why, when Patrick asked me what had changed my mind, I said, "Timothy. He really wants to go." And that was partly true too.

"I have to reimburse the company the tuition fees for the—"

Patrick put his finger on my lips. "Who cares? We're going to be rich!"

Who cares that I quit because I was about to get fired? We're going to be rich!

But first, some minor details needed to be taken care of: I'd have to apply and actually get the teaching job, which turned out to be easier than I'd expected.

With less than a month before the start of the school year, I had to pack from dusk to dawn, a great incentive to get me out of bed in the morning and reflect upon topics that weren't related to me being life's biggest failure.

When I was eleven years old, my sister, Isabelle, joined the army. Her words rang clearly in my ear the morning she left. "American families must be protected. Who's going to protect mine if not me?" For the longest time, I didn't understand what she meant, and when she was dispatched to Afghanistan, I had assumed that, in every family, there was an Isabelle, a selfless and brave Isabelle.

My parents did not take her departure lightly. Every morning for breakfast my mother cried. "We're never going to see her again," she often said, so piously that I believed it too. Then, it wasn't long before we moved into a smaller house, one that fit the three of us just right. That was a decision my parents regretted when Isabelle called two months following her departure to inform us that she *was* coming back. She had "incurred psycho-logical problems," as she'd said so many times, refusing to elaborate.

It wasn't easy, but we moved. Again. To a bigger house. Either that or my mom would have had to tell my sister, "We thought you were going to die, so we took action." Surely Isabelle wouldn't still think we deserved her sacrifice and protection.

As I stood in our bedroom, in the summer of 2018, the pile of clothes staring at me, waiting to be put in ugly brown boxes, I relived that period. What was I going to tell myself every day about the new journey we were about to take on? Was I, like my mom, going to tell myself that we were going to fail, that our families would never see us again? Or was I going to choose a more hopeful mindset, that we were going to succeed, that the best was yet to come? "Choose wisely," said Julio at every meeting, "You're in charge of your own life."

More importantly, Timothy was watching, so what did I want him to believe? I wrote down a promise to myself, "Don't you dare move to a smaller house." It wasn't about the house at all. Rather, it was about my mind. I was done making decisions I regretted.

Timothy walked into the bedroom. Ironically, it wasn't our eleven-year-old who asked, "Dad, do you think they use deodorant in Saudi Arabia? Also, it has to be Old Spice." No, it was my thirty-something-year-old partner.

"What's up, Timothy? Do you need help packing?" I asked, even though I already knew the answer. The boy was so self-sufficient, he often gave us the feeling he didn't need us. Except for his small bladder that forced him to wet his bed, that needed us.

"I was just wondering whose reaction are you excited about the most when we tell everyone we're moving to Saudi Arabia?"

"Easy, Grandma Carla." I imitated my mother-in-law in a dramatic performance. "*My* baby boy is leaving? Who's going to cook for you? Who's going to watch Timothy for you? What will I do with my life? What purpose do I have if you're so far away? Is this the end of the world?" If Carla wasn't moving to a smaller house once we left, she was finally changing Patrick's bedroom from a high schooler's den to an art studio. There, she could paint her cats and crochet outfits for them without the world judging her.

While Patrick and Timothy laughed and applauded me, I bowed to my audience.

"What about you, Patrick?" I asked. "Whose reaction are you most looking forward to?"

"Albert's." Albert was our gay bachelor best friend. Patrick resumed, pretending to be him. "Oh, can I come? I'll marry a Saudi prince and live in a castle. How many camels do you think I'm worth?"

The three of us guffawed.

"When I told Ayden," said Timothy, "he thought Saudi Arabia was in Africa."

So did your other dad, son, that's why he's not laughing.

I took a mental picture of that particular moment. I hoped that, wherever we were, as long as we had each other, we would be happy. The next words that came out of my mouth were, "You know I'm very proud of you guys, right?" I tried to hold in the tear that escaped my left eye.

What's happening to me?

One second, I was laughing hysterically, the next, I was crying. "What we're doing is crazy and scary, and there's no one I'd rather do this with."

Timothy interrupted me before I said anything else. "I dare you to say the same thing when we go to Six Flags."

Every parent thought their child was unique, but ours was extra, extra special. I ran toward him, carried him in my arms, and forced him into a family hug. I closed my eyes shut so hard that I could feel the creases around my eyes. I breathed in my boys' aromas and knew I would have that moment forever, a moment when I loved being both a father and a partner.

"I gotta get back to the kitchen," said Patrick, who'd been preparing a feast for our friends and family. As if announcing our big move wasn't stressful enough, Patrick was also worried that our guests would criticize him for making shawarma, hummus, and other Middle Eastern dishes rather than Saudi dishes. Like they'd know where Saudi Arabia was or what they ate over there.

Patrick was a completely different person in the kitchen. Or should I say, quite the contrary, he was his best self, which looked different from the person he was on a day-to-day basis. He had chopped up all the ingredients he needed the preceding evening. He had organized the sequence in which he would make the dishes to ensure that whatever needed baking went in the oven at once and that he did not use more cooking utensils than he needed to. That way, he saved time, water, gas, and energy—his own and the world's, and he would be able to brag about it the rest of the evening.

"These puff pastries are actually environmentally friendly. The hummus too. I bought dry chickpeas and soaked them overnight instead of buying canned ones," he would boast, and everyone would synchronously say, "Oh," or "Wow," or "Mmmm," as if they were genuinely impressed. And Patrick would then tell a good, intelligent joke and laugh out loud, like it was an award-winning stand-up.

He cherished those moments when he hosted his most loved ones and gathered them around dishes he had prepared with love.

The guests were due to arrive at 5 o'clock. At 4 o'clock, we headed to the bedroom to get dressed. We were filled with mixed emotions; there was excitement and fear, recklessness and ambition, confidence and melancholy. With every passing second, our move to Saudi Arabia became more real. As much as we had read about the country we were traveling to, and watched as many YouTube videos to learn about the culture, we still did not know what to expect. At least I didn't.

Patrick played a random Saudi song, "Ya Omri Ana" by Miami Band, and invited me to dance with him. Typical John would have let him down, but not the new John I was working on. We resembled two seals moving clumsily around each other. Patrick even bobbed his head back and forth a few times. The worst part was that we weren't trying to dance poorly, we were legit trying to look Arab.

When the song ended, I withdrew from the dance floor and stood in front of the mirror. Thinking back to the promise I had made myself the day before, I sought positive thoughts. *I feel thankful*, I told myself.

Seeking attention (and comfort) from Patrick, I said, "How do I look?"

He smiled, came closer, and hugged me from behind, putting his head on my shoulder, so we looked at ourselves in the mirror. "You're gorgeous, as always. Saudi women are going to have a hard time keeping their hands off you!"

Grimacing, I said, "Maybe I should wear a burqa, then."

The doorbell rang. It was Scott and Shay, the gayest couple out there. The most stereotypical. The most punctual. Overdramatic. Overdressed. Over lively. Almost too good-looking. Patrick and I loved them. The four of us had been through so much together; they were the ones Patrick and I would secretly miss the most. Then, my parents arrived, Mark and Hannah Callaway, followed by Leslie and Greg, our straight wedded friends who gave us insight into what happened outside our rainbow world. Just kidding, we loved them for other reasons too.

Then, Joseph arrived (aka Joe) and Carla Mortensen, Patrick's parents. My sister, Isabelle, and our high school friends, Jackie and Albert, arrived last. None of our guests had a clue as to the purpose of the dinner. Thankfully, our living and dining rooms were one room (but not for long, since we were going to be rich soon), so no one saw that we were in the middle of moving, giving Patrick the time he needed before he felt ready to make his announcement.

Yes, we had agreed that Patrick would be the one to break the news. Yes, we had also agreed to disagree that a poem was the way to go. But he had a grand plan, as he said, one where he would keep track of everyone's consumption of wine or whatever else they were drinking, and once they were buzzed enough, he would read it out loud. In my opinion, that wasn't much of a plan, and even if he wrote a kickass poem, the news would probably snap them back to sobriety. And then what?

After everyone complimented his food and finished catching up, the time had come. Patrick stood up and commenced his speech. I did not want to be in his shoes.

"We are gathered here today,

Because we have something to say."

"You're pregnant!" joked Isabelle.

Trying to keep a serious face, Patrick begged, "No interruptions, please, or you'll lose track of the rhymes!"

Right, Patrick, because that's what's going to dazzle their minds, the rhymes...

"We are gathered here today,

Because we have something to say.

Somewhere far, far away,

An opportunity awaits.

We know you'll be hurt,

But it's a great chance.

Out there in the desert,

I'm going to teach English, maybe dance.

Their flag is green,

Movies tell us they're mean.

We know they're rich,

Their language sounds like gibberish.

They don't pay tax,

And eat shawarma wraps.

Their men wear white,

Their women wear black.
John thinks we won't come back,
Because they kill dykes.
I'm surprised he said yes
Which country, can you guess?"

Patrick put the piece of paper back in his pocket. His audience was in shock. The room was so silent that if we dropped a needle, we could hear it. It was more fun when Patrick and I impersonated Carla and Albert. Personally, I did feel a little more sober, so I grabbed the bottle of wine closest to me and filled my glass to the brim, breaking my own rules. I hated to do it, but I had no choice; I chugged the whole thing.

I should have prepared a recovery speech, because I had anticipated this situation, but it was too late for that, so I was going to have to let the alcohol speak. Addressing Patrick, I said, "I'm judging from everyone's silence that they don't know which country you're talking about."

Then, shifting my focus to our family and friends, I said, "Before I give you the answer, I know what y'all are thinking. In fact, I've been thinking about it incessantly for the past few days. We're leaving the nest, and that's a tragedy."

Carla and Joe forgot to close their jaws, so much so that I could differentiate their original teeth from the implanted ones. The image nauseates me to this day.

"But it doesn't have to be a tragedy," I continued, "Patrick and I are looking for a new challenge, one that can take us outside our comfort zone, that can push us to new limits. Honestly, I can already see improvements in Patrick. For the first time, he wrote a poem that didn't make me want to kill myself." I laughed, hoping everyone would jump on the bandwagon, even if they didn't appreciate my joke. Instead, there was silence, again, until Timothy gave it a shot. "In case you're wondering, the country Daddy's talking about is North Korea."

A second wave of shock shook the room, everyone's eyes widened even more. Carla hid her face behind Joe's shoulder.

Guys, have you ever seen a North Korean eat Shawarma? Me neither!

"Just kidding, guys," resumed Timothy. "We're moving to Saudi Arabia. Loosen up a little!" And when they didn't, he said to Patrick, "Daddy, I thought you said alcohol gives people a better sense of humor."

My mom looked devastated, the same way she did when Isabelle left for Afghanistan. "Mom, please remember, we're not going to war. We *will* be coming back. You can even visit us if you like."

Perhaps I shouldn't have mentioned the word "war."

Our parents looked at each other. It was that famous "Aren't you going to say something?" look they gave each other. What could they say? After all, as long as we could remember, they encouraged risk-taking, determination, perseverance, hard work, etcetera, etcetera. I wanted to believe that, deep down, they were proud of us for wanting to start something daring and for finding an adventure that drove us. If not, I hoped they would be proud of us for supporting each other, even in our wildest dreams.

Desperate to break the awkwardness, I pleaded, "Dessert, anyone?" Still no response. "Scott, can you help me with something in the kitchen?"

The kitchen wasn't a far enough distance away, which made me wish we spoke sign language.

"Why aren't you saying anything?" I whispered as low as I could.

"What do you want me to say?" Scott said, mirroring my tone.

"I don't know. Anything!" I spoke that last word too loud, which must have sounded random to the people on the other side of the wall.

"Don't you think you could've warned me about this? Besides, you know how much I dread your mother-in-law." Carla cleared her throat as if to warn us that she'd heard us.

"You've got to say something. Please," I said, walking back into the living room, a tray in my hands.

Scott helped me carefully cut the *kunefe* that Patrick had bought from Trader Joe's. No one touched their dessert. "Guys, you should eat it while it's hot, or the cheese will harden and—"

No one even looked at the plates. If there was an actual elephant in the room, it would have been easier to handle.

Finally, Scott spoke. "I know someone who moved to Saudi Arabia. I can't remember the name of the city for the life of me. Something with a 'D.' Anyway, he went there to manage a construction project for some American oil company. He said he was scared at first, but once he landed, it wasn't much different than the US, really. His wife was surprised at how big the American community was. And American restaurants were everywhere. Their kids went to an American school, so they didn't feel it was too different from home."

Still nothing from our parents, only tears. I looked at Patrick. His lips were glued together. I had one last card I wanted to use, and if it failed, I did not know how else to convince them that we were making a good, thoughtful decision. "All right, everyone, I knew you would all object, so I prepared a brief slideshow, and I hope I can bring the real Saudi Arabia to you." One by one, they shifted in their chairs to face the TV.

This isn't going to work, John. You don't even know what the real Saudi Arabia is.

It was a last-minute idea and finding pictures of expats in Saudi Arabia turned out to be harder than expected. Google was not omniscient after all.

I started with a picture of a white woman in a black dress with palm trees in the background. I made sure the first picture represented a happy minority group, hoping no one would ask me to show them a photo of a happy gay couple in Saudi Arabia. Next on the screen was a picture of another white woman in between two women in burqas and a young boy. Of course, we could not tell if the women in burqas were smiling, but the white woman was, and that was what mattered.

Though I had entered "expats in saudi arabia" in the search bar, the grand majority of pictures did not have expats in them. I kept scrolling until I found a picture that combined locals with foreigners. It was in a business setting, which I thought might transmit the message that women were empowered over there. I clicked on the link to see if I could find more pictures, but it turned out the picture was actually taken in Dubai. Like I'd told Patrick, none of our guests would know the difference, so I used it. For all they knew (and cared), Saudi Arabia and Dubai were the same place.

Halfway through the slideshow, my mother interrupted me, "John?"

"Yes?" I expected a debate, but to my surprise, she was on board. She asked me, "Do you know how long you will be there?"

Not quite believing that my mother was agreeing to our plan, my father jumped into the conversation. "Wait, you're not really agreeing to this, are you? They could die."

"Relax, don't you see the pictures? They're not going to die."

It worked! Wait, it worked?

Patrick had not heard from his parents, so he addressed them. "Mom, Dad, you haven't said anything."

Joe and Carla looked at each other to see who would speak first. Carla and Patrick were particularly close, so she took the lead. "Ricko, I was doubtful at first, but the two of you seem to have done so much research. And honestly, I haven't seen you so passionate in a while. So I can't believe I'm going to say this, but you've got my support. But I want more details on when we can visit you."

Patrick couldn't hold himself. He jumped off his seat and gave a long, warm embrace to his parents.

"Thank you, Mom, I don't know how visit visas work over there, but we'll definitely look into it. Now, everyone, can we please raise a glass for our little big adventure?"

Patrick smiled at me, and with teary eyes, he made the sign for "thank you," which we had learned a long time ago from one of Timothy's nursery rhyme videos. Everyone sat back down and conversed again.

There was one more topic to be discussed. "The moving company is coming tomorrow, so we will need a place to stay. I prepared a game for us to play, and the winner will have the honor of hosting us for a week until we fly out."

Carla, Patrick's mother, volunteered. "If everyone's okay with it, we would love to host you. We would love the chance to see you as much as possible before you leave. Mark and Hannah, you can come as often as you'd like."

My parents nodded in approval. Ecstatic, Patrick raised his arms in the air and said loudly, "All right, it's all set then. Do y'all still want to play?"

"Yeah, let's do it! Games are more fun when you're drunk!" said a merry Albert.

The night should have ended on that happy note, filled with love and support by our favorite people, but I walked in on Patrick and Isabelle having a heated discussion on our balcony. "If you don't tell him, I will," she told Patrick.

If you don't tell who what?

CHAPTER FOUR

It was 2 o'clock in the morning, and I couldn't sleep. How could I when we were leaving the next day? We were leaving everything we knew to go to somewhere we didn't know anything about. I must've rolled over ten times in that single bed.

Why did Carla never refurbish Patrick's bedroom? We were two grown men sleeping—or trying to sleep—in a teenager's bed. I opened my legs into an "A" position to keep my feet from sticking out, as if it wasn't enough to be uncomfortable emotionally.

I clicked my tongue, I sighed, but Patrick was in another world. It was beyond me how he could sleep on such a ground-breaking night. Did Neil Armstrong sleep the night before he was due to go on that rocket? Did Barack Obama sleep the night before the results came out? Did RuPaul sleep the night before his first show? Patrick would sleep through the night before my funeral, which would have been that night if I couldn't control my anxiety.

It was the last day of summer all over again. What would the upcoming academic year look like? Which teacher would I get?

Which kid would bully me? Would my friends share the same classes with me? Not to mention that, after spending three months sleeping at 2 o'clock in the morning, if not later, I was suddenly expected to sleep at eight o'clock at night. I recognized that creeping feeling all too well, and I couldn't get rid of it. My tears pooled in my throat, my mind racing in all different directions, excited for the unknown future, but also upsetting memories of the past.

"If you don't tell who what?" I asked that night on the balcony, looking at Patrick from the corner of my eye for a split second before giving my sister a death glare.

Could it be that Patrick and Isabelle are having an affair, and Patrick wants to move to Saudi Arabia so he doesn't have to see her again?

"It's not what it sounds like," said Isabelle, extending her right arm, so we could hold hands.

When I didn't move, she said, "Y'all made this decision without consulting me first. It says in the egg donor contract that, if the donor deems it absolutely necessary, they can tell the child that they're a biological parent. Y'all are taking Timothy away from me, even though you know that I'm going through a very tough phase in life. But if I tell him I'm his biological mom, maybe he'll want to stay."

"Wait, y'all aren't having an affair?"

"An affair?" said Patrick. "Babe, if I wanted to have an affair, I would've chosen someone more adequate." He winked at Isabelle, who laughed sarcastically. These two have a love-hate relationship I'll never understand.

Faking a laugh, I gently pushed Patrick toward the balcony door. "Can I have a moment with my sister, please?"

"Fine, fine," he said. "Come on, Koala, we're not wanted here."

As the door clicked shut, Isabelle jumped on me, squeezing

35

me in her arms. "I'm so mad at you for not telling me before everybody else, and although I want to punch you right now, I also want to tell you that I'm going to miss you."

Her hair smelled like bubble gum, as it always did. A lot of things about Isabelle stayed the same over the decades, like the fact that she wasn't a crier or that her guards were always up.

She took a step back, placing her hands on the balcony fence, and there she was again, my stoic sister. Gently hitting my elbow against hers, I said, "Apparently you're going through a very tough phase right now, and I don't know about this because?"

Looking straight at the house across the street, she stayed quiet, and so I took the chance to be vulnerable. "I've been struggling myself too." She looked at me as if surprised, but also curious to hear more.

"Yeah," I said, before telling her about my depression and how it had influenced my job performance. For the first time, I allowed my sister into my real world. "I'm also failing miserably as a dad."

I wanted to vent about my relationship with Patrick, too, but it wasn't fair on him. "And so, I'm hoping this move to Saudi will somehow help me become a better person, you know?"

Wiping my tears away, Isabelle said, "I know. Thank you for sharing this with me, I know I never let anyone in on my personal life, but it's not because I don't trust y'all. I just—"

Wiping her nose with the back of her hand, she said, "I just don't like to say the memories out loud. It's hard enough having to see them in my head, you know?"

At that moment, I wanted to stay in San Antonio, if only to get to know my sister better, to help her, to receive help from her.

"You're the bravest person I know," I said, and there was much more on my heart, but that was a conversation for another day, like "Venting to someone or journaling will work wonders, even if it's hard at first," or "I know I haven't been there for you, but that can change. I want to be here for you."

Instead, I focused on what mattered. "Timothy gets his bravery from you."

When she nodded, it inspired me to find the words she needed to hear. "When we asked him if he wanted to move, he said he could make more friends than his friend who's also moving somewhere."

We laughed, because this was also the kind of thing Isabelle would have said as a kid. Or even as an adult.

"I know you're going to miss him, and he's going to miss you too. And as much as it breaks my heart to take him away from you guys, I'm super excited for all the things he's going to gain from this journey. Besides, it's about time you learned how to FaceTime."

Like a couple of drunk, irresponsible teenagers, we sang, "I'll Be There For You" by The Rembrandts at the top of our lungs into the otherwise quiet Texan night.

Great, now that song is stuck in my head, I thought, as I lay in bed the night before our grand departure.

When I did fall asleep, I had a terrible nightmare that I was on some Saudi version of *Who Wants to Be a Millionaire*, and they wanted to send me to the electric chair because I gave a wrong answer. It woke me right back up, and when I'd made sense of where I was, I realized that Patrick wasn't in bed.

It's going to be a long night. I'm dying for a joint right now. And where on earth is Patrick?

I made my way to the bathroom to relieve myself and wash the nightmare off. As I rinsed my face, my reflection stared back at me. *What are you feeling, John? Do you still feel thankful?*

Patrick, who had always taught me that "the only drink you really ever need is wine, it's medicine for the soul" was now sitting in the kitchen, drinking peanut butter whiskey. He had changed into a shirt he had worn in high school (Carla saved his clothes too) that said, "Young, Wild & Free."

"I didn't know crop tops are a thing men do now," I joked.

"I'm bringing sexy back," he replied, half-joking, half-uninterested.

"How long have you been here?" I grabbed a chair and joined him. Pointing at the empty glass that sat next to his, I asked him, "Are you expecting someone?"

"Yes, you. I knew it was a matter of time before you came out looking for a drink."

"Actually, I was looking for you."

Raising his glass, he said, "To the asses. I mean, to the masses!'

"How much have you had?" The bottle was about half full, could he possibly have drunk all that by himself?

"Does it matter? It's technically the same as eating out of a peanut butter jar."

Yep, he did drink all that by himself.

This was the first time since we'd decided to move to Saudi Arabia that I witnessed fear in Patrick's eyes. Was he bottling it up until he could no longer hold it in? Or was he genuinely feeling it all for the first time that night before our flight?

"I came up with a concept," he said, sounding more and more drunk. "I'm going to create a drink, and I'm going to call it 'Drink & Fly.' And my customers will be people who like to drink before a flight."

I gulped my glass and poured myself a second.

"I know you're worried, and that's okay. I'm worried too."

"I know you are," he said, rolling his glass between his hands.

We dove into a childish debate of who was more worried until I'd had enough. "The point I'm trying to make here is that our relationship and our individual strengths are going to help us override our fears."

"Fearful or not, we don't have much of a choice now, anyway."

Thanks for the good talk, Patrick.

"Right," I said. "Listen, I'm going back to bed, why don't you come with me? We have to wake up early tomorrow." We both chugged what was left in our glasses and made our way to the bedroom.

The next morning, I was awoken by the noises of Carla's panicking, which developed into a cacophony, consisting of the washing machine, the dryer, the vacuum, and the dishwasher playing all at once.

"Jump in the shower," said Patrick, which would have been rude if he hadn't clarified, "before my mom offers to wash you. It's a thing she does when she panics. Everything and everyone has to be spotless."

If your dad was more of a maintenance man and fixed her up in the bedroom, she'd have fewer panic attacks. I know, I know, this is super judgmental, coming from the master of panic attacks.

Unlike Carla, I was calm. The anxiety of the preceding month was so extreme, I had maxed out. I was out of anxiety, so to speak, which helped me be mentally present with my family for a change.

"I won't move to a smaller house," I told myself as I walked into the kitchen where both our families sat around the table.

I sympathized with Carla, who was distracting herself from the sorrow of being away from her son and grandson, her entire world. As we gobbled up the typical American breakfast, she remained standing, waiting on us like a professional butler.

"Hey guys," said my sister, "let's take a picture to commemorate this day."

Carla jumped at the opportunity. "I can do it. Do you have a phone?"

"That's alright," said Isabelle. "I can take a selfie, and you can be in the picture."

The poor woman didn't insist. Looking at the floor, she walked toward her seat, gently sat down, and drew the smallest smile. I could never imagine my life without Timothy, and the mere thought of it made me want to cry.

My mother, on the other hand, looked like her natural self, as if it was another ordinary day. Was she hiding it well? Was she going to go through another phase of "They're not coming back?" Or was she also maxed out, having been shocked enough when Isabelle left for Afghanistan that her tolerance for pain had become roofless?

Unknowingly, I stood up, carried my glass of orange juice with one hand and patted the shoulder of my family and friends with the other as I walked toward the other end of the table. Standing behind Patrick's chair, I raised my glass for a quick second and said, "This is not a toast. Erm, I just want to say that we will miss each and every one of you greatly. We are so thankful for all the love and support you have shown us, not just in the past few weeks, but all our lives. I know I can speak for myself when I say that there is not one person sitting at this table who hasn't played a part in the person I've become today and in the decision Patrick, Timothy, and I have made to take on this new adventure. We love y'all."

Joe, Patrick's father, said, "I don't know about having played a part in your crazy idea, but thank you for sharing that. We love you too, and we want nothing but the best for the three of you."

The next few hours flew by. One second, we were in the living room, recounting memories of the past. Not Carla, though, she was still on her feet, serving us tea, coffee, and anything she could. The next, we were in front of the house, wiping tears away. I hugged everyone twice. At some point, I was hugging Patrick, even though it didn't make sense. Isabelle hugged Hannah, our mom. Joe hugged my dad, Mark. And Carla was left alone. Poor Carla. I let go of Patrick and pushed him toward his mom, and they wailed.

It was an adrenaline rush I hadn't known before, caused by a mix of excitement, but also pride that I was doing something brave and courageous. On top of it all, there was fear, fear of not knowing when would be the next time I'd hug these people, and fear of living in a world far from them.

"That's it," said Carla, "I'm coming with you."

For a second, I thought she meant she was coming with us to Saudi Arabia.

My mom followed. "Me too."

And then everyone was dropping us off at the airport. The same scene happened again. We cried. We hugged. We cried some more and hugged some more.

"Joe," said Carla, "go park the car. I'll stay with the boys until they're checked in."

"Mom, you really don't have to. This is making it harder for everyone. If you want, I can keep you updated every step of the way. I'll send you videos." It wasn't easy, but she agreed. No more looking back. From now on, we looked ahead.

CHAPTER FIVE

"You're flying Saudi Airlines from JFK, correct?" asked the check-in officer.

"Yes, that is correct," said Patrick.

"Do you have all the required paperwork for the dog?"

"Yes." Patrick brought out the certificates, forms, and Koala's passport and placed them on the counter. Thankfully, we came prepared. As they stated on the Saudi Airlines website, "The Kingdom of Saudi Arabia allows the entry of hunting/guard/seeing-eye and hearing dogs for blind and deaf passengers only." After much research, we confirmed that our Koala, a Pomeranian, was on the list of breeds allowed in the country.

The reason dogs were generally banned was because in Islam, if someone saw a dog while praying, their prayer wishes would be canceled. Why? Because dogs were considered impure. As Patrick said when we discovered all this information, "Until the prophet said, but not the Shih Tzu, it's just so cute and fluffy. OK, not the Labrador, either. You know what? I'll send you a list of dogs I'll allow. I'll have my assistant pigeon post it to you."

The three of us were familiar with the San Antonio

International Airport. It was the airport we always used. This time, walking the halls, not knowing when we would be back, the feeling was bitter-sweet. Would we find a pretzel shop like Auntie Anne's in Saudi Arabia? What about Cinnabon or Starbucks?

How likely is it that the family grabbing donuts also works in Saudi Arabia? I wish they did, and I wish they could reassure me that it's scary at first, but not only is it going to be worth it, we're going to love it.

Sitting in front of our gate, Timothy watched Frozen on our iPad (it was an old iPad and Frozen was the only movie on it).

Wouldn't it be awesome if the airport employee noticed a mistake in our passports and stopped us from flying? Yeah, right, John, like you could ever be that lucky.

We boarded the plane, and I stared out the window, trying to keep the tears from pouring. I was going to miss my city so much. I was going to miss its people. I was going to miss my life. When the plane took off, I could no longer bottle my emotions and cried like a baby.

"Dad," said Timothy, his hand on my shoulder, "do you want a tissue?" Yes, I needed a tissue. I needed a whole box. A chocolate bar too.

"It's just, I'm just—" I took a deep breath and said, "I feel bad for Koala, you know? Because she's down in the cargo all by herself."

Timothy and Patrick played along.

When we were in the air and San Antonio was out of sight, my weary eyes gave up, and I slept through the flight.

I hated JFK. For a city as international, touristic, and expensive as New York, I expected their airport to represent its grandeur and modernism. Instead, its tiles were old and dark. It smelled stale, even though I had spotted a couple janitors here and there. And despite the ample space, it was closing in on me.

Maybe it wasn't the airport, maybe it was my state of mind. I stood still for a brief moment, observing the world around me: people walking in opposite directions, people stretching across a few seats, a dad running to his gate with his toddler on his shoulders.

Everyone had their own story that led them to be at that airport at that particular moment in time. I wondered how many people, like us, were traveling for better financial opportunities. Were they doing it by choice? If so, many people came to the US for a better life, why were we leaving?

My eyes were hurting. Sitting between Patrick and Timothy, I rested my elbows against my thighs and noticed it had been a while since I bought shoes. They were ripped on the side, like they were tired of walking, of taking me places, like they were ready to retire. And I felt the same.

Patrick said, "Whatever you're feeling, it can't be something a good McDonald's can't fix. What do you say Timothy? Are you up for that?"

I hope they have something similar to McDonald's in Saudi Arabia, or anything that will help me feel like I'm home away from home. Adidas, too.

"This is the final boarding call for passengers John and Patrick Callaway booked on flight SV 20 to Jeddah. Please proceed to Gate 3 immediately. The final checks are being completed, and the captain will order for the doors of the aircraft to close in approximately five minutes' time. I repeat, this is the final boarding call for John and Patrick Callaway. Thank you."

This is the last time we will hear our names together like that. Once we board that flight, we're John Callaway and Patrick Mortensen.

We ran to our gate and were the last passengers to board the flight. Some people gave us a nasty look, as if we had delayed the plane. I didn't care, let them look. Our tardiness and then the adrenaline rush distracted me from the thoughts and feelings that had overwhelmed me at San Antonio International Airport.

Goodbye, USA, I told myself again, *no more looking back, from now on, we look forward.*

I sighed a huge breath of relief, and a spontaneous smile spread across my face. I was now excited for what awaited us. The mixture of emotions I felt in the long twenty four hours leading to that point was draining. I looked for a movie, something that didn't require any kind of focus on my part. *The Greatest Showman* was perfect. I pressed play, but since the plane hadn't taken off yet, I was interrupted by a multitude of announcements.

"Ladies and gentlemen, the text you are about to hear is a supplication, which Mohammed, peace be upon him, used to pray upon traveling. Allah is the Most Great. Allah is the Most Great. Allah is the Most Great. Glory is to Him Who has provided this for us, though we could never have had it by our efforts. Surely, unto our Lord we are returning. O' Allah, we ask You on this our journey for goodness and piety, and for works that are pleasing to You. O' Allah, lighten this journey for us and make its distance easy for us. O' Allah, You are our Companion on the road and the One in Whose care we leave our family. O' Allah, I seek refuge in You from this journey's hardships, and from the wicked sights in store and from finding our family and property in misfortune upon returning."

Patrick commented, "This guy wrote better poems than me."

Patrick, you can't write good poems at all.

"I doubt that he wrote them," I said. Patrick looked at me, confused, so I grabbed my phone and opened the Notes app. I wasn't going to risk being heard and taken out of context. I typed in, "He was illiterate."

It took Patrick a few seconds to make sense of what I was trying to say, and when he did understand, he said, "Well, that doesn't make it any better."

Patrick and I loved flight attendants. We loved their uniforms. We loved the idea of traveling for a living. We loved to hear their stories. Only this time, every time I tried to say something to the comely lady serving us, I froze. What if I said something culturally insensitive? Was I allowed to compliment her uniform or makeup? Would she think I was flirting with her? Would they throw me off the plane mid-flight? The last one was far-fetched, I knew, but I could not ignore the possibility.

That same flight attendant approached our row with a tray filled with beverages. She eloquently said, "Thank you for choosing Saudi Airlines. My name is Farah. May I serve you a refreshing beverage? We have delicious Saudi champagne."

What on Earth is Saudi champagne? Is it like a code for something? Or is it champagne that's made in Saudi Arabia? Or is the word "virgin" so liberal that they replaced it with "Saudi?"

Patrick appeared just as confused as I was. He replied, "Do you have Saudi wine?"

Amused by his honest reaction, Farah laughed. "No, sir, but we do have grape juice."

We were both intrigued to try this mysterious Saudi champagne. Patrick ordered one for the two of us and a glass of grape juice for Timothy. I wondered if they could make Saudi whiskey or Saudi vodka, though the Russians surely would be unhappy about that.

"To the Callaways," said Patrick as we clinked our plastic cups together.

"Oh my gosh, this is just apple juice," exclaimed Patrick. "Why hype it up and call it champagne?"

"Maybe because it's sparkling?" I guessed.

"So? Just call it sparkling apple juice."

"You wouldn't have been curious to try it then," said Timothy.

"I wouldn't be disappointed either. Though I must say, it

would have made a great Prosecco. I guess it's true what they say, Timothy, you don't know what you've got until it's gone."

"How can you have something and not know you have it?" came Timothy's witty observation. Gosh, I loved that boy, especially when he put Patrick on the spot like that.

Patrick, who obviously did not expect Timothy's remark, stuttered before he collected enough words together to make a sentence. "The point is, sometimes, you only appreciate the value of something once you no longer have it."

Timothy did not comment, he raised his eyebrows and slowly turned his head to face the screen, as if he was saying, "Well, that was a useless conversation." I handed him the headphones that the flight attendant gave us earlier, and he sank into his Jurassic Park marathon. What else would an eleven year old do on a thirteen-hour flight?

While the movie played in the background, I couldn't keep my eyes open. I was more emotionally tired than anything else. Exhausted, I murmured, "I think the Saudi champagne is starting to kick in," and fell asleep before Patrick had made up his mind on which movie he wanted to watch. It was not easy being a Gemini...

It was an excellent two-hour snooze, and though the Saudi champagne did not cause a hangover, it did leave me feeling gassy. On my way to the restroom, I noticed two men kneeling in the prayer area. In that small square-shaped space, I was intrigued to know why they weren't facing the wall in front of them.

I noticed a screen that displayed a compass; its arrow followed a small icon. It must have been the shrine Muslims went to in Mecca. As it turned out, they were facing the direction of that shrine, a mandatory rule when praying. Lucky for them, Koala wasn't with me, or they would have had to start over.

How was I going to spend the next eight-something hours? I

grabbed our carry-on bag from the overhead cabinet and placed it on Patrick's lap.

"Well, well, well, what do we have here?" I asked, examining the bag. "Something tells me you weren't the one who packed this bag. Am I right?"

Patrick was an organized man, but he didn't have the creativity to pack the following items into that bag: three toothbrushes, one toothpaste, a sleep mask from Tempur that must have cost sixty dollars.

"Let me guess, this was Carla's doing," I said.

Patrick nodded. "Let's see which snacks she chose."

They were all snacks from Trader Joe's, so I admitted, "Carla did a great job."

I was thankful for her, even from many miles away. And then I spotted a note. "Hey, boys, hope you're having a pleasant flight. I wasn't sure they would allow anything with pork on the flight, but I did my best. We miss you already. Love, Carla."

For that alone, she got extra points, though it did make me wonder if they would have stopped us at the boarding gate for carrying ham, or worse, they would have accused us of smuggling contraband upon our arrival in Saudi Arabia. I made a mental note to look that up as soon as I had an internet connection; things one cannot bring into the Saudi airport—other than 20 breeds of dogs. Oh, and sex toys.

It was the first time I had watched *The Greatest Showman* without the kissing scenes. Even the picture in the newspaper where Hugh Jackman was kissing Rebecca Ferguson wasn't there. I guess they called it Saudi TV. I wasn't complaining, though. It was thanks to this little zombie box that the three of us were able to kill time.

As we flew over Saudi Arabia, the TVs were interrupted by an announcement. We were flying over Medina, which was where the prophet's mosque was located. We were encouraged to pray a special kind of prayer, not one of the five prayers of the day. Some people headed to the small prayer area, others remained seated, and murmurs filled the airplane.

Passengers on the other side of our row were looking down, their lips moving. They looked left, over their shoulder, and then right, over their other shoulder. They raised their pointer finger a few times, and then put their hands on their face, as if doing peek-a-boo. After that, the plane was silent again and everyone carried on with whatever they were doing. For most people, that meant sleeping.

Less than an hour later, the plane hovered over Jeddah. The three of us crammed our heads in next to each other to observe the view out the tiny window.

"It's not such a bad idea to use the things Grandma left for you," said Timothy as he handed us a box of organic peppermints (since when are peppermints organic?). We ignored him.

We were surprised by the beauty of the city under us, not to mention the magnificent aura. It didn't look like a desert at all. If anything, it reminded me of Los Angeles; the city was divided into little squares, which were saturated with buildings. And of course, palm trees too. The city was jammed with cars everywhere. Sitting in straight lines, light poles were patiently waiting for the sun to set.

Jeddah looked lively. Vibrant, even. The familiarity comforted me. Perhaps it wouldn't be as alien as I had imagined. Perhaps if I was pleasantly surprised with my first sight of the city, assimilating would be relatively easy. Perhaps I overreacted the past few days—on many occasions. I closed my eyes and took a long, deep breath in, and when I opened them back up, I whispered, "Welcome home, guys."

Yep, I definitely need to brush my teeth.

JOHN

Hey Scott, We landed safely in Jeddah. Miss me already?

THE GANG (JOHN)

We're at the airport. Goodbye, gangsters, it's been great! Until next time 😊

THE GANG (MARTIN)

See you... next week? How long do y'all think they'll survive over there?

THE GANG (JOSHUA)

Where are they going again? South Africa?

THE GANG (JOHN)

Ha ha... Very funny!

THE GANG (MARTIN)

Seriously, though, you will be missed! Keep us posted and stay in touch

CHAPTER SIX

When the airplane hit the runway, the crowd of passengers applauded unanimously. To whom, I did not know. The pilot? The flight attendants? The prophet?

Then, a few men stepped out into the middle aisle, opened the overhead cabinets, and pulled out their carry-on luggage. A voice on the intercom spoke over the background noise. "Ladies and gentlemen, we ask you to remain seated until the plane has parked and the seat belt sign has turned off. Thank you." Most people sat down. Well, most people, except one man, who accidentally pulled down a duty-free bag from the overhead and spilled its contents onto another passenger. In the US, someone might have been shot for that. Or not, I exaggerate. The two passengers argued until Farah somehow calmed them down.

You go girl!

I loved that my judgment of her was inaccurate. I would've expected a male flight attendant to intervene in the argument, thinking that, in their culture, a woman should be modest and stay away from "manly" things. And I was ready to be wrong in my stereotypes and prejudices, again and again. Like the prejudice that Saudis hated gay people.

The plane came to a stop. I stared at the seatbelt sign, waiting for it to turn off. Meanwhile, a queue formed in the middle aisle, but it was a good ten minutes before they opened the gate.

To our left, a female passenger grabbed a long, black fabric from her purse, and as she unfolded it, she stood up and quietly covered her body in it. I looked for an expression on her face, and somewhere inside of me, I wanted to detect oppression, but it seemed like she'd done this too many times before, and that it didn't matter to her. Then, she grabbed another piece of fabric from her purse and struggled to cover her hair, similar to how I had a hard time wrapping a present. After a few attempts, she put the piece of fabric back in her purse and tied her hair in a ponytail.

Sensing a commotion from behind me, like a silent orchestra, a band of women prepared themselves for shipment, like products in a factory that were about to pass quality control. The only women who'd stayed put were the ones who'd been covered all along, some with their faces covered too, and others veiling every strand of hair with a colorful hijab.

If I were a woman landing in Saudi for the first time, would I have come prepared? I may not have had to cover my body or change my attire, but I did have more in common with these women than I thought. For after all, I did have to hide my identity, which helped me sympathize with these women, especially the non-Saudi ones.

It was an unimportant moment, but very important at the same time, because it was my first sexist experience in the country I'd just called home, and something told me the schism would only grow larger.

Let's say we conditioned American women to cover up, would rapes finally stop? Nah, I don't think so. Maybe I should write a book that tells the story of a world where men cover up to protect themselves from women. Oh, look, the seatbelt sign is finally off!

Every time Patrick attempted to stand up and grab our things, more and more passengers walked down the aisle. He looked at me and shrugged his elbows, as if trying to say, "What do you want me to do?" Seeing him paralyzed in his seat, fear in his eyes, I couldn't make sense of what he was feeling. But then, as the passengers walked past us, it clicked—how did it take me so long to realize—the scene was all too familiar. The plane. The angry people mumbling in a foreign language. The black dresses. Hatred for freedom. Hatred for Americans. Hijacking. A bomb.

When they opened the gate, even more passengers walked down the aisle, including a woman who hadn't cover herself in a dress, just a long-sleeve shirt that almost went down to her knees, and loose cotton pants. Had she forgotten her dress? Was she a VIP of some sort? Was something bad going to happen to her?

"Um, guys," said Timothy. "What are we waiting for, exactly?"

For your other dad to grow a pair.

"I'm not sure, son. I think your dad is waiting for the plane to fly back to the US."

"What can I do?" asked Patrick. "They're either staring right at the floor or pretending to be focused on something, so as to avoid eye contact with me."

"So?" I asked.

"So they're not stopping, even though they know we're trying to get out."

"So?" I asked, again.

"They look so exhausted. I don't want to stop them."

"Well, I'm exhausted too. Just get up and force yourself out, and whoever is behind you will have to wait."

It was too late anyway. At that point, the plane was already empty. It was just us, a few elderly people and passengers with disabilities waiting to be escorted. But, hey, we had the aisle to ourselves. I knew for a fact that, if we were in the US and the same scenario had happened, which it often did, Patrick would have reacted differently. He would've stood up and pushed his way through. But we weren't in the US. Our racist attitude was against our will, for it had been the result of years, decades, of false ideas being shoved into our heads.

Except this wasn't a movie, and what happened made me question which side hated the other. And why there were two sides to begin with.

Standing before a set of foldable stairs, I felt like a president waiting to be handed a pair of scissors and cut the red ribbon to mark the beginning of a repaired relation between two countries. We were the only ones up there, and I was tempted to wave to the crowd downstairs, like a leader would. I didn't do it. I did, however, take a deep breath before I took the first step down. I wanted to breathe in the moist air and let it fill my body. I could almost touch the humidity.

I grabbed Patrick's carry on, because I didn't know how well he could see behind his fogged up glasses. "Stay next to your dad," I told Timothy, and I took the first step down.

"Dad, don't move."

"What's going on, Timothy?"

"Just trust me. Don't move."

I felt a heavy hand on my shoulder. Black gloves.

What the...?

I turned my head in slow motion. It was a woman wearing a burqa and black socks under her black rubber sandals. If that was not a fashion statement, I did not know what was. My only guess was that it was an elderly woman who needed support. I didn't want her to fall, but I also didn't know if I could hold her arm to support her, so I imagined her little body bowling down the stairs.

Okay, slowly, slowly. You can do this. But what if she stumbles? Can I blame it on her dress or is that offensive? Am I allowed to catch her? What I really want to know is why she didn't choose Patrick or Timothy. And why did she have to be a woman? Is this a test? If I pass, can I become a national hero? John, the man who helped Fatima, Saudi's sweetheart, down the stairs. Rumors say he's gay. What a controversy! Am I racist for naming her Fatima? She doesn't look like a Barbara to me. Okay, John, one last step! You made it.

When my feet—and then hers—touched the ground, I let out a huge sigh of relief.

"Thanks for trusting me, Dad." Timothy had the biggest smile on his face.

I was disappointed in myself, though. Why did I react like that? I had to unlearn everything I knew, or thought I knew, about this culture. Patrick and I both.

"Hey," said Patrick softly, "Where do you think the airport is?"

We were standing in the airplane parking lot. At least we weren't by ourselves. A large group of passengers was standing there, and if anything, we had the elderly women by our side. Surely it wouldn't be hard to keep up with them.

"What are they waiting for?" Patrick rubbed at the sweat dripping down his face and covering his upper lip.

For the camels to pick us up.

He walked toward one of the employees and asked, "Excuse me, do you speak English?"

The man nodded.

"Do you know what we're waiting for?"

The man pointed toward a bus that was moving our way.

"Oh, thank you."

The bus was packed within seconds. There were only a handful of seats, which were saved for elderly and pregnant women. Cramped up like sardines in a can, the men standing

55

around me were holding on to a latch that hung from a bar above us. I could almost visualize the stink traveling from their armpit and up into my nostrils. In fact, I detected another odor that reminded me of the time I had woken up from surgery. That smell of bad breath. If one man (or woman) yawned from a yard away, I smelled it. All of that was to be expected after a thirteen-hour flight, combined with the ten minutes we were standing outside. I wanted to faint.

At last, the airport. Everyone turned to face the door closest to them. This time, I was not going to panic, I wasn't going to be passive. I was getting out ASAP. If Timothy and Patrick wanted to take their time, good for them, but I wasn't waiting.

We walked into the airport and our co-passengers divided into two opposite directions. We had no clue which way to go, right or left. There was a small group of police officers standing behind a desk, but for fear of being interrogated about our rela-tion to each other, we didn't ask them for help. On the wall behind them, there were large pictures of the king and—I guessed—his sons. I must have looked so stupid when I bowed down to the pictures.

"What are you doing?" asked Timothy.

Even my eleven year old thought I was an idiot. I replied, "Maybe he will give us a sign which way to go. Left or right."

An airport employee, who was dressed in the traditional white dress (the thobe), came our way. He asked us, "First time?"

Patrick jumped in. "Yes, it's our first time here." The employee signed with his hand, which we interpreted as "follow me."

Left was the right answer.

Everything was white; the shining floor, the soaring arches towering over us, the thobes of the passport control employees. The whiteness matched the cleanliness of the airport. The pleasant Arabian smell was a great contrast to the bus ride.

"How can they run if they need to catch someone?" asked Timothy, out of the blue.

"What do you mean, son?"

"The guys who stamp passports. Aren't there people who use fake passports or whatever? What if they catch one, and he tries to run away?"

"Yeah," said Patrick, "and they're wearing sandals."

I didn't follow their discussion after that. Instead, I focused on the big billboard advertisement that discouraged visitors from smoking. It was signed by J. C. Decaux, an international advertising agency. Underneath it were the passport control desks, occupied by male employees only. If they could not see the face of a woman dressed in a burqa (like the one I helped come down the stairs), how could they verify her identity?

Every foreigner to have ever stepped in this country walked the same steps I did. It was clear that the Saudi authorities had invested a great deal of money to make sure that our first impression of this country was positive. They weren't a secluded nation. In fact, their airport was built by foreign engineers like me.

The local passengers who were on our plane were nowhere in sight. They probably turned right when they entered the airport. I wondered if that was a representation of how things worked in Saudi Arabia. The locals and the expats lived in different worlds that almost never met. The expats provided the expertise, and the locals provided the space and the money. It was a win-win situation, under one condition: we respected and obeyed their rules and culture.

"Huh?" I said, not having a clue what Patrick had been blabbering about for the past minute or so.

"I said, you go first with Timothy. And if he raises the issue of how we know each other, tell him we're colleagues. Make sure your passport is open on the page that shows your visa, that way, you go through as fast as possible. Let's hope he doesn't ask you about Timothy's mother."

"Are you suddenly afraid of dying?" I teased him. He smirked and shooed me, like he did with the neighborhood cats.

"Hello," I said to the officer sitting behind the desk.

"Hello," he said while pointing toward a small machine that registered fingerprints. I wiped my sweaty fingers against my shirt and placed them on the scanner, one by one, submitting the one thing that made me unique from everyone else on the entire planet. It was like they wanted me to know they were watching me, that I better be careful with my every move.

But it wasn't like that. A gentle smile on his face, the officer stamped our passports and signed for us to move forward. Smooth as butter. I wished we treated Saudis in our airports as well as they treated us. Even Patrick, who looked like he was on ecstasy or something (his eyes open wide, gnawing on his lips, his body rocking from side to side) made it past customs without a single question asked.

"See, that wasn't so bad." I tapped my elbow against his.

"Yes, but it could have been," he said.

Timothy looked up to Patrick. "Daddy, our plane could have crashed. Or Koala could have died. Or—"

"I get it, guys," said Patrick. "I think I'm allowed to feel fearful every now and again. I don't shove it in your face when you do."

We found the baggage carousel that would deliver our suitcases, but it was still empty. The three of us were startled when a loud noise filled the airport. The voice on the speakerphone was calling people to prayer. So far, that was the only aspect of the culture that Hollywood got right. All the airport employees disappeared, as did some of the passengers. There we were, standing incapacitated in front of the immobile baggage belt, the big exit sign in sight behind it.

"What's happening, Dad?"

"It's prayer time, son."

"What does that mean?" asked Timothy.

"I'm not sure how it works, but I'm getting the impression that there's a prayer at this time every day. So people stop what they're doing and go to the mosque, which is like a church, but for people of another faith."

Timothy carried his backpack.

"Where are you going, son?"

"If the airport is closed for prayer, we'll have to come back tomorrow when prayer time is over, no?"

I fought back the urge to laugh for fear that Timothy would think I was laughing at him, not at his innocence.

With Timothy on my lap, I sat next to a woman who was fully covered. She might have been the one I helped down the stairs, there was no way to tell. Actually, there was, she got up to sit next to a woman, which meant she didn't feel comfortable being around a man. Either that, or I was so stinky, she couldn't bear my odor.

I grabbed my phone and took a selfie. I tried to connect to the Internet, hoping I could post my picture on social media with the caption, "I found a place for men to fight against sexism #meninism," but without a connection, I was on my own.

Fifteen minutes had passed before employees and passengers reappeared. Before we knew it, we could no longer see the belt. Was it moving? We didn't know. Had our bags arrived? We didn't know. How much longer before we were finally home? We didn't know. Gosh, I hated airports, even fancy ones.

After another forty minutes, we had Koala and our luggage. We emptied the carts, placed the bags on the x-ray baggage scanner, then put them back on our carts, and walked out the sliding door, two hours after having left the plane. I made a mental note that, going forward, we would either plan our trips so they didn't collide with prayer times, or we would fly without luggage.

We were told the compound chauffeur would be waiting for us, holding a sign that had our names on.

"There's no way we're going to find him," said Timothy, looking at the multitude of men waiting to pick up other travelers from behind the low, metal fence. Thankfully for us, the king, or the prophet, was on our side. We walked toward the final gate and found a man with a sign that read, "John Callaway and Patrick Mortensen."

Behind the sign was a tall man in his forties. He wore a short-sleeve shirt, loose black pants, and slippers, but not the kind we were used to, rather something you would see an actor wearing while he played Jesus.

"Welcome, sirs," he greeted us in broken English. "My name is Raj. I am the compound driver."

"Hello, Raj. I'm John, this is Patrick, and that's little Timothy. Thank you for picking us up. It's really so good to meet you, you have no idea." I wanted to jump on the guy and hug him.

He wobbled his head, tilting it from side to side.

We had been traveling over twenty hours, and we finally walked out the airport walls. No heat or humidity would deny me what I was feeling. Unconquerable. I was exhausted, both mentally and physically, but I was also victorious. I promised myself that I would reach out to the guys at Amazing Race and suggest Saudi Arabia for their next challenge.

I let the world around me sink in. The new smells, the line of taxi drivers who tried to negotiate a good price, the yellow lights coming from the poles, the fog that surrounded the light, the private chauffeur who carried luggage into a luxurious car while the arriving family relaxed, the two dark men in a traditional Indian dress, holding each other's pinkies.

After a short walk, we arrived at the compound bus. It had a big sticker across it that read, "Belleview Family Compound." There was only one other person aboard, who spoke into his earphones.

Is he speaking Arabic?

Patrick, Timothy and I sat in three different rows, so we would each get a window seat. It was showtime.

MARTIN

Hope y'all made it to your new home safely. How was your flight?

JOHN

Thanks for checking in on us. On our way home with our own private driver. Ha ha just kidding

MARTIN

Any chance you can send me pictures?

JOHN

Knew you missed me!

MARTIN

Not of you, you self-centered egomaniac. I meant of your new hometown! Smh

CHAPTER SEVEN

"Thank God for your safety," said our neighbor on the bus. *What do you mean by that? Did the embassy send you to make sure nothing bad happened to us?*

"Excuse me?" asked Patrick.

"Oh," said the stranger, "I take it you're new here. That's how we greet someone in the Middle East when they return from travels."

So you're not from the embassy, I thought we were special for a second.

"Then thank God for your safety too," said Patrick.

The other guy laughed and said, "You're supposed to say, 'May God keep you safe.'" He paused and continued, "So, anyway, are you American?"

"Yes, we are," Patrick and I replied simultaneously. Gosh, we sounded so gay. We might as well have worn shirts that read in capital letters, "I'm not gay, I'm SUPER gay." We had to learn to tone it down if we wanted to keep our identities hidden. Or maybe not, my gaydar couldn't make its mind up about our neighbor.

He smelled like he had just walked out of a candy shop, even though, in reality, he had been on a plane and then had walked through a sauna for an airport. He should've smelled like us. Nobody smelled that good unless they cared enough to carry a bottle of perfume, and it was my understanding that straight men didn't do that. Also, he traveled in a polo Ralph Lauren shirt, for goodness' sake. This wasn't Hollister or Zara. I know a gay man would stereotypically keep his buttons closed, but he was clearly the type to use fashion to express himself. Aside from his fashion choices, my instincts were telling me he wasn't gay. After all, what were the odds that the first person we met would be gay? It was Saudi Arabia, not San Francisco.

"Welcome," said the perhaps-gay-perhaps-not-gay man. "I'm Elie," which he pronounced *eh-lee*, as opposed to the American *e-lie*.

Just like that, we had made our first friend, a Lebanese expat who grew up in Jeddah.

Luck was on our side that night, because Elie knew Jeddah better than he did his hometown in Lebanon, and a knowledgeable friend was precisely the kind we needed.

"It's funny, when I go to Beirut, I feel like a tourist, but here, I'm more indigenous than a local."

You're not moving to a smaller house, I told myself, fearful that, if we stayed in Saudi longer than intended, Timothy, too, would feel like an alien in the US. I withdrew from the conversation and observed the city. I almost fell off my seat when I saw a Baskin Robbins. And then I saw another one. And then another one. Like a four year old overtaken by excitement, I screamed, "Burger King!" I lost count of the local burger joints we drove by.

Looks like the city was built by foreigners.

The streets reminded me of San Antonio. They were wide and clean, yet bumpy because of the many potholes. I even noticed a couple of women driving.

"Hey, I thought women aren't allowed to drive here."

Elie said, "That used to be the case, but they changed that law in 2017. Let me tell you, I definitely don't miss being the family driver."

It took me a minute to understand what he meant. I couldn't imagine chauffeuring my mother and sister whenever they wanted to go grocery shopping, get their nails done, or visit a friend. Not to mention San Antonio's horrible traffic on highway 281. If anything, I would understand if men were the ones demanding women's right to drive.

So many questions came to mind, but I didn't want to overwhelm Elie. I would save them for another day. Like, how do such laws come to change in this country? Do people protest? Do people vote? What else are women fighting for? Are they fighting at all? Are they allowed to? Do men fight for them?

Then, as if it was a sign, we drove by a roundabout with a large sculpture of a bronze iron fist as tall as a single-story building. It wasn't the first roundabout that had been decorated with an artistic sculpture, but it was certainly unique.

"I know I'll always choose paper," teased Timothy, using his hand to pretend he was playing rock, paper, scissors against the sculpture.

But seriously, what was the message behind this sculpture? It symbolizes strength, but whose strength were we talking about? The people's? The government's? The strong unity between the government and its people?

As if he had read my mind—because gay minds think alike— Elie said, "Wondering what's behind the roundabout?" I nodded. "It's the Prince Sultan Al Saud Palace. This street was named after him."

Maybe we didn't think alike after all, because he was talking about what was behind the roundabout. Literally.

Elie continued, "And he donated the fist sculpture to the city.

Other than being the crown prince, he was also the defense minister."

"Oh no," said Patrick, having a blond moment. "What happened?"

"Uh," said Elie, prolonging that syllable, "he died. Anyway, want to guess how many wives he had?"

We both shrugged, so Elie answered excitedly, "Fifteen. Not simultaneously, of course, but still! I can barely find one woman to marry. He had thirty-two children! Can you imagine having to remember their names?"

"Was he black?" joked Patrick.

"Whoa," said Elie, so surprised that his head accidentally hit the window behind him.

"Oh, you'll have to excuse him. He tends to make racist jokes, but believe me, he's not racist. It just means that he's feeling comfortable around you," I said.

Well, good job, Patrick. You may have just cost us our first friendship.

"No, I get it, I'm not racist either. In my culture, we still use the term 'slave' to refer to a black person. It's so bad."

How did we get here?

To lighten the mood, I continued, "But man, I thought they only married this many women in ancient times."

"Saudi Arabia is still in ancient times, my friend. We're still in the 1400s according to the Islamic calendar."

I laughed a little too hard for such a silly joke, desperately trying to give a good impression to Elie.

"So, back to the palace. I think it's empty now, as are so many of the palaces in this city. This one alone is dispersed over 100 acres, can you imagine? I remember, whenever we passed by here with my dad as kids, and if we wanted to mention the prince's name, we had to whisper. My dad believed that there were spies who listened through people's radios to check that they weren't talking about the prince. Of course, there was no evidence to prove that, but the older generation, God knows how they think, right?"

"Maybe they used the same technology that Facebook uses to listen to our conversations," said Timothy.

"Good point," said Elie. "That stuff is creepy. Like, I'll tell my friends that I'm craving KFC, and YouTube will play a KFC ad."

OK, so, people in the Middle East like KFC too?

It had been a mere fifteen minutes since I'd seen the city, and I was already under the impression that it was underrated. If the authorities opened abandoned palaces up to the public, as the French did with Louis the Fourteenth's, or the Indians with the Taj Mahal, tourists around the world would be flocking to visit this country. After all, who wouldn't want to time travel and still enjoy a Whopper?

Perhaps that was the answer to my question; the fist sculpture symbolized the strength of the government to keep the people under their control. Our government did the same thing, it just played by different rules, theirs preferred the iron fist, ours preferred the invisible hand. But then again, this was all my interpretation, based on the many prejudices I had to unlearn.

Raj parked the bus outside the compound gate and requested, "Sirs, what apartment numbers?"

"Oh, we don't know yet, we're staying in a furnished apartment until our stuff arrives," Patrick said.

"Okay, you're staying together?" investigated the compound employee.

"Yes," said Patrick, having learned from the school administrator that it was not uncommon for bachelor staff to share an apartment.

"Okay. The security at the gate will need your IDs."

Patrick jumped out of the bus. Poor thing, he looked terrified, and I could not blame him. The security guards were dressed in soldier-like uniforms. Some were sitting in a 4x4 beige military vehicle and were armed with AK-47s on their chest. The others were sitting in a small office. Patrick headed toward the window and handed our passports to the security guard. I could not make out the conversation, the guard picked up a landline phone and shortly thereafter returned our passports to Patrick and handed him a key.

Who are these guys supposedly protecting?

The gated community was like a city within a city.

Elie said, "That's a restaurant, we have parties here sometimes. Do you guys drink?" Before we could answer, he resumed, "Of course you do. Anyway, that's the bowling alley, there's a small cafeteria there too. There's a mini-market over there. That's the small pool, I don't think we will be passing by the big pool. As you can see, that's the tennis court, the basketball court, and iron-ically, next to them is Dunkin' Donuts. I love this compound. It's the best in the city. You know, in the beginning, it was only acces-sible to the staff of the school. Now ordinary non-Americans can live here too. Hehe, I'm just teasing."

The few women I spotted were wearing shorts and t-shirts. There were townhouses, villas, and apartments, but something about them was different from the typical American-style home. First, they were made with concrete, no bricks or combinations of basalt and portacabin materials. Also, the roofs were flat, which was a nice change from the dark, ugly gable roofs.

We had no idea the compound would be this luxurious. I would have rather imagined a small estate with a maximum of twenty homes, and maybe a community pool, if we were lucky. But perhaps, because the world outside the compound walls was limiting, and because they needed to give expats a strong reason to stay, the community was extraordinary.

The bus stopped in front of a two-story villa that would be our temporary accommodation. Elie offered, "Hey, let me give you my cell number and my home number. If you ever need anything, let me know, really. I'll be more than happy to take you around town some time."

Our first night was weird, to say the least. I had another nightmare wherein Timothy and Patrick secretly converted to Islam. When the call to prayer woke me up, it took me a minute to realize where I was and what was happening. I was sweating, like I'd just run a marathon (not that I'd ever know what that's really like). Timothy called for us from his room, and my bets were on Patrick was pretending to be asleep, so I'd have to check on our son.

"What's that, Dad?" asked Timothy, standing on his bed, his legs on either side of the bed frame.

"That's the call to prayer, son. Remember we heard one earlier at the airport. Think of them as church bells."

"What are church bells?" he asked.

We're definitely going to hell.

I invited Timothy to sleep in our bed, partly to console him, but mostly because I needed him around; I was just as scared as he was. What if I had another nightmare?

"I peed the bed, Dad. I'm sorry," confessed Timothy.

"What am I supposed to do for you," I said, trying to stop the next words from coming out of my mouth, "we're in a freakin' guesthouse. I have no idea where to get extra sheets from. Gosh, Timothy. Just go sleep downstairs on the couch or something. I don't know. You figure it out."

As I walked out of his bedroom, the image of my son scared of me, scared of being left alone, and it pushed me to turn back to him. He stood in the same position I'd left him, the room suddenly too big for his small body.

"I'm sorry, son," I said, my arms opening wide for a hug, "I'm sorry I said those things. This isn't your fault. Want to sleep in our bed? It's too big anyway."

With my arm over his shoulder, I walked him to our room.

My doubts were well founded; Patrick was awake. He lay down with the light of his smartphone shining against his face. "It's the only call to prayer that's in the middle of the night. The next one is at noon. Looks like we're going to have to get used to it."

Timothy went next to Patrick. Timid, and still shaken by the nightmare, I whispered, "Um … guys," and then found the courage to chirp, "can I sleep in the middle tonight?" I did not wait for them to respond or ask why I wanted to sleep in the middle.

I tucked myself tight next to Patrick, who whispered into my ear, "There's no way we're doing anything with Timothy in the bed with us."

Yeah, you can think that's what this is about.

Three hours and about a dozen kicks in the stomach from Timothy later, we woke up. The three of us cuddled and played in bed for a good half an hour, as we always did on the weekend. We then migrated to the living room downstairs to check out the channels on the TV. Half of them were in Arabic, the other half were American—Fox News, Fox Sports, MSNBC, HBO, etc., and we weren't paying $160 per month for the service. In fact, we weren't paying for it at all.

Patrick joined us with a brochure he had discovered in one of the kitchen drawers. It introduced the variety of services offered by the compound management. Free daily bus shuttle to different malls and supermarkets in the morning. Free home repair services from 9 o'clock to 5 o'clock, as needed, and until 10 o'clock at night for emergencies (I wouldn't have to touch another toilet flush valve or fix another sink). Tennis, football, swimming, and martial arts classes at an affordable price.

"What is this place? Heaven?" said Patrick.

As if those amenities were not enough, I then spotted a

barbershop, and as I pointed at its picture, I said, "It looks like we never need to leave the compound. It's almost too good to be true."

"Wait a minute. This isn't heaven. This is a Scientology camp!" joked Patrick.

"Seriously, though. Do you think that it's so bad outside the compound that they had to provide everything inside it?"

"It didn't seem so bad to me yesterday on our ride to the compound," said Timothy.

"What about the security guards and their AK-47s?" asked Patrick. "Whose side are they on?"

We silently stared at the TV screen. At 14 minutes past 12 o'clock, the second call to prayer filled the house. We listened closely, though we did not understand a word. We had no choice really. The *muadhan* (the one who performs the *adhan*, or the call to prayer) started with the famous, "Allahou akbar, Allahou akbar."

At first, I didn't mind the adhan, but then another adhan started from another mosque, and then another, and as the sheikhs sang asynchronously, I caught myself in a web of mixed feelings, forcing myself to shut off my own disrespectful thoughts.

Ugh, Gosh, if you're going to hire someone for the whole country to hear, at least make sure he has a nice voice. I can't believe this is the voice of someone encouraging people to go to the mosque. It makes me want to run in the opposite direction. I'm sure even God wants them to shut up. Do we really have to listen to this five times a day? Shush, John. Happy thoughts. Happy thoughts. Happy thoughts.

We couldn't hear the movie, apart from Kevin Hart, who was always loud. #shortmansyndrome

The adhans finally came to the actual sermons, which lasted forty-five minutes each. One muadhan's speech struck me as more passionate than the other two, loud and aggressive with occasional squeaks like he was crying. Even without a visual of him, I could tell some of his words were accompanied by spit.

Disgusted with myself for picturing him as an ugly, unintelligible man, I tried to talk about the movie. "Kevin Hart is so funny."

"I know we're supposed to respect other religions or whatever," said Timothy, and my heart raced with fear of what he might say next, "but this is really annoying. Like, what if I don't want to hear the prayer?"

What do I say? What do I say? What do I say?

"Timothy," said Patrick, his face firm, "why would you say something when you know it's disrespectful?"

"It's not like that! I have nothing against their religion. I just wish—"

"You don't wish nothing," said Patrick, which wasn't like his usual self. "We are the ones who came here, so it's our job to embrace their culture."

"That's not going to solve anything," I said, grabbing the remote to decrease the volume. "This is a safe space to talk about this. Right, Patrick?"

"Yes," he said. "This is a safe space, but—"

"I won't lie," I said, "I'm feeling conflicted too."

With Timothy's eyes focusing on me, a small smile on his face, as if relieved he wasn't alone, I confessed my own thoughts. "I've met a couple of Muslims before, and I never had a problem with them or what they believe in. And I'm really scared of discovering that I might actually be racist if I don't like the way they do certain things like their Friday prayer. And I mean people have died for criticizing their religion so having any kind of thought frightens me. But I can't shake the feeling that I just listened to something against my will."

Now Patrick was looking at me, too, which inspired me to keep going. "And I don't even know what they're saying, but it sounded hateful. It's nothing like the compassionate speeches I grew up with every Sunday at the Catholic church. Oh my God, I can't believe I'm saying these things out loud. I'll just shut up now."

"No," said Timothy. "Keep going."

"OK." Closing my eyes, I pictured myself alone in the room. "Imagine they're saying awful things about us, like Americans, or people who don't believe in their religion. And everyone who speaks their language hears this every Friday. They end up believing the words these leaders are saying. Like we believe the movies we watch, never questioning their factuality. The people behind 9/11 and Charlie Hebdo and—" I stuttered, searching my mind for other terrorist attacks. "I mean, what if they were listening to these leaders, week in, week out?"

I jumped off my seat at the sound of Patrick's mug being placed on the table forcefully. "Enough," shouted Patrick, as he stood up. "This is all theoretical, and instead of comforting Timothy, you're scaring him even further. If he becomes agoraphobic, we'll know who to blame!"

"Dad," said Timothy, holding onto his hand so he didn't leave the room, "Aren't you the one who always says that our thoughts and emotions are valid?"

Taking Timothy's hand in his, Patrick sat next to him and said, his voice calm this time, "Son. Yes, I do say that, but you also have to remember that differences scare us. We can't be jumping to conclusions like that. Who knows, maybe this man was angry with terrorists, and maybe he was begging his listeners to share love instead."

"Either way," said Timothy, looking at his hand, "Is it okay for me to not want to hear it?"

Patrick giggled briefly, "Yes, it's OK, and it's normal for you to have these thoughts. You're not the first, and you won't be the last. But remember—"

The doorbell rang out of the blue, surprising us all, even Koala, who jumped off her pillow bed.

Oh, my God, is there a bug in this house? Are they actually listening to our conversations? Are they here to take us because of what we just said?

CHAPTER EIGHT

It wasn't the feds, it was Elie, who came to wish us a "morning of goodness" and invited us to join him at the pool.

I expected Patrick to request a rain check, considering:

1. We'd have to look through our six pieces of luggage to find swimsuits.
2. It was 102.9°F outside, but no, when he heard that there was a restaurant by the pool, mister had FOMO, and I'm not talking Fear Of Missing Out, I mean Food Or Meet Ogre.

Personally, I was insulted by Elie's comment when he said, "I told you, man, this compound was built for Americans, and the whole world knows just how important food is for you guys."

It wasn't what he said, but how he said it, grinning, as he looked at Patrick's stomach, which was considerably larger than Elie's, a bachelor, who probably ate lots of junk food.

Gosh, are there body shamers even out here?

"Oh," said Elie as we made our way to the staircase, "and take this. The compound may have been built for you, but not this desert sun." As he threw the bottle of sunblock to Patrick, he winked at him, which was either a sign of arrogance or flirting, and I needed to figure out which ASAP.

I couldn't make up my mind about Elie. Picking us up on his way to the pool meant he was thoughtful. The previous night, he had opened up about using the term "slave" to refer to black people, which showed honesty. But he had three traits I couldn't stand: arrogance, flirting with my partner, and a poor sense of humor.

In the car, I asked him, "Hey, do you know what this morning's sermons were about? The speaker sounded so angry."

In a casual tone of voice, he said, "He's fed up with non-Muslims coming into the country. He's fed up with Muslims who befriend non-Muslims. He explained why it made perfect sense to kill non-Muslims." With no expression on his face, he tapped his fingers against the steering wheel to the beat of the music playing from the radio.

Patrick's eyebrows rose so high that the wrinkles on his forehead resembled those of a Shar Pei. And this was someone who took care of his skin in a desperate attempt to postpone the signs of aging as much as possible. His jaw dropped and his mouth remained open for a good thirty seconds. "Erm, is—is that normal? H—h—how do you feel about that?"

"The same way you do," said Elie, "I'm Christian."

"First of all, I thought Arabs were Muslim, and second of all, doesn't that scare you that they want to kill you?" I asked.

Elie laughed. I had no clue why. This was a serious matter.

"Guys, oh my God." Elie laughed some more, having a hard time containing himself. "You should've seen the look on your faces. I don't know what the sermon was about. He was just speaking passionately. Haven't you ever heard a priest speak passionately? What are you, Greek Orthodox?"

What are you, a jerk? Who jokes like that? I'm going to kill you if I have nightmares about this tonight!

I couldn't help comparing Elie with our friends back home. They would never have made such a joke. No American would, not after 9/11. Making a friend from a different culture came with its own challenges, but I couldn't be picky. It wasn't like I could go to a shooting range or a bar nearby, like I did in the US, simply because these kinds of places didn't exist in Saudi Arabia.

At the same time, I didn't want to be friends with fellow Americans only because the whole point of traveling to Saudi was to get out of our comfort zones, to expand our horizons, to face new challenges. But who would have thought that friendship could be so complicated? Especially one that was still at its conception.

Once we pulled up at the recreation center, I sped to the trunk of the car, the sunblock melting down my face and droplets of sweat racing down my spine. I grabbed a towel from my duffel bag and as I wiped my eyes, moisture filled the air, making it hard to breathe. If I didn't drink soon, I would suffer from a heatstroke.

We walked into the recreation center, and right above the door, there was a split air conditioner. My shirt instantly froze, and I did not want it to touch my back because the difference in temperature would be too painful. I scanned the area, looking for the cafeteria. There was a lounging area with two TVs, a ping pong table, and an office. No sign—or smell—of food.

I followed the guys out the other door. The scene in front of my eyes was nothing like the Saudi Arabia we saw in movies. I was getting used to the misrepresentation, and quite frankly, I was relieved to know Hollywood had gotten it wrong.

The pool was surrounded by artificial turf, a smart move, because no one wanted to play an actual game of The Floor Is Lava. Not even Timothy. At one corner was a small restaurant café that served cold drinks, food, and shisha. "Wake Me Up" by Avicii was playing on the loudspeaker. The lounge chairs were occupied by women in bikinis and men in—

"Speedos!" exclaimed Patrick, thrilled that many of his neighbors wore swim briefs.

"Oh, no, you've got to be kidding me," I taunted.

Taking his swimming trunks off, Patrick burst out, "Surprise!" as he revealed the Speedos he was wearing underneath.

"What? How? I took those out of your suitcase while we were still in San Antonio!"

"I know, now this suddenly feels a lot more like home."

"It does," said Timothy. "It shouldn't be so hard to make new friends. I'm so going to win this contest against Ayden." Heading toward the pool where a group of kids his age were hanging out, he shouted back, "Call me when my hamburger is ready!"

Patrick was right, it did feel a lot more like home, and Timothy's confidence boosted my mood tenfold. It almost distracted me from judging Timothy's arrogance for thinking hamburgers were on every menu around the world.

Elie wrapped one arm around my shoulder, and the other around Patrick's, before leading us to his group of bachelor friends. "John, Patrick, that's Mohammed, that's Talal, this is George, and this is Tony. It looks like our group of bachelors is expanding." It wasn't *mo-ha-med*, it was *m-hamad*, and it took me a minute to realize that.

Tony, who wore a big cross pendant around his neck, asked, "Your wives didn't come with you?"

Reluctantly, I replied, "My wife died when Timothy was born." It may have felt like home, but it was not home after all. At home, I could be who I wanted to be, but not here.

"Oh, I'm sorry to hear that," he said, his eyes meeting mine for a fraction of a second, before he mixed water and 7Up in a plastic cup. "Here, Elie." He stretched over and handed the cup to Elie as he browsed around the pool area.

"I never got married," said Patrick before going on and on about the benefits of sharing a house with a friend, rather than living alone, even though no one had asked him. "Besides," he said at the end of his long speech, "I also kinda get to see what it's like being a dad, and we'll see if it'll make me want to have one of my own one day. John and I have been friends forever, so maybe, if I play my cards right, he'll give me Timothy in exchange for Koala."

Patrick's attempt at being funny was a disguise to hide his fear.

"Okay," said Elie, addressing me and pulling me away from the group, until I couldn't hear Patrick anymore. "I want to show you something. I know it's nothing like whiskey or gin, but if you can stand this, you can officially be a part of the pack." He handed me the plastic cup that Tony had given him moments ago, accidentally spilling some on my fingers.

Wait, is he handing me alcohol? Isn't it illegal?

I sniffed it to check. "2016 Pinot Noir," said Elie.

"There's no way, it's transparent."

"Exactly, so why are you smelling it? Just drink, man!"

I took a small sip and could not help but gag. *What is this? Poison? 100% alcohol?* Disgusted, I gave the cup back to Elie, who laughed and said, "You remind me of my first time, but I was sixteen. Bro, this is called 'Ced.' It's moonshine that's made in dodgy rooms by workers from Thailand or Pakistan. This is how all expats are surviving in this country."

George, the one covered with a chest full of hair (come to think of it, all four of them were hirsute) said, "You mean this is how Filipinos in this country survive. Ninety percent of them are gay. And how else will they numb the pain if they're going to take it up the—"

Elie quickly jumped in to interrupt his friend, "Shall I pour you a glass?"

"No, please, not today, not ever. I think your friend George might need one." My blood boiled, smoke billowed out of my ears.

"I've already got one," he said calmly.

"Good, because how else will you numb the pain when I shove my foot up your—"

The Filipino waiter interrupted me, asking us if we were ready to place our order.

"Would you like a hot dog?" George asked the waiter with a look on his face I knew too well. All my life, I dealt with the likes of him, arrogant homophobes who took pride in their sickening, hateful jokes.

"John," said Patrick, "I think I saw Timothy waving your way. Want to go check on him?"

Timothy was clearly in another world, happy to be jumping in and out of the pool. I went along with Patrick, so I took my shirt off, walked toward the edge of the pool, and jumped feet in first.

"Oh," I said to Patrick. "Looks like Timothy is having a blast. This is so refreshing. Why don't you jump in?"

Soon as Patrick's head came out of the water, I whispered, "I wonder what Elie is telling his friends. I hope he's telling them to stop their stupid jokes."

"John," said Patrick, a serious look in his eyes, "I know how you feel, I'm just as angry as you are, but remember, we can't blow our identity. You have to learn to let those jokes go in one ear and out the other, like we've done all our lives."

Although Patrick was right, that kind of self-control would take plenty of practice.

"I mean," said Patrick, "I can only come up with so many distractions to help you calm down."

"I've got to admit," I said, moving my arms in the water, "I kinda like this distraction."

As the waiter placed the plates on our table fifteen minutes later, Elie called out our names as he waved for us to get out of the pool. I searched around to find Timothy, but he was already digging into his fries. My hands still damp, I grabbed my burger, taking a big bite, like an animal feasting on its prey. I couldn't help but moan at how delicious it was, or maybe it was an okay burger that tasted extra good because it was my first meal in over twelve hours.

Then, Elie apologized to me on his behalf, hoping that I wouldn't leave the pathetic pack.

We ended up finding a common topic of interest: alcohol. We agreed that the closest flavor to Ced was nail polish remover, and just as my mood turned jolly again, Elie said, "But listen, you're American."

Is this some kind of racist joke? What are you insinuating? Am I going to go from liking you, Elie, to hating you? First the lame joke about killing non-Muslims, then the homophobic friend, then a joke about Americans.

I took another bite of my burger, so he resumed, "You're American, so you can probably access some whiskey at your embassy."

Let's not hate you just yet. Man, this hamburger is good!

Though whiskey was not our first choice, it was better than Saudi champagne and the death in a bottle I had just tried.

"Really?" I asked, curious to know more.

"Yeah, sure. But before I tell you about that, tell me, man, what's up with Patrick's swimsuit?"

Patrick jumped into the conversation. "I've been dying for someone to ask me this. Are you ready for the answer?"

Say no! Say no!

Patrick puffed out his chest, and began to speak as if he were on stage. Thankfully, no one around us was paying attention.

"Have you seen *Home Alone 2*,

The scene where he jumps in the pool?

That's the problem with swim trunks,

They don't properly hold your junks."

Patrick put his hands in V shape around his private parts. Embarrassed, I focused on my hamburger.

"I don't like my eggs to be cage-free,

They're saved for one pair of eyes to see."

Elie interrupted Patrick at the perfect time, just before his poem got even cheesier. He took a few steps away from our spot so his friends couldn't hear him and signed for us to follow him. "Don't take it the wrong way if I misjudged. Are you two together?"

I was ready to answer, "No," plain and simple, but Patrick took a different route. "Are gay people not allowed in the pack?" he asked, probably because he didn't care if he'd potentially lost homophobic friends.

"No, man, my brother is gay."

He is? Then why would you allow another man to make homophobic jokes?

"But I think we will introduce a new no-Speedos rule. Hey, you want to hear a funny joke I always tell my brother?"

Depends, is it going to be the same type of joke George just told?

Elie continued, "Life without women would be a pain in the ass. Literally."

Okay, that one was funny.

There were some parts about Elie that I liked and others that I couldn't stand. Yes, he was kind, but he was also offensive. For all I knew, he would have laughed at George's joke if Patrick and I weren't there. And that meant he lacked integrity, which is a core American value. A feeling of homesickness washed over me. I didn't want to make new friends. I didn't want to feel judged. I didn't want to try and fit in. I wanted wine—lots of it.

Patrick asked, "So, you think it's okay for us to tell people we're gay?"

And there it was, as Elie answered Patrick's question, I saw him for who he was, a human being, and if I expected people to accept me with my flaws, I should reciprocate.

It was absolutely not okay to tell anyone outside the compound about our sexuality, especially not a local. Inside the compound walls, and at the school, however, it was okay, as long as we trusted the person.

I knew he was right when he advised us, "Oh, and unless you plan on getting fired or going to jail, you're going to have to tone it down, so next time someone makes a homophobic joke, you keep a poker face."

As I noticed Timothy having a blast with his new friends, jumping off the springboard again, and again, and again, I made my way to the water, which appeared mighty cool and refreshing but was as warm as piss.

Holding his arms against the edge of the pool, Patrick smiled at me, so I grabbed my phone with my wet hands and took a selfie. I made sure the two women tanning behind me were in the picture because our families wouldn't have believed us otherwise.

"I wish I'd brought my hat," said Patrick.

"Next time, we're not going anywhere, are we?" I said smiling, and I didn't know if that was a good thing or a bad thing, but despite the nerve-wrecking moments of that day, I was glad it was Elie at our door earlier and not the feds (yes, I did wish for a moment they'd come and take us back to the US).

"No, we're not," acknowledged my spouse, and we clinked our cups of Sprite together.

JOHN

Hey buddy, tried calling you. Let me know what time suits you. Really miss you

SCOTT

Yeah sorry

JOHN

In the meantime, feel free to send me your updates! And by that, I mean pls send me updates!!!!

CHAPTER NINE

I wasn't a social media kind of guy, but there was no other way to kill time while we waited for Elie to pick us up. "Listen," he said earlier when we were at the pool, "why don't I pick you up for dinner later? Everything is closed until 5 o'clock anyway, because it's Friday. I'll take you to the Saudi version of KFC. Be ready at 6, okay?"

Though I had had enough of Elie to last me at least a week, I was curious to try the local interpretation of an American product.

It was half past 6, and there still wasn't any sign of Elie. After I had caught up on my newsfeed, deleted useless emails, called my mother, and browsed the pictures we'd taken since our arrival, I was out of things to scroll through. Patrick and Timothy were still invested in their screens.

Patrick, as usual, was watching Shaun T's stories and videos. He admired the fitness guru who used social media platforms to shine. Shaun and Scott were his "#relationshipgoals," as he always said. Timothy was probably learning fun facts about Saudi Arabia.

I, on the other hand, was wishing I hadn't cut my nap short for the sake of punctuality. It was the kind of two-hour nap that felt like five minutes. And, though I was scared I'd have nightmares about a terrorist attack, thanks to our new friend Elie, I didn't have a single dream. But I did wake up covered in sweat.

"Do you think he forgot about us?" I asked, but both Patrick and Timothy ignored me. I stared at Patrick, hoping that, if I looked long enough, he would notice I was burning a hole in his head. I asked again, "Hey, Pat, do you think Elie forgot about us?"

"Huh?" he said, without looking away from his screen. He was ignoring me again. I wanted to snatch the phone out of his hand, but that would lead to an argument, and I was too hungry for one of those. Besides, I knew what he was going to say, and I wouldn't know how to fight back. "It's not because you're done using your phone that we now have to put ours down too."

Yes, but then don't be surprised when you tell Timothy it's bedtime and he ignores you.

I picked up our corded landline phone and dialed Elie's extension. After a few attempts, he finally picked up. "Hey, John, what's up, *habibi*?"

"Excuse me?"

Why do I have a feeling he just called me a faggot?

"*Habibi.* It means 'my dear one,' but you can literally call anyone habibi, even a stranger you're mad at for driving slow on the left lane."

That's right, you better not call me a faggot. You can keep your Arabic pet names for Patrick. Man, I'm getting hangry.

"I was just calling to touch base, and see what time we were going to head out, since it's half 6 already."

"You're now in the Middle East. When someone says 6 o'clock, they usually mean 7 or half 7."

Before ending our brief chat, Elie asked what I was wearing, and though I anticipated another one of his sick jokes, I answered, sounding like Jake from StateFarm, "Erm, khakis."

"OK, great, and what about Patrick?"

"He's wearing Bermuda shorts."

"Oh." The sound of disappointment was clear in his voice. "That's not good. Ask him to change into pants."

"Excuse me?" *This has to be some kind of fetish. Maybe it's time to tell Elie things aren't going to work out between us.*

"Well, if men wear something above knee-level, they might not allow him into a restaurant. Or anywhere else for that matter. I'm just looking out for you, bro."

Okay, maybe I keep misjudging Elie. I haven't had to make a new friend in a long time. I already know all my friends' flaws. I love those guys to pieces. I can't recreate that anymore, not at this age.

Elie showed up thirty minutes after our phone call, at 7 o'clock, right on time, according to his watch. He rolled his window down to greet us. "Evening of goodness."

"I'm guessing the right response is evening of light," said Patrick.

"That's right!"

Flashbacks of this morning raced in my mind and the mixed feelings toward Elie left me conflicted. There wasn't a doubt that he was kind and serviceable, but he was insensitive. Or maybe he just didn't know any better. Like Patrick, and his racist jokes.

One thing that wasn't up for debate was that he was charming. He was dressed in a turquoise short-sleeved shirt, which brought out his eyes, even though they were dark. Again, the first few buttons of his top were undone, proudly showing off his chest hair, which I really wanted to pluck with a pair of tweezers. I came to the conclusion that his self-care routine was the reason for his tardiness. When we met him, there were whiskers going in all directions, but not that night, which, if I were to guess, meant he did a beard mask, brushed it, and then moisturized it with oil. And if I were to bet, I'd say his brother taught him how to do it.

Elie pointed at Patrick. "What's that?"

I said, "That's Patrick."

"Ha ha! What's that in Patrick's hands?"

"Oh, *that*. It's a booster seat. Haven't you seen one before?"

Elie shook his head, so I explained, "It's for big babies like Patrick to sit in when they're on the road."

Elie laughed and replied, "You Americans and your safety measures. Okay. It's not going to ruin the seat on my Tahoe, is it? Because you can't buy an SUV anymore if you're a bachelor expat."

Though I thought it was some kind of incentive to get married and pop babies like rabbits (because why else would you ban expats with less than five family members from buying SUVs with seven seats or more), that rule was targeted at residents who bought SUVs and used them for unofficial purposes. Trucks, which could only seat five people, were included, because they were considered commercial vehicles.

It was a smart, iron fist move, but for a Texan like me, it was devastating news, and when I shared my perspective, Elie said, "You sheikh, without devastating, without watermelon." I had no idea what he meant, so I stayed silent just in case.

"I can't believe I'm saying this," said Timothy, his eyes closed, "but I'm actually happy I just saw a Chuck E. Cheese." Then, raising the palm of his hand in my direction, he said, "Please, don't judge."

A cackle escaped me as I recognized Patrick's love for drama in Timothy. "Don't worry, son. No one's judging here. In fact, I get why you feel this way."

Timothy opened his right eye, as if to check for sarcasm in my face.

Timothy didn't like that place or that obnoxious mouse, but it reminded him of home and gave him hope that, if they had a Chuck E. Cheese, maybe they'd also have a House of Air or a Six Flags. If that was the case, we wouldn't have to stay inside the compound all the time, as if we were protecting ourselves from a migrating disease. That would be crazy, though, if one day we had to stay inside the compound because of some disease that's airborne.

The further we drove, the more familiar names we saw; Holiday Inn, Starbucks, Movenpick Hotel, Dunkin' Donuts, Honda, just to mention a few. And to think that we were afraid we wouldn't find deodorant or keto coffee, to think that there was a limit to the American influence on the world.

We drove down the main highway, where people honked their horns more than I was used to. Even though it was evening, all the shops were still open and every store added extra light to the city, with big billboards that showed off their names. We could see through the glass of tourist offices, print shops, pizzerias, barbershops, and occasionally, we would see a woman shopping at a bakery. Flower shops and car rental shops looked abandoned.

Inside stores that sold traditional clothing, the mannequins dressed in thobes looked lonely. The female mannequins didn't have heads. There were employees standing outside the stores, waiting for their next customer. Drive-thrus were only at American fast-food chains, it seemed. The movement of people from their cars to the stores made the city vibrant. There was a joy in going to a place in person rather than ordering it at the click of a button, at home, behind a screen.

"Everyone's trying to run their errands before shops close at prayer time," said Elie.

"What's that?" I asked Elie, referring to a store behind opaque glass.

"That's a lingerie store. Men aren't allowed. Just like they're not allowed in women's hair salons, and vice versa."

"What about the hair salon in our compound?" asked Patrick, who preferred female barbers.

"What do you think?" asked Elie.

"I think the world inside the compound walls plays by different rules," said Patrick.

"That's right!"

Many of these shops were on the ground floor of a residential building. These people had no other choice than to live on such noisy property. One particular building was so old and dirty, I first thought it had been painted brown. Some of the windows were broken and replaced with cardboard. Through another, a lightbulb hung from the ceiling, putting the dull white walls of that apartment in the limelight.

Can it be? Poor Saudi families? It almost feels like an oxymoron. Or are these the houses of refugees or other sorts of immigrants?

Elie explained, "People think Saudi Arabia is all rich, but there is a lot of poverty here. The streets are a lot cleaner now though. Traffic lights used to be invaded by beggars, many of them kids. You know, you would see them get off a bus and one kid would occupy this traffic light as his territory and his sister, or father, or mother would get another traffic light. And if you ever tried to talk to them, they would immediately receive a phone call on their old Nokia phone. They would hang up and get away from you. And these people are usually from Afghanistan and those countries. I don't know how the crown prince did it, but he did a really good job cleaning up the streets. He managed to get rid of all those annoying kids who try to sell you stuff on the sidewalk."

Elie, Patrick, and I simultaneously took a few deep breaths in and out as we allowed the sadness to sink in.

"Hey, Elie," said Patrick, pointing at a store we'd passed, "any chance we can go to that currency exchange office? I need to convert my dollars."

"Of course, habibi," said Elie, as he turned right. "Anything for the American dollar."

Like the master of a maze, Elie drove us back to that shop, finding a parking spot in front of it. When Patrick left the car, I endeavored to lighten the mood. "I've noticed that the city is quite Americanized. It's almost like Saudis love Starbucks more than we do. I didn't know that was possible."

"Oh, it's definitely possible. What *I* didn't know was possible was how complicated coffee could be." Doing an imitation that looked like Paris Hilton to me, Elie said, "Skinny, 37% fat, half-sweet, half-caff, triple shot, soy latte at 90 degrees. Or whatever that is in Fahrenheit. May Allah have mercy on your grandfathers, who had to grind their coffee manually."

This was the kind of moment with Elie that I needed to remember; our similarities could outshine our differences.

"I agree, it's so overrated," I said. What is it that made people feel so cool when they walked out of Starbucks? And why was this a global phenomenon?

Of course, Patrick came back to the car holding four drinks, all from Starbucks, and as he explained what each one was, he sounded exactly like Elie's imitation. Elie, Timothy, and I burst out laughing.

"What's so funny?" asked Patrick.

"Inside joke, Daddy."

Elie parked in front of a double-story building. Next to the restaurant's name, Al Baik, was the logo, a white chick—an actual chick, not the "sexist" way to call a woman—that wore a bowtie and a cowboy hat. Why wasn't it wearing the national white dress that the airport employees were wearing? Why was the chick smiling?

"It looks like they closed for prayer," said Elie, because the curtains were down and the lights inside were dim. "Normally, they will allow you in a restaurant if prayer has already started but will only serve you after they have reopened. But the guys know me here, so they won't make us wait."

"Did you work here?" asked Timothy.

Elie gasped and put his right hand on his chest as if he was insulted by Timothy's question. "Me? Work *here*? Of course not. They know me because I eat here on the regular."

"Oh, but why do they close during prayer time?"

"Because you're supposed to go to the nearest mosque and pray."

"Then let's go to the nearest mosque and pray," said Timothy, but no one answered him.

There were so many aspects of that sentence that bothered me. Something told me it had to do with my being an American, and so valuing freedom. There was no point in raising a debate, since Elie was neither Saudi nor Muslim. Rules were rules, and I had to learn to follow them, whether they made sense to me or not. Also, if I distracted Elie any longer, Patrick was going to eat me alive.

Outside the restaurant, there was a long line. Not a lot of people were heading to a mosque.

Elie must have noticed my confusion, as he told me, "There used to be something called the Islamic Police, or the Committee for Promotion of Virtue and Prevention of Vice. And if they caught you outside during prayer time, they would load you into a bus and force you to go to a mosque."

"But like," said Timothy, "if these police officers were out catching people for not praying, then when did they pray?"

"Good point, T. I have no clue. Anyway, it happened to me once when I was a teenager. I was the only Christian guy with my friends, and we were waiting for the driver to pick us up and take us home. Meanwhile, these two sheikhs walked out of a white van, and behind them was a policeman who walked out of his car. Anyway, they asked us for our ID, and he totally misread my name, because it was written in Arabic. I think he read it ee-lee. And mind you, he read on my ID that I was 'non-Muslim.' So he asked us why we weren't at the mosque, and I think my friends made up some stupid excuse. He told us to get in the van. I tried to tell him I wasn't Muslim, and I didn't know the rituals. He said to do as my friends did. So we jumped into the back of the van where there were other guys. Once we got to the closest mosque, I just copied my friends, first washing my arms and feet, and then, inside the mosque, I kneeled and moved my head around as they did."

"Sounds like a nightmare," said Timothy, which was exactly my thought.

"It was fine. I was fine. My mom, though, she never let them talk her into anything. You see, back in the day, if a woman's abaya was higher than ankle level, they would ask her to go home and wear a longer abaya. Or if she went to the mall with her hair uncovered, they ordered her to cover her hair. So one time, my mom was walking around the mall, and she already caught every-one's attention, regardless of the length of her abaya, because she was blonde. So, same thing, a group of sheikhs approached her with policemen standing behind them, and they started telling her about how she was going to hell and stuff. And she just shouted at them, telling them that they should be ashamed of themselves for looking at women, that they should find more honorable jobs. And guess what? It worked! They left her alone!"

"I love your mom!" said Patrick.

"I love her too," said Elie, "and here's the best part. My dad, when he saw the sheikhs and the police approaching my mom, he told her he would be waiting for her in the car, and he ran away!"

While Timothy, Elie and I laughed our butts off, Patrick did that thing where, instead of laughing, he said, "That is hilarious." *If it really is, how come you're not laughing?*

"Man, I'm glad times have changed," concluded Elie. "This

way, guys. Welcome to the one and only, Albaik." Elie showed us to a door with a sign that read "Singles Section."

Since we were unaccompanied by women, we couldn't access the Families Section, and unless I made female friends, I never would.

Though there was a long queue outside, the employee let us in, thanks to Elie's loyalty. In his honor, they should launch a loyalty card, "Ten Access Vouchers If You Come During Prayer Time."

Patrick and I were further surprised when we entered the dining area. There was a spacious counter with four different cashiers. Above them were four screens that displayed the menu in Arabic and English, the calorie count, a picture of every meal, and home delivery information. All the employees behind the counter wore a hair net. I thought of taking a picture, uploading it onto Twitter, and tagging KFC, with the caption, "Here, you might want to learn a thing or two from the Saudis."

When Patrick reached into his pocket to pay for our bill, Elie put his hand on Patrick's and said, "No, *wallah*."

"Yes, wallah," said Patrick.

Elie insisted, "I swore to God first." Then, whispering, he continued, "In the Muslim religion, if you swear and you don't do it, you have to fast for three days."

"But you're not even Muslim," said Patrick.

"Just allow me, please," insisted Elie again.

As we waited for our food to arrive, Elie told us a few anecdotes. "This is my favorite Albaik branch, because I have so many memories here. I had my first date ever here. In the Families Section, at least. And my first break up. You have to understand that this restaurant is iconic for everyone who grew up here. All families eat here at least once a week, from the richest of the rich, to the poorest of the poor. It's probably the only place in Saudi where nationality doesn't matter. I remember

93

clearly, I used to love opening the fridge the next day and eating leftover bread with the garlic dip. I would invite my neighboring friends, and we would feast on it. And anyone who leaves the country will tell you they miss this place the most. You know, Anthony Bourdain ate here. That was before he—" Elie motioned his hand in front of his neck, as if to say "cutting one's throat."

He continued, "A Saudi prince offered the owner a partnership, but the owner refused, so the Saudi prince banned the opening of Al Baik all around Saudi. So, you'll only find it in Jeddah. We've been blessed with a great privilege, my friends."

"Again," I said, "a classic example of the iron fist, isn't it?"

Elie tilted his head sideways and lifted his hands. By now, I knew exactly what that meant.

Maybe Timothy would have his first date here one day.

Less than fifteen minutes later, our food arrived in aluminium containers that were covered with a white piece of cardboard with the white chick stamped on top, the smile still on its face. *What are you smiling at? That's probably your mother in there!*

"Make sure you try this garlic dip. It's divine," said Elie.

At the rate we were eating, there was no chance we were going to leave anything. After each bite, Patrick, Timothy, and I nodded our heads in approval. The crust was the perfect thickness. It was crunchy and not greasy. The meat was so moist. Either the Saudis made better chicken wings than we did, or we were so hungry that this meal tasted like the closest thing to heaven. For whatever reason, the chick was smiling, and I was definitely smiling back.

Elie must have thought we were savages who ate without taking a breath between bites. He taught us, "This is how you do it, you take the bread, and snatch a small piece. You use that to break the chicken apart, or you'll burn your fingers." Fingers? Who was using fingers? I held either side of the chicken and bit right into it. There was no time to waste. Savages, we were.

"You hold that and take a fry and dip them all in the garlic sauce. And then you can thank me."

Fine. Fine. I'll try it your way. Bread. Chicken. Fry. Garlic.

"Oh, my God! You're right! Patrick, try it the way Elie said."

Patrick's container was already empty. Timothy had finished his sandwich, too, and he was already invested in his gaming device. To avoid Patrick asking to have some of my meal, I dived back into my container. It was every man for himself.

Patrick looked out the window and noted, "Whoa, look how many people are standing outside."

Yeah, right, if this is your way of trying to get me distracted so you can steal some of my food, it's not going to work!

But he was right, there must have been ten times as many people as there were when we'd first arrived, and it was nearing 8 o'clock.

"You call this late?" asked Elie, "People will eat at 2 in the morning here. Wait until Ramadan arrives. It's my favorite time of the year, because people wake up at 4 to eat before they begin their fast."

"But you're not even Muslim," said Patrick, for the second time that night.

"Trust me, bro, when Ramadan comes, everyone's Muslim. It's a month of giving and selflessness. Just before it's time to break fast, you'll see the youth giving out water and dates on traffic lights. Mothers will stand for hours in the kitchen to prepare the most delicious meals. Families and friends gather around the dinner table. After supper, everyone in the country sits in front of the TV to watch the best comedy, *Tash Ma Tash*. And then, once we've rested and had a cup of Turkish coffee or tea, we go to malls and walk around, sometimes until 3 in the morning, just in time for the last meal before fasting again. You wait and see. There's a completely different vibe in Ramadan."

"Do you fast during Lent?" Patrick asked Elie.

"Are you kidding? And cut meat for forty days? No way, man. I'm a better Muslim than a Christian."

Did I say this guy has a poor sense of humor? Scratch that, this guy is hilarious.

"Are you guys free for a ride around town?"

"Let's do it!" Patrick and I said simultaneously.

"Actually," said Timothy, "let me check my calendar."

Haha, you got me for a second.

Although it started on shaky grounds, the night was about to get more impressive and more impressionable.

CHAPTER TEN

T here it was, the city's icon, the King Fahd Fountain. It shot water up 984 feet in the sky, the world's tallest fountain— it was even taller than the Eiffel Tower.

What a beauty! It looks like it touches the sky.

Elie suggested, "Why don't you guys go down while I find a parking spot?"

The corniche was jam-packed; there were families picnicking, children rollerblading, men and women jogging in their abayas. Food trucks were busy catering buttered corn, ice cream, popcorn, and cotton candy. Were we so different after all?

"I love the smell of the ocean," said Patrick as he took a deep breath in to appreciate the environment around him.

"Yeah, reminds me of our summer vacations at South Padre Island. It's going to take a while to get accustomed to everything, but for the most part, it looks like we have more in common than we were taught to believe."

Meanwhile, Timothy pulled at my shirt relentlessly, repeating, "Dad, Papa," even though I had asked him to wait until I was done talking.

"What is it, Timothy," I said, my tone more aggressive than intended. "What do you want?"

"Do you think I can ride the camel over there? I just saw another kid ride it."

"Definitely, kiddo," said Patrick. "Let's just wait for Mr. Elie, so he can help us talk with the camel's owner," which was a wise choice because for people with glowing white skin like ours, the ride would've cost double.

When Elie addressed the camel's owner, he started with, "Mohammad," before speaking in their native tongue. "OK, bro, I was able to bring the price down to 20 riyals."

"Cool, thanks, man," said Patrick as he reached into his pocket for money. "You guys seemed to hit it off. Do you know him?"

"No."

"Didn't you call him Mohammad?" asked Patrick.

"I did. Here, you refer to a stranger as 'Mohammad.'"

"I can't imagine calling strangers 'Jesus' in the US," said Patrick. "It definitely would work in Latin America, though, because every other guy's name is Jesús."

Spoken like a true gringo.

Elie laughed at Patrick's joke and confessed that, "At first, the guy said he was willing to let Timothy ride for free if I found him a beautiful American bride. His way of persuading me was by bragging about his five camels, and he claims he has three happy wives. He says he's confident he can please an American lady, who would be blessed to be the fourth, hence the best. Especially if she was a real American, white like you."

While the camel was sitting down, the owner pointed to Timothy and signaled for him to sit on its dromedary, which was where a cloth had been placed. Timothy, who was both scared and excited, followed the man's instructions. The large animal stood on its back legs, carrying Timothy's body forward. Our brave son let out an anxious giggle as he tried to grip on to the animal as best as he could.

Patrick, who was holding his phone up to take a picture, said, "Yeehaw, camel boy!" That was when the camel released a big pile of excrement that had a nauseating smell.

When the five minute ride was over, the camel slowly sat down, bending the lower half of its front legs and then the lower half of its back legs, causing Timothy to struggle to stay on its back—again. Then, with skin around its mouth jiggling, it finally slid its tongue out. "It looks like the slime you like to play with," Patrick teased our son, who was disgusted.

"Would you like to try it some time?" asked Elie.

"What? Riding the camel? No, I'm fine." Patrick replied.

"Not riding it, eating it. Don't worry, you can eat the tongue too."

Patrick pretended to gag, then looking at me, he said, "Can you imagine going back to San Antonio and opening a Kentucky Fried Camel?" He took a few steps forward until he was eye-to-eye with the camel that Timothy had just ridden. "Yeah, there's no way I'm trying this."

Elie drove along the corniche, which gave us the chance to observe the beautiful mansions. Pointing to a particular one, he turned to us before hitting the brakes at a roundabout. "It's a duplicate of the castle of Versailles. I don't know if it's true, but they say it's owned by the lawyer of someone in the royal family. Not bad, huh?"

"Not bad at all," murmured Patrick, before he commented, "People seem to be nocturnal here."

"Oh, yeah, Arabs in general are. People stay out until 2 in the morning."

"Look, Dad!" said Timothy, referring to a roundabout that displayed a wave sculpture.

"I never would have thought Saudi Arabia to be a country that appreciates art," I said.

"It depends on the kind of art. For me, I work in the advertising industry, and believe me when I tell you we're very limited in the creations we're allowed to make. You would think it would make our work easier, but it makes it much harder."

"I can only imagine," said Patrick.

"But there's an up-and-coming generation of young artists making a splash. They're studying abroad and pumping their creativity into the country. We never had exhibitions or comedy clubs or book clubs until very recently."

"It must be interesting to have watched the country change," said Patrick.

"I guess so." Elie turned right at another roundabout that displayed a carpet that seemed to fly in the air while carrying a car.

I stared at the piece of art. "There definitely is something magical about this city. What is necessary to change a person is to change his awareness of himself—Abraham H. Maslow."

"What does that mean, Papa?"

"It means that our perceptions and prejudices can be wrong. We've been living in an era where everything is about race. But what is race, really? It seems to me that there are so many fights being fought in the world because people focus on differences. And then there's a bunch of people who try to counteract it, try to change the status quo, but they don't realize that the damage has already been done, and there is no going back. And we never really understood what all this meant, because we were lucky enough to be born the way we were. Boy, how did I get here? Sorry for ranting."

Elie said, "No, I totally understand what you're saying. History is always written by the winners."

"And the winners work in Hollywood," Patrick added.

Timothy surprised us all when he summarized it better than all of us, "Saudi Lives Matter!"

"They prefer the term 'ISIS' over here." Elie had a smile on his face.

Timothy didn't understand Elie's joke. "Oh, I'm sorry," and with a passionate voice, he raised his fist and said, "ISIS lives matter!"

I hope with all my heart that you don't repeat this when we call your grandparents.

> **JOHN**
> What's it like having a woman on top?

> **MARIANA**
> Bro, Johanna is GOOD! Never thought I'd like saying her name so much

> **JOHN**
> Great, I feel so much better -_- You do remember she was my archnemesis, right?!

> **MARIANA**
> What are you sad about? It's not like you have experience being on top LOL

> **JOHN**
> Remind me to never confide a secret in you 😶

> **MARIANA**
> Haha! How's your new life in God knows where?

> **JOHN**
> Saudi Arabia, look it up sometimes. Or actually, don't

CHAPTER ELEVEN

"**G**ood morning, Raj, is this the bus that goes to the mall?"
"Yes, sir." This was not the Texan "sir" I was used to; it sounded more like "sahr."

We hopped on the bus and made our way to the vacant seats at the back. The engine shook the bus, causing my body to vibrate like a buzzing mobile phone. At least Raj had successfully replaced the unpleasant, musty smell of the bus with sandalwood.

When someone made eye contact with me, I nodded as a way of greeting them. I remembered the days we went on the school bus, but instead of cliques that separated the nerds from the jocks, ethnicity was the common denominator. The Westerners sat on one side, Arabs on another, Eastern Europeans on yet another. And, alone, in the back, there were the Callaways. Or, should I say, the Mortensen and Callaways. Lonely and isolated, I empathized with Rosa Parks—not that I was heroic or anything, but I did wonder if anyone knew about our big little secret.

Patrick had picked out a paper that listed the bus schedule. "Today," he said, "we're going to the Mall of Arabia. It says here that's where Panda Supermarket is."

"We're going to buy a panda?" asked Timothy with sarcasm. Coincidentally, that was when everyone on the bus fell silent for a few seconds, and the voices in my head made me believe they thought my boy was stupid. A sudden fear washed over me, the fear of being judged, and Timothy was to blame for it. So to fix it, I had to discipline him.

Is it just me or are these tiny air vents making it hard to breathe?

"What do you think?" I asked Timothy. "That we're going to be some kind of panda kings? That they'll create a docuseries about us and portray us as crazy people? That's just absurd!"

Everyone was looking at me, even Raj through his rear-view mirror.

I wasn't always a bad dad, but according to my therapist, sudden outbursts of rage were common among people struggling with depression. Just before I started my sabbatical, Julio was teaching me to recognize and cope with triggers, but I hadn't practiced; I should've known the extreme heat, the strong smell, the tight space would overwhelm me.

"Calm down, John," said Patrick. "Who got on your bad side this morning?"

"Sorry, Timothy, I don't know what got into me."

Timothy nodded, without saying a word, and I couldn't blame him, it was starting to sound like a script I repeated every time I did or said something wrong.

I'm sorry I humiliated you, buddy. I hope I don't tame your great personality when I react like this. Don't ever stop asking questions. Don't let anyone steal your sense of curiosity away from you, not even me. Please, because if you do, then I have failed as a father.

"Hey, guys, check this out," said Patrick as he held his phone so Timothy and I could see the screen.

Fast & Furious 8 Starring Up-And-Coming Bus Racer, Raj.

In a picture with the cast of the movie series, Patrick added an Indian-looking man whose only common trait with Raj was the mustache. He wasn't good at photo editing, but he *was* good at making us laugh when we needed it the most.

Patrick was right, though; Raj was driving way too fast, and other drivers honked at him for passing them on the right lane. In the row before ours, an infant sucked on his pacifier, his head on his mother's shoulder, staring at me as he fought to stay awake.

What if Raj hits the brakes too hard? What will happen to this baby? What will happen to my baby? Oh God, oh God, this was a mistake, how can we be such irresponsible parents?

A billboard showed an endless road in the middle of the desert and its slogan was "Own Your Path." Ironically, Raj was stuck at a roundabout and, although priority was his, cars drove past him. Raj blocked the road, resulting in at least ten cars lining up behind us.

"It's almost as if they take it literally," I joked, referring to the ad. Patrick let out a brief laugh, as if he didn't understand the joke and wasn't interested enough to ask.

Among the cars lined up behind us, one driver reversed, colliding with the car behind him. The two drivers exited their cars and verified whether there was damage. One of them seemed to be Timothy's age. They then had a brief discussion, shook hands, and returned to their cars.

"I'll be right back," I said to Patrick.

"Where are you going?"

I moved to the single passenger seat behind Raj. "Hey Raj, did you notice the accident that happened behind us?"

"Yes, sir," he said.

"One of the drivers looks so young. Do you think he has a driver's license?"

"I don't think so. But maybe his mom needs to go some-where, so he is taking her there."

Hello, it's supposed to be the other way around!

"What if the police stop them?" I asked, still trying to understand how things worked.

"He can tell them he's only driving in his neighborhood, and when they see his mom is with him, they will not tell him anything."

"Okay, but he hit the other man's car. Aren't they going to report it?"

Raj laughed. "No need."

"What do you mean?"

"Police will take a long time to come, maybe one hour, maybe more. The drivers don't want to wait. Maybe the man is going to work."

"He's still on his way to work at 10 o'clock?"

Raj laughed again. "Yes, and then he will eat breakfast in the office and go home when it's *salat al duhur*, noon prayer."

"One more question, so if that kid hit our bus instead, how would you have dealt with it?"

He tilted his head and raised his hands, the same way Elie had the previous night. "Sir, he is Saudi, and I am from India."

"So? What does that have to do with anything?"

Before Raj answered, the passenger behind me jumped into the conversation. "What he's trying to say is there are different rules for different nationalities. Saudis are at the top of the ladder, and so, the law applies differently to them. You're American, right?"

I nodded.

The passenger continued, "You're right after the Saudis."

I didn't say anything, as it was a lot to process, so I went back to my seat and continued observing the city. Actually, I wasn't focusing on anything, my thoughts running in all different directions. I was raised to follow rules and systems.

How can I integrate here? This isn't what I signed up for. Is it? Is Timothy going to learn that someone is more or less valuable because

NADIA SAKKAL

of the passport they own? What if he starts treating others with less respect and dignity just because of the color of their skin? What if he learns that he can get away with breaking the rules?

Kids were playing soccer in flip flops on an empty lot. I thought that sort of thing only happened in Africa. Or in Latin America. Not in a rich country like Saudi Arabia.

"Look, Dad!" I couldn't make out what Timothy was pointing at.

I need to remind Patrick not to answer when Timothy calls out "Dad."

"You missed it," he said, "I just saw a woman driving!"

"Yeah," said Patrick, "I saw one earlier, too, but I guess I forgot that it was something special."

"I wish I took a picture, she would so go viral on my TikTok."

The scene took me back to the summer our parents took us to Cancun and I saw a topless woman for the first time. "Boobs!" I shouted, which made Isabelle laugh hysterically. I wondered which one would get more views, Timothy's picture of a woman covered from head to toe behind the wheel or a topless woman at the beach.

At one point on the ride, there was a bus driving next to ours, and it was occupied with East Asian laborers in uniforms. They reminded me of the airport employees who carried passengers' luggage. The ones on the bus had an unforgettable expression on their faces, one that reminded me of the pictures I once saw at the Holocaust Memorial Museum of San Antonio. Behind that bus was a man in a Ferrari. He held a phone to his ear, and his smile stretched wide, as if he was without a worry in the world. I asked myself which one would get more views, the bus with the sad, poor laborers or the rich man in his luxurious car.

There was a garbage man cleaning up the sidewalks and a good Samaritan pulled up next to him, handing him a box of biscuits and a bottle of water. There were many stray dogs and cats that seemed to prowl around in search of food.

The city had so many stories to tell, stories that made mine relatively irrelevant.

Be thankful for your circumstances. Lots of people have it worse than you do. You can always go back and visit your friends. Not everyone has that option.

Just as I encouraged myself with positive thoughts, I heard the sound of vomit coming from behind me. I turned around, as did everyone else, and saw it was Timothy. "Oh, no," I said. "What's wrong, Timothy? Are you okay?"

He pointed toward something, a butcher shop that displayed dead animals in its windows. The head of a cow with its tongue sticking out hung from the ceiling outside the shop.

At least everyone on the bus knew we weren't flesh-eating monsters.

The vomit landed on the floor. "It's OK," I said. "We will figure out a way to clean this up." Raj took peeked at us while keeping an eye on the road. "Sorry, Raj, we will clean this up."

"Okay, okay," he said, picking up a box of tissues, waving it in the air for me to grab.

The mother with the infant in her lap handed Timothy a box of wipes. I grabbed the trash can, and we managed to do a quick clean up. Once Timothy had calmed down, Patrick said, "I guess you're a vegetarian now."

"Yeah, I guess you are too," said Timothy. Patrick was not smiling anymore.

Mostly made up of glass, the Mall of Arabia looked more like a university than a mall. The main entrance sat at the top of a long stairway, surrounded by greenery. On the right side, a beige wall read "Mall of Arabia" and underneath it, "HyperPanda" both in English and Arabic.

"Still want to buy a panda?" I asked Timothy to see if he was feeling better after his incident.

He smiled at me and shook his head. "No way!"

Raj followed the signs to the underground parking lot near Gate B. As everyone exited the bus, he reminded us all, "Half 11, you come back here, okay?"

By the time Patrick, Timothy, and I had hopped off the bus, all our neighbors had vanished. As we walked through the sliding doors, strong waves of cold air washed over our heads. A security guard standing next to the door addressed Patrick, who could not make out what he was saying.

Confused, Patrick explained, "I'm sorry, I don't speak Arabic."

The Saudi man said, "*Amreeky?*"

I whispered in Patrick's ear, "I think he wants to know if you're American."

Patrick bobbed his head as if to say. "Yes, do you like Americans?" The employee pointed to Patrick's shorts, which were above knee level, and then he shook his pointer finger from side to side.

Right, Elie did tell us we wouldn't be allowed in certain places if we wore shorts.

"What do we do?" I asked Patrick. The employee signed for us to follow him. "Where is he taking us?" I asked, panicking.

This is it. This is the reason we're being deported. Or worse, incarcerated.

I was sweating, partly because we were in the underground parking lot, but mostly because I was anxious. He led us right, then left, then right again, until I lost count of the turns. Knocking on the door of what I thought was his supervisor's office, he opened the door and gave me a gentle push on my back, so I walked into the portacabin, Patrick and Timothy following my lead. Although the supervisor held a phone against his ear, the security officer explained the situation in Arabic. The supervisor spoke gently with the person on the other line and put the phone back in the cradle. His smile disappeared and turned into a frown, as if we had just interrupted a phone call with his life-long love.

Yeah, we're definitely in trouble.

"What's he saying?" I asked Patrick.

"He's asking his colleague what he wants for lunch."

"Really?" I asked. "How do you know?"

"I don't. I'm being sarcastic. What makes you think I know what they're talking about?"

"We'll just go home, we didn't mean to cause any trouble," I said to the officer behind the big desk.

"*Amerkan?*" he said, looking at the employee who had brought us there. When that employee nodded, the supervisor got angry, his tone of voice getting higher and higher. He threw his arms in different directions and then bounced the tip of his fingers against his forehead.

Oh my God! He's more upset because we're American. We're screwed! I wish I never came here! I want to go back. This so isn't worth it. We only just landed, though. If we go back now, I'll be hearing, "I told you so," for the next two years from all my friends and family.

The supervisor stood up, and just when I thought he was going to arrest us, he reached out his hand to us. Confused, I shook his hand. He explained in broken English, "Please excuse him. Him new. Amreeki." Then, he raised his thumb.

Did I just hear him right?

I could have sworn the picture of the king hanging on the wall behind the supervisor was moving. The king looked down at me, a long smile across his face, his teeth sparkling, and winked at me with his left eye.

That's right, we are Am-freaking-reeki!

He opened the office door for us and said, "Him take you gate." We silently followed the officer, Timothy trailing at the back, still shaking from the adrenaline. So much had happened in the span of less than an hour. I was ready to go home and curl up in bed. First, though, we needed to do what we were there for: shopping. I used to get excited about that word, but that day's experiences might have ruined it for me.

We walked through those sliding doors again. I was so overwhelmed, my senses had shut off. I desperately wanted to take in the smell of butter that came from the kiosk that sold corn, but how could I? I wanted to point out the incense burner that was almost the size of Timothy, but how could I? My mind hadn't processed yet that such a benign incident had shaken me to my core, as if one small "mistake" would determine my destiny and send me back to the US, quicker than it had taken me to get to Saudi.

When the salesman tried to hand me a small piece of paper that he had sprayed perfume on, I unwillingly ignored him. And even though I wanted to stop in front of the shops that sold traditional clothing, take a picture, and send it to my parents, teasing them that I knew what to get them for Christmas, I wasn't in the mood for being jolly.

We took the travelator to the first floor, and as if we'd ridden a magic carpet, we'd entered a new, more familiar world. GAP, Sephora, Swarovski, Zara, H&M, Crocs, Adidas, Carter's, and many more brands from around the world. Not to mention the mall was spacious, freeing me from the claustrophobia I felt in the parking lot.

I could almost see the frown on my face through my reflection on the shining marble floors. The names of the shops were mirrored onto the floor, making it look as though there was a third dimension beneath our feet.

The ceiling stood high above, welcoming in direct sunlight. The day was still young, and it deserved a second chance. I took a deep breath and released the tension in my shoulders. It was time for my favorite kind of therapy. Retail.

It's all about perspective. You can choose to look down and see the world through an unrealistic lens. Or you can look up and appreciate the newness around you. You are safe. Remember, you are not moving to a smaller house. You are expanding.

"It looks like the shops are still closed," said Patrick.

Of course they are.

"The grocery store's open," said Timothy, pointing to HyperPanda.

I stopped and looked around, examining whether Patrick's shorts caused unwanted attention, but the lady in the niqab outside the Starbucks was more invested in quieting her toddler than anything else, and the East Asian janitor didn't even look at us as we walked past him. Relieved that no one seemed to care about who we were or what we wore, I was ready to move on with my day. "Do you guys want to walk around or do you want to go grocery shopping?"

Without hesitation, Patrick proposed, "Well, we only have an hour and a half." Then he whispered, "And we all know how gay men feel about shopping. I say let's hit HyperPanda."

We were now whispering the term "gay" like antipathetic people did when they wanted to say "fat" or "slut." We should have taken this into consideration when initially contemplating our move to Saudi Arabia.

The supermarket looked like our local H-E-B. All fresh produce that was imported from the US was significantly more expensive than their local counterparts. Patrick was overjoyed to find the Bisquick pancake mix and keto coffee. He went down the men's personal hygiene aisle three times, like a police dog, persistently trying to spot the Old Spice deodorant.

"Dad, come on, you might find it at another store.

Remember when H-E-B was out of your favorite creamer, but you found it at Walmart?"

Patrick ignored Timothy.

"Fine. You can stay here, but we're going to the cash register. Bye."

Patrick followed us.

If you throw a tantrum, we can officially call you a toddler.

We put our items onto the belt, and the cashier, who looked Saudi, tried to communicate something. It looked like something was wrong, but what exactly? It was our first outing by ourselves, and it was clear that we needed to learn Arabic.

The woman standing in line behind us, who was covered from head to toe, suggested an answer. "He's saying that you didn't weigh your produce. You can't do that here, you have to do it in the produce section."

She speaks English! I found my way to the fruits and vegetables section. There was a short queue, where people placed their plastic bags on a counter and an employee would weigh and tag them. I stood in line and followed by example. Then it hit me, it was the first time I saw a female employee since we landed in Saudi.

With all our produce tagged, I ran back to Patrick, who comforted me. "Raj says it's okay if we're a little late since schools are off, so he's off after this."

We paid and bolted outside the supermarket. The translucent doors of the grocery store rolled down behind us. Prayer time. As we carried our bags onto the bus, Patrick apologized. "Thank you for waiting for us, Raj. Sorry we're late, everybody. We're still trying to get the hang of things."

A stranger on the bus replied, "It's all right, mate. We've all been there."

"Really?" I wanted to ask. "Does it get easier? Do you always feel like a silenced minority? I feel like, as long as I'm outside the compound, I am afraid. Is that normal, or am I overreacting?" Only time would give me the answers I was looking for.

It was 12 by the time we reached home, and I had felt, seen, and thought too much in our outing. I needed to reboot, so I placed only the perishables in the refrigerator and lay on the couch with my family. We flipped through the channels on the TV until we found something we all liked.

"Alright," I said, "I guess I'm ready to make our first home cooked meal in this country. Thanks to Timothy, who found the box of lasagna sheets at the grocery store, we're having everyone's favorite dish tonight. Anyone want to keep me company in the kitchen?"

"Sure, I'll come," said Patrick.

Grabbing my phone, I played the song *Sweet Dreams* by Eurythmics, Annie Lennos, and Dave Stewart. It was time to focus on the future, so I shared with Patrick what would occupy my mind for the next twelve hours. "Tomorrow is our first meeting with the principal. What if he suspects that we're gay?"

John, you're triggered. You might want to try breathing before your anxiety takes control of you again.

Patrick's eyes were sweet and warm. Sympathetic. Soothing. But his words betrayed him. "You should be more worried about the fact we don't have teaching certificates. I told him we were gay when I applied for the job."

"What? And you never thought it was a detail worth mentioning to me?"

Why do you always keep important things from me? How many times have you invited friends over for dinner without consulting me first? How many times have you failed to tell me that Timothy had complained of painful urination? Why am I the last to know these things? I thought we were great communicators.

"You never asked…"

Don't give me that. What a stupid answer. I shouldn't have to ask.

More important than rebutting that argument, I went on with the discussion. "He didn't have a problem with it?"

Breathe in. Breathe out. Repeat. Release. Prioritize.

"No, he said we aren't the first gay teachers he's imported. Just the first gay couple." He winked at me and continued, "I know you love being the first at everything."

He was right, I *did* love being the first, and everybody should have a taste of this rewarding feeling. In first grade, I was the first to bring jaw breakers to class. In high school, I was the first in our school's history to graduate with a perfect score in math, physics, and chemistry. In college, well, I didn't do much in college, but after that, I was the first among my gay friends (and among my straight friends) to be a parent.

"Okay, so he knows we're gay. Aren't you anxious?"

"About starting a new job or about meeting the principal?" He didn't wait for my answer. Looking cool as a cucumber, he came close to me, reached his hand out, and we slowly danced along to *If I Ain't Got You* by Alicia Keys. Then he sang my favorite part: the chorus.

Wrapping him in my arms, I teased him, "Oh, yeah? And what is it you want?"

His eyes focused on my lips. "You know what I'm looking for."

"Old Spice?"

Patrick laughed. "That, and a hot date with your sister."

We laughed like two teenagers experiencing love for the first time. Once the song ended, Patrick sat down, and I opened up about everything that had bothered me the preceding days. The homophobic comment that Elie's friend made. The inappropriate jokes Elie made. Timothy vomiting on the bus. The security guard who scared us half to death. Patrick reciprocated.

We reconnected, and I was relieved that Patrick had experienced a similar culture shock. And just when it was time to serve dinner, he concluded the pillow talk. "Whatever circumstances we go through, you are not alone. You'll always have Timothy and me. Together, we can conquer any mountain. I don't like that it took us so long to have this talk, so maybe next time, we can open up to each other from the beginning. What do you think?"

I nodded, adding, "And please, don't keep important details from me. Not even mundane ones, for that matter."

The hug we shared touched me to my core, because it confirmed that, even in my vulnerable moments, I am heard, I am accepted, and I am loved. I fell in love with Patrick all over again—not that I had ever fallen out of love with him. I wasn't an ant crossing the earth aimlessly, I was John; brave, funny, and resilient. Even if I didn't matter on a grander scale, the people around me who relied on me and cared for me deeply, as though I was irreplaceable and uncrushable, were enough fuel for me. To them, I was irreplaceable, uncrushable.

Timothy walked into the kitchen. "Hey, guys, Grandma Carla's asking why we almost got arrested today."

You can keep me out of those mundane details, though.

JOHN

Tried calling you again. Starting to think you're avoiding me. Is everything OK?

JOHN

Scott? IDK what to make of your sudden silence. Everything okay at home?

CHAPTER TWELVE

It was a short—yet eternal—fifteen-minute walk to the school, which was accessible from the compound through a back gate. Although we wore light-colored cotton shirts, there was nothing that could help us against the merciless sun. My skin was burning. I wanted to stop and take a deep breath, but that meant more time spent in the heat. Patrick and Timothy's faces were so flushed, I expected them to faint.

As we forced ourselves onward, we didn't talk. We saved our precious breath for whatever oxygen we could catch. I was going to take another shower later (water bills were paid by the compound, by the way), preferably a cold one, but there was only lukewarm water.

We crossed the gate and walked past the empty parking lot. To our right was a football field and to our left was a dull white concrete building. Unsure of where to go, Patrick pointed. "I guess we should try the building."

"Water," gasped Timothy, "I hope we find water."

We found a water cooler and rushed to take turns. We refilled our cups many times, but we were still dehydrated.

I found the restroom before returning to the cooler where I'd left Timothy and Patrick. Patrick had dropped his cup, so he bent forward to pick it up. I smacked his round butt in the tight pants. Surprised, he jumped. Before he looked back, I noticed Patrick approaching from a distance.

If Patrick's there, then who did I just smack? This isn't even a white man, he just happens to be wearing the same color pants as Patrick.

"I'm so sorry, I thought you were someone else," I said, taking a few steps back in case the man wanted to hit me.

"I take it you're John," said the man, with a deep voice that gave men and women alike the confidence that they could conquer anything in the world if he just uttered the words, "You can."

The principal, Tom Knowles, was the type of man Patrick would fantasize about— before he met me, of course. A tall, muscular, pulchritudinous black man, who had tucked his green t-shirt tightly into his black dress pants, his buff shoulders and chest making me thirsty for more. In contrast, Patrick, Timothy, and I stood drenched in sweat.

"Guilty, as charged. And you are?" I asked, swallowing, hoping for any name but Tom.

"This is our new boss." Patrick half smiled. "What on earth are you doing?"

I've got sweat everywhere. I smacked my boss on the butt. My stomach's making funny sounds because of the water I drank. Humiliated.

"Good morning," said Tom, a smile on his face, as if nothing had happened. "I see y'all haven't bought a car yet. Nothing like a real local experience, huh? Welcome to Saudi Arabia."

I extended my sweaty hand to shake his. "Well, I'm Jo—"

"NONSENSE! That's not how men greet each other in this country."

My hand still in his, he grabbed me with his strong arms, so close that his face was a strand of hair away. He tried to bring himself closer, but I pulled back.

"Oh, come on, don't worry. I won't bite you. Put your forehead against mine."

I hesitantly followed suit.

"Look me in my eyes."

I followed again.

Boy did he have beautiful dark eyes. Eyes that looked like they had seen death in the face and weren't threatened by anything life had to offer.

He put his nose against mine, before instructing me to blow a kiss in the air. I opened my lips, pronouncing the letter "p" rather than blowing a kiss, as I didn't want to risk accidentally hitting his lips with mine.

"Ahlan wa sahlan," he said, in a strong American accent that even a newbie like me recognized. "That's Arabic for welcome," and I was relieved that he wasn't bullying us because we were gay.

Standing behind me, Patrick was practically drooling. Luckily, Timothy had gone to the restroom and missed the whole thing.

"How about y'all follow me to my office? I promise it's colder and more comfortable there."

It looked like a typical American school. Lockers. A small window on the classroom doors. Graduation pictures on the walls. Pictures of sports champions. There was an indoor basketball court. And then, at last, the principal's office.

Tom sat comfortably in his desk chair, like a king on his throne, and it suited him. We, on the other hand, sat on old wooden chairs that made it look like whoever was responsible for the school's furniture was a hoarder.

He briefly described the school's history and its curriculum before detailing the typical day-to-day tasks of English and math teachers. Then, he took a deep breath before saying, "So, a couple years ago, a student went to his teacher and asked him for advice about coming out. The teacher told him to follow his gut and do what made him most comfortable. When the kid came out to his crush here at school, he got rejected, and that caused him to be bullied. When his parents found out, the teacher was fired, and the kid left for another school."

"That's messed up," I said. "I wonder what happened to that kid."

"It is messed up, and I want to make sure that you know that under no circumstance can you discuss anything on the matter of homosexuality. Ever. Not even with a student off school premises. And if you hear people using any kind of terms, you are not to interfere. The only thing you can do is come to me about it."

"Let me get this straight." I was hardly able to keep my body in my chair. "If I were black, and someone made a racist comment, I would be expected to stay silent about it?"

Now I feel more like Rosa Parks.

"No, then you could say something about it. I know it doesn't make sense, but it is the way things work around here. And your jobs depend on it."

"I get it, a typical example of the iron fist. I've got used to it by now."

"Gotten," said Patrick.

"What?" I asked.

"I've gotten used to it."

"Whatever, you know what I mean."

I guess this is what we signed up for. I'm being asked to hide my identity in front of my eleven year old. I want to move to a smaller house.

I sank into my chair and crossed my arms, like a teenager who'd been called to the principal's office for causing trouble.

"Now," said Tom, "Patrick, you said you wanted to teach dance, is that correct?"

119

"Yes, sir, I would love to do that."

"We don't currently teach dance, so what we can do is introduce it as an extracurricular activity. We will have a trial period, and if enough people sign up, and they want to continue, we will make it official. How does that sound?"

"Challenge accepted."

"Great. I don't have anything else scheduled for today, so I can show you around campus, if you like."

I wasn't in the mood, as I was trying to process the status quo at the school, and I sure didn't want to have to walk any longer in the heat. Patrick, though, was ecstatic. "We sure would like that. Very much so. Thank you."

We walked out the building. "That was the building with classrooms from pre-K to Kindergarten, and as you know, my office."

Further down, there was a square garden. "This is where we get all the school pictures taken. Advantage of having summer all year long is you can take pictures outside all the time."

Around from the garden were the other divisions; on one side were the classrooms for grades one to five, on the other were grades six to eight, and on the third side were grades nine to twelve.

This is what your students are paying $14,000 for every year? You can get much better than this for free in the US.

"All right," concluded Tom, "that's pretty much it. Thank you for coming, and we will see you in class next week."

Patrick extended his hand to our boss. "So, are you going to show me how men greet each other here?"

My God! The audacity!

Tom laughed. "Good one," except Patrick wasn't joking.

As Tom walked away, I whispered in Patrick's ear, "You're such a pervert, it's because of people like *you* that the media portray us as hypersexual!" When the principal was no longer in sight, I held

Patrick's elbow until he stopped walking. Gluing myself to him, I danced around him, and mocked him. "Oh, Tom, show me how it's done, Tom. Touch *my* nose, Tom. Come closer, Tom, with your perfect six pack."

"You're such a kid, Dad." Timothy rolled his eyes, as if I was overreacting, which I was, but instead of apologizing, I overreacted even more.

"If being a kid means being like you, Timothy," I said, unable to control my words, "then, please, spare me the insult."

Our walk back home was silent, but this time, it wasn't because we were fighting for air. It was because we were fighting, period.

CHAPTER THIRTEEN

The only person I trusted my familial problems with was Scott. I downloaded a VPN app (because calling through apps like Messenger and WhatsApp was banned) and tried calling him multiple times, but then I remembered it was about eight hours earlier in San Antonio, so he must have been sleeping still. I left him a dozen messages, which I did not dare replay, because I sounded panicky and desperate.

"After all the time it took me to trust him after he cheated on me with Mr. You-know-who, he does this right in front of me and Timothy. Gosh, I hate him so much right now."

"I know he's an awesome partner, and I might be overreacting, but like, what if he's only supportive so I'll never doubt his loyalty?"

"I'm sure he loves me. I'll tell you who doesn't love me. Timothy. And I can't blame him."

"Coming here was just a real big mistake. Like does he really expect me to say nothing if someone calls me a fag? I shouldn't have to deal with this."

"I'd really appreciate it if you could reply to my messages. I really need you. I'll stop harassing you now. Bye. Waiting for an answer. Bye for real now!"

The only other person who might have been awake was my mother, and though I wasn't going to talk to her about my issues, it was the perfect occasion to let her think she was on my mind, when in reality, I just needed someone to talk to about anything. That, and I didn't want her to worry about me.

Hannah (my mom) told me how surprised she was to see my name pop up on her screen, even though I said I'd call her once a week, but seeing how short that phone call was, once a month seemed more reasonable. She asked me about our trip, about Timothy, and how I was feeling, and then said she was going to move on with her day, as she was about to jump in the shower when I'd called.

Frustrated that my best friend wasn't a phone call away, I threw my phone, not caring where it landed, and covered my face with my pillow. Patrick was my partner, but he wouldn't understand me if I confided in him. The words were ready to come out of my mouth like puke, but how could I tell him, if he didn't show me an ounce of care?

"I apologize," said Patrick, as we ate lunch later that day. "What I did was way out of line. You didn't deserve that."

All I had to say was, "Thank you, I appreciate that," but I didn't, because my family was my safe space where I could act out and be stubborn, like a toddler is with their mother.

"Sometimes," I said, accepting that the monster inside of me was uncontainable, "I wonder if you're autistic 'cause like, do you have feelings?"

"Dad," shouted Timothy, food flying out of his mouth, "that's super offensive. And so untrue! People on the spectrum have feelings, they just—"

"Can't you see that I'm talking?" I threw him the meanest side-eye. "Don't interrupt me. Also, don't talk with your mouth full." I was becoming my dad, though I'd vowed to myself I wouldn't.

I know Julio said I should take a few breaths, but he doesn't know what it's like to be inside of my head. I'll show you, Patrick, I'm about to make you respect my presence once and for all.

"After everything I do for you two, and this is what I get in return. I moved across an ocean for you, and you can't even consider that you're hurting me. And this isn't the first time; ever since I took my sabbatical, it's like you think you're better than me. And you, Timothy, I can't get you out of bed without hearing you complain about how hard your life is. And then you show me this attitude and talk to me like I'm your friend. I'm not your friend, okay? I'm your father. How about a freaking thank you every once in a while?"

The worms are out the can. The dragon is about to spit fire.

"And you know what, Patrick? If you don't want me to care that you freaking flirt with the entire universe, fine, I won't care. Sleep with them for all I care. But don't expect my love. Don't expect my sacrifice. And don't freaking expect my shoulder to cry on in the middle of the night. I don't want you to show me you love me in front of our family, only to stab me with knives now that we're so far away."

"Dad—"

"I'm not done yet," I said to Timothy, and then to Patrick, "Say something."

"Dad—"

Tears ran down my cheeks.

"Come on," I said to Patrick, my voice higher, "say something!"

"Dad—"

"What, Timothy?" My words echoed around the house. "If you want to call me a horrible father, then please save your breath."

"I'm sorry, okay?"

Hyperventilating, I closed my eyes and silently counted to ten, but when I opened them, the embarrassment and weakness still felt heavy on my heart. My eyes focused on the San Antonio River painting as I tried to think of happier times.

Slow down, John. Everything's going to be alright.

Unable to stop my head from nodding, I wished the earth would swallow me.

And once I'd gathered the courage to turn my head toward Patrick, I found him staring straight into my soul. "I'm sorry," I whispered, "to the both of you, I'm sorry. Patrick, please say something.."

"What do you want me to say?" He gently put his cutlery down. "I apologized, and in return, I got a big fat speech about respect from someone who can't respect me. You think you're the only one who's having a hard time, but let me break it to you: we all are. It's not just you. So for a moment, stop asking and start giving."

This used to be the part where we got off our chairs and ripped each other's clothes off, our vulnerability magnetizing our bodies, but with a child living in our house, we had to wait until after hours.

"Listen," I said to Patrick, "I'm sorry, okay? I just got a little insecure, and it triggered all kinds of other insecurities. And you're right, all this time I thought I was the only one fighting my own demons, believing all kinds of lies about our present and our future. About my love for you."

"You know there's no one else I desire. I'm sorry, too, for being so inconsiderate. Sometimes I forget how much of a jealous man you are."

Happy tears.

"I love you, Dad," said Timothy, for the first time in a long,

long time. "Don't worry about forgetting who you are. We won't let that happen."

"Oh, son," I said, my heart full, "I owe you an apology. I'm so proud of you. I just—"

"Shhhh," said Patrick gently, like a parent calming their newborn, and as he extended his hand to me and Timothy, our energy was unmatched, strong, unbreakable.

Timothy's eyes sparkled, a trace of light, a trace of hope.

Overwhelmed with a variety of emotions, the next words that escaped my mouth were "Thank you."

Patrick grabbed a bottle of Saudi champagne from the fridge, filled three glasses, and raised a toast. "Here's to love and forgiveness."

JOHN

Hey Elie, are we going to a public place tonight? Can we bring Koala?

ELIE

Hey bro, if you take Koala out in public and a cop sees her, he'll tell you to go home and if you don't, he'll take your dog away

ELIE

This isn't America habibi...

CHAPTER FOURTEEN

E lie was picking us up at 6 (hopefully) for lunch—as he said —and surprising us with a local experience.

Usually, when we tried new cuisine, we packed a snack for Timothy because kids have a superpower that allows them to judge that a meal is nasty without even trying it. Patrick and I wanted to try something different this time, or our son would turn into "that guy," who'd be known for doing weird things, like bringing orange juice to a bar, so if he refused to eat, we'd say, "You've got to be open to new experiences and cultures, Timothy." That, and they didn't sell his favorite snacks in Saudi.

As Patrick snacked on a local brand of flavored yogurt, I folded up all our Bermuda shorts and placed them in a box labeled, "Not To Be Worn In PUBLIC." I put them away in our closet, like a teenager hiding his first collection of porn magazines.

"How can we expect him to be open to new cultures when we're constantly comparing the local culture to our own as if we're in a competition?" said Patrick, as he placed his empty yogurt box on his nightstand, which was right next to the trash can. I wasn't sure if that was a subliminal message intended for me.

"Speak for yourself," I said, staring at the box. "I'm not the one who considers threesomes with the black principal as being open to new experiences and cultures."

The incident of Patrick flirting with Tom was behind me, but I kept my guard up, considering how often they'd run into each other at school. If he thought of how cute and sexy he was every time he lay eyes on him, it was only a matter of time before Tom became a temptation. The last thing I needed was to lose my partner to a straight married man in a country where being gay was forbidden.

Before Patrick and I committed to each other, we had discussed our deepest fears and darkest secrets. If one of us had feelings for another man, the deal was to come forward about it from the beginning, so we could figure it out together. Whether it one of us was growing weary of our relationship. Whether it was a temporary emotion led by a tough phase in life. Whatever it was.

But that was then, over a decade ago. I was going to keep my eyes open and stalk Patrick at school, if need be. I wasn't going to risk losing my relationship.

It wasn't long before Elie knocked on our door. Koala ran down the stairs with me, and when I scanned Elie from top to bottom, he said "You must be wondering why I'm wearing a traditional Saudi dress." I nodded, so he continued, "I'm coming straight from the office. I usually wear a suit, but today, we had an important meeting with a prince, so this is me building rapport." With his palms facing upward, he waved up and down at his dress.

"Smart, right?" He raised his shoulders and fixed his collar.

What's it like knowing a prince? Would he be interested in marrying Albert by any chance?

In the car, Elie pumped up the music. "Alright, who's ready to party?"

"I am!" I shouted. "Is it true that there's a party every weekend in different compounds? I'm curious to see what they're like."

Elie laughed. "Hold your horses. I was just joking. I'm not taking you to a party. I was just asking who's ready to party in the car, because once it's prayer time, we have to turn the music down."

Oh.

He continued, "Patrick said you guys want to buy local SIM cards and maybe buy a car, so that's what we're going to do after lunch. We're lucky that tomorrow's the weekend. There's one more prayer, and then everything will be open until eleven or midnight. If you guys want to party, I need to talk to my friend, who'll talk to his friend, who'll talk to his friend, who can put us on the list. There's an entrance fee. 500 riyals per person. And I don't know if kids are allowed."

500 riyals, that's like 130 dollars.

"I don't know if it's worth all the trouble if we're going to end up drinking ced," I said.

"Who said anything about ced? They serve whiskey and vodka, I think, it's like two hundred riyals per glass."

Fifty dollars per glass? So it's going to cost me an arm to get drunk? I'll pass.

Patrick said, "Alcoholics should move to Saudi, and they'll be sober in no time. No one can afford to be an alcoholic here."

If we wanted to witness the partying scene, explained Elie, we were a gym membership away. Gyms were separated into the "Men Only" and "Female Only" sections, and over time, they became an underground hub for the gay community to mingle. "It's like a silent disco where the attendants are hyenas looking for prey. #imtop!" He snapped his fingers from left to right, moving his head in the same direction, as if he were gay.

Since the partying scene wasn't for us, we were left with two options:

1. Do the usual boring things straight people do, like going to the mall, walking by the corniche, eating at American restaurants, visiting friends, or cruising around the city.

2. Live like the people of the desert, who liked to picnic in random places, like an empty parking lot or behind a loop, wherever there's an inch or two of grass. Those were the same people who drove with their toddlers or infants on their laps.

"This makes me so angry," said Elie, referring to the irresponsible dads, "I don't know how they can be so reckless. Whenever I see that happen, I roll my window down and scream at them, begging them to be safe, but bang water, and it stays water. There's no point."

Talk about culture shock.

Elie parked the car in front of a minimarket, and before exiting the car, he said, "I've been to Gold's Gym once and couldn't finish a workout because a guy kept hitting on me. I never went back."

"Are you sure it's not because you're lazy?" asked Timothy, which made us giggle.

Elie came back and gave us each a bottle of Bison energy drink, a local version of Red Bull, both of which tasted awful. Elie believed (as did everyone else, apparently) that it contained bison sperm, and yet he drank it religiously.

Does Red Bull have bull sperm in it? Would that make it more popular if it did?

An electric pink sunset painted the sky with a majestic aurora that reminded me of my hometown. I missed being in my comfort zone, which was where everything made sense. Since we'd arrived in Jeddah, we were so busy that I'd forgotten all about my depression, I'd forgotten to feel, and for a brief moment, I longed for my sorrow, because it was familiar and safe.

We crossed a bridge that gave us a peek into some of the mansions that hid behind walls: expensive cars, beautiful modern architecture, pools. These kinds of houses existed in the US, too, but it wasn't common to see them, at least not up close. You'd have to go to a rich neighborhood in a city of rich people. These mansions were surrounded by ordinary apartments belonging to the middle class.

At the end of the road was a roundabout decorated with giant metal copies of a set square, a compass, and a protractor.

As if he had read my mind, Patrick said, "This city keeps getting more and more interesting."

"This thing has been here for the longest time," said Elie. "The problem is that many accidents happen at roundabouts."

I nodded. "I can see why. Priority is given to the person on the outside."

"Right," resumed Elie. "So, now, they're replacing all these beautiful roundabouts with traffic lights. And as you can imagine, it's going to take away from the city's artistry. All of that because people have trouble respecting rules."

It didn't make sense. In fact, it sounded chaotic, but it wasn't up to me to decide if removing roundabouts was the right or wrong thing to do. Just like me, those decision-makers were adapting to the culture around them, and that was, well, chaotic. That didn't mean that roundabouts were worse than traffic lights.

CHAPTER FIFTEEN

"Where's the table? Where are the chairs?" asked Timothy once we had reached the dining area of the restaurant.

"Where's your sense of cultural openness," said Patrick sarcastically, raising his hands in the air and drawing a large smile on his face. He was just as unhappy as Timothy was.

A changed man, I didn't complain. Instead, I chose a spot, sat cross-legged, and sucked my stomach in. Next to me, Patrick indiscreetly unbuttoned his pants and rested against the thick velvet cushions that matched the rug. In front of us, Elie and Timothy looked perfectly comfortable. Elie, thanks to the baggy, white cotton pants that men wore under their thobe, and Timothy, thanks to his size.

"Don't look so sad," Elie told Patrick, "in some cultures, men squat while they're eating."

I tried to picture myself eating like that, and I couldn't think of one good reason why someone would do it.

In the middle, on the floor, a waiter placed a disposable plastic table cover that was decorated with "Happy birthday," "Congratulations" and "Please enjoy." He shortly came back and put a tray on the cover, the heat from the rice and camel meat fogging the letters.

Old John would have been disappointed, he would have thought Elie had made a big fuss about an ordinary dinner. Not the new John, though, who was curious to know how they got the rice to be beige and who wasn't afraid to admit his fondness of the unfamiliar spices. (New John didn't look for the sign that said "BPA Free" on the table cover.)

"So, guys," said Elie, "I don't know exactly how they cook this, but I know for sure that they cook it in a pit underground. And they let it simmer overnight. You'll see, it's going to melt in your mouth."

"Doesn't it make it haram when they cook it underground," said Patrick, laughing alone at his own joke.

"What," said Elie. "No. Halal refers to the way they kill the animal—"

If Elie's explanation got graphic, Timothy was sure to vomit all over our food, so I interrupted him, "Son, would you like a salad or something?"

"Why? Is he on a diet or something?" Elie asked.

"Erm, no."

"Then why waste that space in his stomach on salad?" Elie used his right hand to cut through a piece of meat and combine it with a handful of rice. He opened his mouth wide and dumped the big ball of food in. "Oh, my God," he said, his mouth full. "This is really good. The meat is so tender!" He then collected another handful of rice and meat and brought his hand close to Timothy's mouth. "This is actually really good, habibi. Try it."

Timothy squinted his eyes, the food right under his nose. He shook his head, and knowing my son, he must have thought of the camel he'd ridden a few weeks prior.

"Come on, trust me, be a man."

"Or don't," I said, my words intended more for Elie than Timothy, "up to you, really."

Timothy's face paled. He gagged and turned his face toward the customers sitting closest to us. The men had taken their shoes off, and they played with their toes while waiting for their food to arrive. I'd be surprised if Timothy didn't ask us to move back to the US after this. This was worse than any Survivor or Man vs. Wild episodes he'd ever watched, and there were many.

Failing to speak, Timothy typed a note onto his phone and showed us the screen. "Can I wait for you in the car? Please!!!!!!!!"

When I agreed, Elie opened his eyes wide in surprise, but I didn't care if he thought I was raising a wuss or that I was a soft parent; men were allowed to be those things. Elie grabbed his key out of his pocket with his pinkie and handed it to Timothy.

Copying Elie, I created a ball in my hand with equal portions of rice and meat. As I chewed, I evaluated the flavors in my mouth; clove, cardamom, and other unfamiliar spices. The meat was incredibly tender. Old John would have complained, preferring the way Asians cooked rice (or at least the way Asians in the US cooked it), but new John was open to new flavors and textures. New John finally understood that something different wasn't bad, or good, or right, or wrong.

Good job you didn't move to a smaller house, John. You're getting better and better at this.

With forty-five minutes before the next prayer, Elie drove off as fast as he could. Even when a traffic light turned yellow, and then red, he drove past it, and then spoke in Arabic, sounding frustrated.

"What's wrong?" asked Patrick.

"I don't know where that policeman came from, I have to pull over somewhere." He exited the car and walked toward the police car, which was apparently a normal thing to do.

"If this was in the US," said Patrick, as surprised as I was, "he would've been tased by now."

"Dad, with the dress he's wearing and his beard, he would've been shot. No doubt."

Elie's hands waved in all directions. He laughed. A few minutes later, he shook the policeman's hand and returned to the Tahoe, a big smile on his face.

"What happened?" asked Patrick.

"Nothing, I just told him that I have new guests coming from America and I'm showing them around the beautiful city. Then I told him I grew up here and started praising this country. He asked me where I was from, I told him Lebanon. I'm so happy I'm not from Egypt or I would probably be in the back of his car right now. And if it wasn't for you guys being in the car with me, he would've fined me. So, thank you."

"What? That doesn't make sense." I was confused.

"Yeah, man, that's just how it works in this part of the world. Your nationality matters big time," said Elie, as if he were discussing the color of the sky, "and it determines how the law is applied."

"Well, you'll be surprised that it's not so different in the US. Not with your nationality, but your skin color," said Timothy.

The streets were bustling with people, whether on the highway or on the sidewalks.

Elie said, "We are now on Tahlia Street, it's one of my favorite streets. I used to hang out here a lot as a teenager."

The design of the buildings was different from San Antonio, but everything else was recognizable; IKEA, Texas Roadhouse, Starbucks, Cheesecake Factory. The streets, too, were clean and neat.

"You know, before WhatsApp and all the different social media, there were not many ways that men could meet women. So, men would drive expensive cars around this street and spot women sitting alone in the back of a car, while her driver chauffeured her. He would follow her, and once he got her attention, he would sign for her to roll down her window and if she did, he would throw a phone to her. That way he could call her. Crazy, no? You'd think that a bearded man wearing the thobe would throw a ticking bomb into your window, not a brand new iPhone."

No comment.

A few minutes after we collected a ticket at the cell phone shop, curtains rolled down, indicating that the store was closed. An employee went around the store and closed all exits.

When do the people with the guns show up?

Elie clarified they were not necessarily praying, but they may have been smoking a cigarette or having a quick flirtatious call with a girl they met through Snapchat or Instagram. "Because how else can boys meet girls in this country if they're separated all the time? Imagine, in some Saudi families, they won't allow cousins of opposite genders to play together starting at a certain age for fear that they would mingle or something."

"What if your cousin is ugly?" I asked.

"You know what we say, a monkey is a gazelle in his mother's eye," which I interpreted as an Arab way of saying, "Beauty is in the eye of the beholder."

Our turn came a couple of minutes later. Elie and I sat at the two chairs opposite the employee desk, while Patrick and Timothy remained standing. The man serving us had light brown skin, his facial features were accentuated—beautiful big dark eyebrows, a slim nose, and perfect cheekbones. His thobe shined bright. The *shemagh*, or the white cotton cloth on his head, stood perfectly symmetrical, with a triangle in the middle, just above his forehead. His fingernails were clean and trimmed. And he spoke fluent English.

Talal, as his name tag indicated, answered all our questions.

He also explained that, after a few years, if we remained with the same provider, we would each receive a new phone for less than a third of its price.

By the time we were done, prayer time was still going on, so an employee opened the door for us, and I tripped on a curtain as I exited, but it didn't stop me from walking out impressed and satisfied with the service I'd received.

It was 8 o'clock. "Do you guys want to check out cars? I've got to warn you, though, it's probably a forty-minute drive from here."

"Maybe another time," said Patrick. "Thank you so much for everything, we really appreciate it."

"And even if?" asked Elie, but I didn't understand his question.

"Oh, we say *Walaw*, which literally means 'and even if' but it actually means 'don't mention it.' I don't know why we say it like it's a question, though."

As we drove home, we turned onto King Abdul Aziz Road, and Elie noted, Elie's favorite road, which was named after the founding father.

Elie pointed at different palaces and explained that they usually belonged to people who worked for the royal family. He then elaborated, "You know? This is the only street in the city that was built with an underground water system. When they built the city, they thought they would not need an underground water system, because it barely rains here, until they started praying for rain. Let me tell you, it has rained cats and dogs for the past ten winters or so, and this road was the only one in the city to remain intact. Bridges drowned. People lost their houses and their lives. Now, they pray for no rain, and when they feel rain is coming, most of the time, they will either close schools and some offices for a few days, or if rain comes and people are already out, they will send students and employees back home. And I'm talking rain, not a thunderstorm or anything."

As a new song played in the background, *Wavin' Flag* by K'naan, Patrick pulled out his phone and put on his "I'm writing a poem" face. I waited patiently until he was done before I asked to see it.

Nobody looked at the piece of paper
The stranger had just handed him.
He wasn't a beggar,
But an extra penny helped a body so slim.

He identified with it;
Overused, broken, old.
Dirty, unwanted, ripped.
Replaceable, forgotten, sold.

Somebody, have mercy on me.
I've cleaned your street,
I've stood in the sun,
What else must be done?

100 riyals a week
Would make anybody weak
I've got ten mouths to feed.
The tears in my eyes are starting to bleed.

Somebody drove by.
How could Somebody notice Nobody?
Nobody felt like a dead body.

Anybody couldn't help but cry.

Nobody, Somebody, Anybody,
Poor, rich, average,
Unfair division of equality.
Unfair division of advantage.

For the first time, Patrick had written a poem that didn't suck. Since he hadn't titled it, I took the chance to add, "The Land of Opportunity" at the top.

Elie parked in front of our villa, and as I was leaving the car, Elie pulled my arm, "Want to run an errand with me? Just me and you?"

Patrick's sole condition was that we didn't drive past a red traffic light.

Is he taking me to Gold's Gym?

When Timothy left the car, I asked Elie, "You're not taking me to a drug dealer, are you?"

"That's exactly where I'm taking you."

"No, seriously, where are we going?"

"Seriously, we're going to see my dealer."

Smaller house. Smaller house.

CHAPTER SIXTEEN

P oker face. Poker face. Why did Elie ask me to join him in an illegal activity? Was he going to tell me about our destination if I hadn't asked him? Am I some sort of legal pass that keeps him out of trouble? Is that the price I have to pay for his kindness? Where's he taking me to next, the Family Section of a restaurant?

"Why didn't you say anything?" Fidgety, I was unable to remain in my seat.

"You look like I just told you we were driving to hell," said Elie.

"Erm," I said, my right leg tremoring, "I won't lie to you. I do have a thousand questions going through my head right now."

"I understand. You must be judging me, aren't you? You know, I'm sorry I suggested this, I can drop you home right away."

"I don't care that you smoke weed, I did, too, at a certain point in my life. I'm just wondering why you would take me with you to see your drug dealer." My seatbelt tightened against my chest, and after four angry attempts, I finally loosened it.

"If you're worried about us getting caught, I totally understand, but the question is, do you trust me?"

I didn't say anything.

"Listen, bro, I've made this trip hundreds of times. Besides, if there was anything to worry about, I would know it by now. We all warn each other when a dealer's caught and the cops are on the lookout. But, like I said, if you want to go home, I can drop you. Just know that I would never put you in a dangerous situation."

"No, yeah." I shook my head, embarrassed. "You're right. I guess I do trust you after all."

"Oh," he said, his smile suddenly disappearing. "I didn't say that you should trust me. I don't even trust myself."

"Okay, now I'm confused."

Elie laughed. "I'm just teasing you, man. Of course you can trust me."

One thing I loved about Elie was his honesty; he wasn't greedy with his thoughts and emotions. He also stopped me in my tracks if I said something that bothered him—a quality I did not have. That to me meant he was well intentioned, open minded, and a "what you see is what you get" kind of guy. I did have to do something about his punctuality—or the lack thereof.

"Do you mind if I ask you a personal question?" asked Elie, which I usually interpreted as "I have a potentially offensive question, and I don't know how you'll take it."

"You're not going to ask me who the woman in the relationship is, are you?" Elie laughed at my joke. "No, I already know who that is. I was going to ask you if Timothy is your adopted child."

"Wait, what do you mean you already know who the woman is?"

"Let's just say the man wouldn't wear Speedos, would he?" Elie winked at me.

He did make a valid point, but I wasn't going to get into the details of how every gay couple was different and there wasn't such a thing as a man and a woman in a gay relationship. There were just two men or two women. Or more than two, in some cases. Just like plenty of straight men like to wear Speedos too. I laughed and made a mental note to tell the joke to Patrick and relish in his embarrassment.

Next thing I knew, I couldn't stop talking. I'd told Elie about my sister donating her eggs to us, about the stillborn baby who would've been Timothy's twin sister, and about Timothy being our greatest gift. There was something about Elie, the way he responded to me, nodding and listening, that made me comfortable about sharing personal details. That was until he asked me if my sister was hot, and if she was interested in making pretty babies with him. He raised his right hand from the steering wheel, showing off what could have been a bicep but had been replaced by fried food, and I pictured my sister beating the kebob out of him.

And then it was Elie's turn to talk a lot; his mother made it her life mission to find him a bride, it didn't matter who the bride was or what she looked like, his mother described them all as "beautiful, blonde, tall, well educated."

"If I'm going to spend my life's savings on a wedding ceremony, I have to make sure the return on investment is worthy, you know?"

It was the same in the US, where more and more weddings were turning into a show, a demonstration of wealth and social status. Elie was lucky enough to have life savings; I had numerous friends who had to apply for loans. The worst part was that some of those marriages ended in divorce.

Elie had talked to his parents about adopting a child, "and they nearly had a heart attack, kind of like you did when I told you we were going to see my dealer."

Elie didn't have the option of finding an egg donor, and much less of hiring a surrogate, because that was unheard of in the Middle East, just as having children out of wedlock was.

Although our worlds were far apart, although our cultures were alien to each other, the things that made us human brought us together, and however different we were, our worlds were the same in their essence.

"International Medical Center," I read softly. "I thought this was a hotel, not a hospital."

"You should see the inside." Elie took a few turns, and less than a minute later, we were in a poor neighborhood. There were no street lights, so it was hard to see. Every house was a concrete box, each a different color that looked more like a big stain than painting. Some weren't even painted. The cracks in the walls told stories of poverty and struggle. The window air conditioners hung by a thread. Children walked outside, way past dark, unchaperoned. There was trash everywhere. Puddles, too, even though it hadn't rained.

Even Elie didn't know who lived in those houses, whether they were Saudis or "expats," or how many people shared that small space, the size of a food truck.

Elie parked in front of a two-story villa that hid behind a washed oyster pink concrete wall. Opaque windows. They concealed the lives within. Or they protected women and girls from the wildness outside. Or both. The same could be said of the security bars, and I couldn't decide whether they kept victims in or if they kept bad people out. Perhaps a better word would be *insecurity* bars.

I had never met a dealer before, so I was curious to see whether a Saudi dealer looks like a local version of Snoop Dogg. After a brief conversation over the phone with the dealer, Elie took off his seat belt and leaned toward me. "Okay, he's invited us in. Do you want to come with me?"

"Yes." There was no way I was waiting in the car by myself.

"Okay." Elie brought his hands together. "So, there's only one rule you have to follow."

Don't call the cops?

"Don't, under any circumstances, talk about the women of his family."

"What? Why would I do that?"

"I don't know, man, but I have to make sure you don't. You have to understand that if you just know his sister's or his mother's name, it's like you've seen her naked. I'm not exaggerating. It'll bring him shame, and he'll never want to see us again."

I mean, you'd think being a dealer would be shameful, but who am I to judge?

It was my first time entering a Saudi home. As a man opened the door, Elie said to me, "Step in with your right foot first."

"What?"

"Just trust me, man. It's proper Muslim etiquette."

Proper what?

"B—" I didn't finish my sentence. What I really wanted to say was "But this is a drug dealer's house. It's not exactly the most ethical job." I remembered the scene in *Cop Out* where Guillermo Diaz kneels in a church and says, "Bless me, Father, for I'm about to sin," before pulling the trigger at someone.

Unlike I'd expected, Otbah didn't wear a thobe or a shemagh, and he wasn't surrounded by ladies in burqas. And there definitely was no tiger at any point.

Instead, Otbah, the dealer, wore black polyester capris that were below-knee level, which was proper Muslim etiquette, and ironically, matched it with a Queen t-shirt. He extended his olive hands, his fingernails a dark yellow, a result of rolling too many joints made of Afghani hash.

As I shook his hand, Elie took his shoes off, so I followed his lead, hiding my left foot with my right one so they wouldn't notice the big hole in my sock. Then Otbah said something to me in Arabic, which Elie translated, "He's honored to have you in his home. That's a common greeting in this part of the world."

"Are you a fan of Queen?" I asked Otbah, pointing at his shirt.

He looked at Elie, furrowed his brows, and with a smile on his face, he tilted his head. They conversated in Arabic, and I tried to think of a reason why I'd ask this man his mother's or sister's name, when I couldn't ask about the shirt he was wearing.

We walked down a narrow hallway. There was a strong smell of incense that made me sneeze a few times. The walls were decorated with Quranic texts on black background in golden picture frames. There wasn't a single picture, which made sense, they wouldn't hang pictures of women covered from head to toe, like that picture I showed to my family the night of the last supper. The floor tiles were brown with green floral patterns from the nineteenth century that matched the furniture, which looked— and smelled—just as ancient. There was no Playstation, no gang members, but there was a joint waiting for us. Otbah picked it up, along with a counterfeit LV man purse, and walked back in the direction of the front door.

Cool, cool, let's get out of here.

Otbah wasn't escorting us to the door, though. He led us to a tent on his front veranda, which had a big, velvet rug and cushions to support our backs and arms. For the second time that day, I sat cross-legged.

Otbah passed the joint to Elie, who said, "Allahou Akbar," before lighting it up.

"Elie? What are you doing?"

"What does it look like I'm doing?"

"But you're driving. That's not safe, let alone illegal."

"Relax, man, I've done this a million times."

145

Yeah, well, people who get in car accidents have driven a million times, too, but that doesn't decrease the risk.

Elie lit up the joint while Otbah increased the volume of the TV—yes, there was a TV in the tent, so concert music filled the room. It was a Saudi singer, dressed in the full traditional costume, standing in the middle of a stage. Behind him was an orchestra dressed the same way. The camera zoomed in on some of the players, who had mastered beautiful, unfamiliar instruments. The scene was everything but gangster, anything but Hollywood, and I was glad. Elie extended the joint to Otbah, who pointed at me.

"Want to smoke, John?"

I was hesitant at first, so Elie asked, "You said you trusted me, right?"

Yes, he was right, so I took the joint and inhaled. I coughed for a good minute, which gave Elie and Otbah a good laugh. The dealer then grabbed a big piece of something that looked like a chocolate bar, cut off a piece, and handed it to Elie. Elie smelled it and brought it close to my nose. "Afghani hash. Now *this* will give you wings."

Elie stuck the piece in his pocket while Otbah slit a cigarette and let the tobacco fall onto a bill of five riyals. He then cut off a pea-size piece of hash and stuck it to a Swiss Army knife. He burned the piece and threw it onto the money bill. He mixed it together, like I did when I tried to crumble down a stubborn piece of brown sugar into my homemade cake mix. Otbah's fingers turned brown.

At the bottom of the rolling paper, he added the tip of a cigarette, where we normally used filters. He filled the rolling paper with the tobacco and hash mix and then sealed it with his tongue. He lit the joint, which meant we had two joints among three men, and although one hit had already gotten me high, I didn't want to seem like a wuss, so I inhaled again. This time, I accidentally swallowed tobacco, which tasted awful, but I didn't want to make a fool of myself again, so I didn't react. I passed the joint to Elie, who took a few puffs and passed it back to me.

I was high. Very high.

Elie grabbed his phone from his pocket. "It's Patrick," he said, handing it to me. "He probably wants to talk to you."

I picked up the call, "Hey, what's up?"

"Why aren't you picking up? I called you over ten times!"

"Called me where?" I asked.

"Your new number, John."

It took me a second to realize what he was talking about. "Right. My new number. I forgot about that." I laughed, even though it wasn't funny.

"What's the matter with you? Where are you?"

"I can't really tell you, but you trust Elie, don't you?"

Elie's eyes popped out. He snatched the phone from my hand. "Hey, Patrick, we're just at a friend's place." I couldn't hear what Patrick was saying.

"No," said Elie. "He's fine. We will be back home soon. Alright, bye." He hung up the call, even though I could still hear Patrick's voice.

"Sounds like you're in trouble," he said to me.

"Relationships 101," I said.

"See?" he said, passing me a joint again. "I knew Patrick was the woman. They're always on our backs. They can never let a man just relax a little."

Next thing I knew, I passed out. I couldn't help it. All the tiredness from the traveling, the unpacking, the jet lag, the emotions, the overthinking, the past two months, and the high.

"John, John!" I heard Elie's voice as he pinched my arm. "John, come on, man, wake up."

Where am I? Why do I hear Elie's voice telling me to wake up?

I opened my eyes.

Where am I? Oh my gosh, I'm still at the dealer's house.

"What time is it?" I asked Elie.

"It's 4 in the morning. Come on, let's get home." I grabbed my phone and found thirty missed calls and twenty text messages, all from Patrick. I was definitely in trouble.

CHAPTER SEVENTEEN

*H*ow is Elie still awake? How many joints did they smoke after I fell asleep? Hm, my mouth is so dry. I'm so hungry!

"Elie," I said as we walked out the tent. "I'm really hungry."

"Say no more. We can pass by McDonald's. I remember when I was a teenager, I'd come home late at night, and my mom would be waiting for me with her slippers in her hands. Soon as I walked through the door, she'd throw them at me. I miss those days."

"I can see Patrick doing that tonight." I opened the metal gate of the villa, the sunrise hitting me with the truth that I'd stayed out overnight. "Today."

I sunk in my seat and closed my eyes. I didn't sleep, but I drifted, the lyrics of *Three Little Birds* by Bob Marley playing in the background. I let the smell of leather sink in, taking me back to my adolescence, back when my dad bought a 1967 Ford Mustang. I missed those days too. I imagined the car lifting me into the air as I flew past the empty streets of Jeddah, passing one light pole after another.

During that short ride to McDonald's, I allowed myself to

escape reality, to feel not a care in the world. I let myself be John for a little bit, not Timothy's father, not Patrick's partner. Just John. I didn't care that Elie was speeding. I didn't care if there were cops. I didn't care that a huge fight was waiting for me at home.

I missed me. I didn't miss my old job, but I missed my old friends, especially Scott.

In an attempt to eat my emotions away, I gobbled my hamburger by the mouthful, not allowing myself to indulge in the flavor of home. I even finished the extra sandwich Elie got, but that hadn't solved any of my problems.

To my surprise, Patrick hadn't locked me out. I made my way up to the bedroom, took my clothes off, and snuck into bed. As soon as I closed my eyes, I was asleep.

"John, wake up," said Patrick, "John, come on."

"What? What's wrong?"

"It's 1 o'clock already. Don't you think it's time for you to wake up?"

I ignored Patrick and rolled onto the other side of the bed.

"Suit yourself, I'm taking Timothy to the pool."

I slept for another hour, which gave me time to recollect my memories from the previous night and think about what I was going to say to Patrick. There was no doubt I was going to tell him the truth, it was more about *how* I was going to say it, without giving him a heart attack. I didn't know whether I should tell him that we went to a drug dealer's house first, or that we smoked so much I passed out on the couch. Maybe I could spin the scenario, as if it was my attempt at "being open to new cultures and experiences."

Patrick gave me the silent treatment, the most torturous form of communication, once he got home from the pool. Afraid I'd say something upsetting, which I excelled at, I started the discussion with, "Have you ever heard of a Big Tasty?"

He ignored me, so I continued, following him into our bath-room. "It's a burger at McDonald's, and it's so good!"

Then I went on and on about how the Big Tasty was a metaphor for my life. It was an American product that was created by Americans, for Americans, and yet, it can thrive outside of America. It can actually recreate itself, it can adapt and blend, becoming a better version of itself when it takes in the things it likes about another culture.

"Does it make it less like McDonald's?" I asked. "Absolutely not. Is one version better than the other? Maybe, but that doesn't matter. What matters—"

And then I'd lost my train of thought, forgetting the point I was trying to make.

"Erm, Patrick, can we talk about yesterday?"

"I believe you're the one who should do the talking, not me."

I'd gotten him to reply, so that was a good start.

"Right, right." I nodded, trying to figure out the right words to say. "Erm, well, I'd like to start by saying I'm sorry. I'm sorry that I didn't call to tell you where we were going. I'm sorry that I didn't update you as the night went on. And I'm sorry I came home so late."

I'm sorry for not saying sorry enough.

I waited for a reaction from Patrick, who bolted down the stairs, and if I didn't know any better, I'd say he enjoyed that I was running after him. Once I caught up with him, I held his arms and turned his body so we were face to face. Without making eye contact, he asked, "Can you just tell me where you went? Why were you out so late?"

"Yeah, I really want to, but first, can we sit down?"

"I'm fine standing here." That was a lie, no one was "fine" arguing at the front door.

"Come on. Please?"

"No, John," he said, his eyebrows pulled close together, wrinkles appearing between them. "What if you're dirty from an affair? I don't want to be anywhere near you."

He looked at me, his face filled with disgust. Although I carried the symptoms of an affair—the late return home, the lack of communication, the presence of another man—I couldn't believe what I was hearing. I was more likely to end up in prison last night than in bed with someone else.

"What?" I asked, hoping he would say something else. Anything else.

"If you were having an affair, then you definitely aren't worth how worried I was. I thought of all the worst case scenarios. What if you got into a car accident? What if Elie drove through another red light, and you ended up in prison?" He paused. "It's easier to think that you were cheating on me with Elie, because then what would I do if you got in some sort of trouble? Who could I call? How could I reach you? How could I find you? We're alone here, no one can help us."

"Patrick," I said, relieved. "I'm terribly sorry. Really. Can we please sit somewhere, so I can tell you what happened?" Preferably a place where Timothy couldn't hear us.

"First, tell me you weren't cheating on me." His eyes were focused on the floor, like he'd caught a hair against the white marble.

"Of course I wasn't cheating on you. You know that's never going to happen. Besides, I know Elie is a cool guy and all, but you know how I feel about chest hair."

Maybe a little humor will help.

Patrick smirked, which comforted me, because it meant he was slowly calming down. "That's what I kept telling myself. Of all people, would he really cheat on me with a man who's proud of his chest hair?"

"You've set a high benchmark, babe. If he looked more like his friend Tony, though…"

"Ha ha ha, not funny," said Patrick, his shoulders loosening gradually.

"OK, tell me *this* isn't funny. Elie thinks you're the woman in the relationship."

"Me? What? Why?"

"The Speedos, first and foremost." Patrick laughed, unable to deny that the Speedos did give way to part of his effeminacy.

I held Patrick's hand and led him back to our bedroom. I told him the whole story, not in chronological order, though. With little thinking, I let the words out of my mouth and tried to depict as accurate a picture as possible. He gasped and said, "What? Really?" a few times, and when there was nothing left to say, I apologized again. "I'm sorry for putting you through that. I wasn't thinking. Do you think you can forgive me?"

"Only after you explain to Timothy why you weren't home this morning."

My world was once again full.

CHAPTER EIGHTEEN

If I'd known that my job came down to saying things like, "1 + 1 = 2 buggers," or "6 - 4 = 2 butts," (I'm kidding, I didn't actually use the word "butt," although it'd have earned me a standing ovation) then my first few nights of the new school year would've been slumberous. But no, my mind wandered, coming up with worst case—borderline irrational—scenarios, like what if the children hate me? Or what if I have to take them on a field trip and lose one of them? Or worse, what if I lose control over my emotions because one of the kids keeps disrupting the class, so I carry him by the neck and choke him for a few seconds? I wouldn't ever do that, of course, but what if?

My job wasn't as hard as Patrick's, who taught the more difficult age groups, high schoolers (aka the real bullies). The creative activities he came up with put my funny words to shame. Once a week, he played a song by a trending artist and the students filled in the missing words in the lyric sheet. That alone made him teacher of the year, in my opinion. If my students asked me who The Weeknd was, I'd say, "Do you mean to say, 'What is the weekend?'" as if I was on *Jeopardy!*

All I had to gain from those sleepless nights was … nothing. Worrying didn't change anything, it only meant that I wasn't practicing my mantra, "Don't move to a smaller house." Besides, integrating was easier than expected, probably because being gay didn't matter. Oh, yeah, that was another thing I was worried about, what if the children found out about my sexuality and cast stones at me?

At first, I constantly looked over my shoulder, fearful of "getting caught" for doing something wrong, but investing my energy in that downward spiral was a waste of time. I could have—nay— I should have celebrated how great life was about to get. At the compound, people believed Patrick and I were roommates. At school, we were colleagues. No one asked us why we lived together, or whether our wives would eventually move to Saudi. And for the record, the children were adorable beings, who told me I was "cool." So no choking was involved.

The first two weeks after school had started, I'd approached Timothy to try and find out if anyone was bothering him for living with two men, but when he'd told me, "There's nothing that I didn't tell you yesterday, Dad," I stepped down from my interrogation.

And so, until further notice from Timothy:

1. His classmates knew that I was his dad.

2. They thought Patrick and I were life-long friends who decided to make life abroad easier by sharing a house.

3. Timothy didn't tell anyone about having two dads.

It was an ordinary life, just like it would have been anywhere else. Except for the part where we fed twelve stray cats that lived in our compound and took them to the vet if they were sick.

We memorized the prayer schedule and learned how to organize our lives around it whenever we made plans to eat out or go to the mall. We still hadn't bought a car and relied either on Uber or Careem (the Middle Eastern Uber) to go places.

One time, after I sat in the back seat of a Ford Fusion, I greeted the driver (or "Captain" as Careem called them) in poor Arabic, "Al Salamou Alaykom."

He looked at me in the rear-view mirror but didn't reply, which was odd and rude. *You, sir, just lost a star.*

He pulled out his phone and typed something, not caring that he had a customer in the car, waiting to be taken to his destination. He then pointed the screen toward me, but I couldn't read the Arabic text. That was when he turned his body and brought his arm closer to me, raising all kinds of red flags. He must have an awesome gaydar, and because of his homophobia, he wanted to slap me. That was the scenario in my head, at least.

The Captain pulled a board out of the backseat pocket that read in Arabic and in English, "Your driver is hearing impaired. Please communicate with him via text."

In that split second, I became the rude one. What a jerk. Me, not him. I apologized. He pointed at his screen, and I couldn't believe how dumb I was; he couldn't hear my apology.

I typed in a text but couldn't press send. I erased it and typed again, not knowing if I was condescending or offensive. I kept it simple, "Al Salamou Alaykom. I apologize for the mishap." *Thank you Google translate.*

He nodded and drove off.

To distract myself from the guilt of being the world's most insensitive, egocentric, and judgmental person, I admired Careem for providing equal job opportunities. I grabbed my phone and Googled "Careem KSA," the latest news being that they were training women to become Captains.

If I stick around, I might be driven by a Saudi woman one day. Man, Jeddah has so much more to offer than I ever could have imagined. The same city that Patrick thought didn't have pancake mixes is working just as hard as the next city to bridge the inequality gap in the workplace.

156

Timothy seemed to love school too. Whenever we asked him, he said, "Everyone loves me. They keep saying that it's so cool I'm American and how they all want to study in America one day." Who would've thought, my son, Timothy, would be the popular kid. *What if they find out he has two fathers? Would they feel the same about—no, John, stop.*

It wasn't long before Timothy was invited to birthday parties and to hang out at his friends' houses. It only made sense that he wanted to invite his friends over too.

"Timothy." I asked him over dinner, one night, "How do you think your friends would feel if they found out we were gay?"

"I don't know." He separated the onion pieces from the other vegetables on his plate. "I never thought about it."

"I don't think they'll be very pleased," I said, sipping on my soda, which was in a wine glass. "And even if they don't care, I don't know how their parents will feel about it. So we just have to be careful about it. I know I always tell you to be yourself, but this time, we have to change the rules a little. Just so we can protect ourselves and our jobs."

Patrick nodded. Timothy didn't say anything, so I didn't know what he was thinking. Just in case he thought we were hypocrites, I suggested, "Here's what we're going to do. We're going to take away any pictures that might hint that the three of us are a family. And if your friends ask, you'll tell them that Patrick is our housemate, that he and I are life-long friends."

"You can call me Uncle Patrick. Anyway, I imagine that your friends will want to spend their time at the recreation center, where all the girls are."

Why do you assume all of them are into girls? Oh, wait, never mind, you're probably right.

"It's fine." He put his fork down, defeated by his vegetables. "I like it better when we go out with Elie anyway."

157

"Yeah," said Patrick, "Elie is a funny guy. You're funny, too, little man."

"At least he knows you're gay, and he doesn't mind it," said Timothy as he put his plate in the sink. "So at least I can be comfortable when he's around. But anywhere else..." He walked toward the table, and just as I thought he was finally going to let us into his world, he pushed his seat under the table. "It doesn't matter. I'm tired. I'm going to my room. Good night."

Our son was struggling before our eyes. Since when did children have to carry the weight of their parents' lies? The money we made in Saudi was going directly into his therapy sessions two decades down the line.

Part of me doubted whether we were doing the right thing, and part of me didn't want to think too much about it. This was the epitome of parenting, feeling guilty for not knowing the right answer. It wasn't the first time we had to hide our identity. Growing up, we did it all the time, but I didn't want that for Timothy, I wanted him to be his true self, regardless of who his parents were.

I didn't want him to learn that to gain friends, he had to hide the "ugly" parts of himself, or worse, that if he had the right reasons, he could hide things from us, his parents.

One time, as we walked home, he told me the kids who waited with him at the school's multipurpose room (aka "The Saddest Place on Earth," think overused books, a TV that didn't work, board games with missing pieces, and a mean old supervisor) felt like they were abandoned by their parents, or at least, that they came second to their parents' job.

"Is that how you feel, Timothy?" With sweat dripping down my forehead, my eyes started to burn, but I had to focus on Timothy, considering he'd also had to spend a couple hours there every now and then while Patrick and I worked overtime, grading tests, planning lessons, or attending (parent) teacher meetings.

He shook his head, but I knew it was a stupid question, because he wouldn't admit it. If Patrick was on pickup duty, he'd comfort Timothy with the right words, but my wonderful chef of a partner raced home every day to make us a home-cooked meal. He was superman, and I was Good And Not Great.

At least I was good at being punctual, except for that one time when a female colleague walked into my classroom just as I was preparing to head out.

Her voluminous, dark curly hair framed her face, adding three inches onto her height. Her facial features were symmetrical, as if God had taken extra time to draw the details, erasing and correcting, until He was surprised with his own work. Her dark eyebrows accentuated her piercing eyes. The dorsal hump on her nose put today's beauty standards to shame; it told a story of ancestry and culture. *Her pink, plump lips—Whoa, John, stop, what are you doing?*

Her floral dress fit her curves with pride (or perfection), an icon of the "love your body" types on social media.

"Hi, John," she said in a soft voice. "Is this a good time?"

"Erm, yes, yes. Erm, how can I help you?"

Suck it up, John! You're gay, for goodness' sake! Besides, it's not at all a good time, Timothy's waiting for you!

"I know you're new in town, and I just wanted to be a good host. I know when I first moved here, the culture shock hit me hard."

Where did you move from? The Garden of Eden? Did they mourn your loss the day you left them?

Her lips moved, but my mind paid no attention. I dared look below her face, at the necklace laying gently across her collarbone, my favorite bone in the human body. The pendant was a blue eye, which my Mexican friends used to protect themselves from the evil eye, and I'd never seen it in a more deserving place.

The pendant stared back at me, as if there was a camera hidden in there, analyzing my every move.

I narrowed my eyes to focus better on the details of the eye.

What are you doing, John? Don't bring your head closer to her, she'll think you're looking at her breasts! Abort mission. I repeat, abort mission!

"Anyway, I was just wondering if you would like some company."

What did I miss?

She looked straight at me and paused, as if too shy to continue.

Is she asking me out on a date?

In all my years living in the US, never did an American woman walk up to me so openly. Never did I consider the fact that Middle Eastern women were so empowered as to do so. I was shaken. It took everything in me not to bow down to this goddess and kiss her feet.

"Erm, erm." My body short-circuited. "I don't have a car." There it was, the lamest excuse in history.

"What does that have to do with anything?" she asked, and I didn't know either.

"Oh, erm. I was just thinking, if we were to have dinner together, how can I pick you up if I don't have a car?"

"I guess you don't know," she replied, before laughing, as if I was a six-year-old who'd made a gullible comment. "Women can't ride in a car with a man unless he's her brother, husband, or father."

I stared into the distance, focused on the word "husband."

"Oh." I attempted to tame my body language. "Well, I guess that solves our problem, doesn't it?"

"What could a single father possibly be busy doing on a weekend in Saudi Arabia?"

She was right, what could he possibly do?

"Finishing a whole bottle of Saudi champagne," the six-year-old in me said.

As she laughed at my joke, I took the opportunity to admire her graciousness and come up with reasons as to why her ex-boyfriends weren't good enough for her. They bought her flowers, even though she didn't care for them. They never learned how to brush her curly hair. Worst of all, they asked her to straighten it.

For obvious reasons, I wasn't good enough for her either, but why was she interested in me? When she proposed that we meet at an Italian restaurant at 6 o'clock, I knew Patrick had something to do with it, because that was my favorite cuisine.

It was a trap, and I was going to play dumb. I wasn't about to miss a date with the world's most beautiful woman.

"You didn't write your name down," I said as she stood by the classroom door.

"I know." She walked out, grabbing her abaya from her purse.

Just like that, I had a date with an ineffable, anonymous Lebanese woman in Jeddah, Saudi Arabia. I carried the piece of paper she'd left the details of the restaurant on and smiled at it, as if it was a good luck charm. I put it in my wallet.

Even though there wasn't a chance we could build a relationship of any sort, this piece of paper would encourage me in times of self-doubt. That is, every day, when I ask myself, "Am I a handsome man?" I can confidently say, "Yes, I am." Maybe I should frame this piece of paper and hang it above our bed.

Oh, no, no, no! Timothy! It was quarter past 5, so I was fifteen minutes late, which, in Timothy's world, meant I'd forgotten he even existed. He was going to be so mad! I ran to get him. The mean old lady was indeed so. "Mr. Callaway, where have you been? You should have been here 20 minutes ago. The world isn't going to stop and wait for you, we have families of our own to tend to."

"I'm sorry, it won't happen again."

She shooed me with her hand like I was an unwanted cat. She called Timothy, locked the door behind her, and left without saying another word.

"Hey, buddy." I put my hand on his shoulder. "I'm so sorry I was late. You won't believe what happened—"

"Please, Dad, if you're really sorry, then don't make excuses."

"Fine, I just thought you'd want to know that a colleague asked me out on a date." Raising my eyebrows up and down, I showed off. "A female colleague."

"A woman asked *you* out on a date? Why?"

"It's a game your dad and I are playing," was the best I could come up with, because it sounded better than, "Why are you so surprised that women would want to date me?"

After lunch while Patrick secretly caught up with the Kardashians, danced, or did other Patrick things (goodbye black-heads), Timothy and I cleaned up the kitchen. To fill the silence, I asked him simple questions like, "Did anything funny happen at school today?" or "Was there any moment that made you wish I was with you?"

And although he was hesitant at first, a few weeks in, he let me into his world, and what an amazing world that was. He'd made a friend, Laura, who was either English or Australian and lived in our compound, but she went to a British school. In my eyes, she was the perfect friend:

1. She liked girls.

2. Timothy had finally found a person he could trust with his biggest secret—his two dads.

One time, I had said to him, "Why don't you invite her over for dinner?"

"I'm not sure. I think it's inappropriate in their culture here to invite a girl friend to your house when you're a boy. At least, that's what Haya says."

"Haya?"

"She's the first friend I made at school. When I introduced myself to my class at the beginning of the year, I'd told them my mom had passed away when I was a baby and that I'd never met her. She came to me after class, telling me she'd lost her mom, too, when she was really young. I cried because of how sad her story was, but she thought I cried because I missed my mom. I should've told her the truth, but how? I feel so dirty. Most of the time, I can't look her in the eye, and she thinks it's because I'm sad. It's not. I guess it's a good thing her dad won't allow her to come over."

"Because you're a boy?"

"There's that, but also because I live with my dad and a male teacher. If Isabelle or grandma was with us, he would let her." His back facing me, I was left with his tone of voice to make out that this subject bothered him; making friends, lying to them, and something else, but I needed to peel the onion.

A few weeks and many simple questions later, I got him to tell me more about his friends. "Today, me and Haya talked about what life is like without a mom," and as my heart sank, he paused. "And we imagined scenarios of what it would be like to have one. Like going to the mall together and stuff."

As much as I wanted to scream for Patrick, so he could come to the rescue and teach me the perfect words to say, this was a moment between Timothy and me. And even if I didn't know what to say, just having my presence close by, my listening ear, meant I was there for him.

A lot of days, all I got was, "It was alright," or "I don't really want to talk about my day," and as hard as it was to respect that boundary, I really wanted to know what he was hiding, and why he was hiding it from me. I had to trust that, some things, he had to do alone, and they weren't my burden to carry.

In a similar way, my burdens weren't his to carry, but in my case, I'd taken advantage of a listening ear whose mere presence made my world better. I had to learn to open up to Patrick before it felt like my life was going down the drain. What I felt when Timothy didn't let me into his world, Patrick experienced a hundred times and more with me.

CHAPTER NINETEEN

Every day, we waited until Maghreb (Sunset) prayer was over before taking Koala for a walk. We learned the hard way that walking outside during prayer time resembled walking into a horrible opera. If you didn't like the music, you wanted to tear your ears off. We made one stroll around the compound before heading to the recreation center and engaged in small talk with neighbors along the way.

It wasn't until we moved to Saudi Arabia that I discovered how individualistic our society had become and how obsessed it was with appearing busy. In fact, when we took Koala for a walk in our cute San Antonio community, a wave hello or a quick nod was the most we would expect from neighbors walking by. Timothy wouldn't dare ask if he could pet other neighbors' dogs for fear of being ignored.

In Saudi, though, things were different, especially with our Arab neighbors. For example, the first time we met Ali, his eight-year-old daughter, Yasmine (the Arab equivalent of Jasmine, pronounced Yass-meen), ran out of their front door to pet Koala. It was thanks to Yasmine that we met Ali and Asma. Ever since, when we walked past their house, they insisted we enter their home for a cup of delicious Moroccan tea and addictive bite-sized Middle Eastern sweets. It took me a minute to understand that when he said "bet," he actually meant "pet," and from then on, it was a fun game deciphering his words.

Ali always joked, "So, have you decided about Yasmine and Timothy's wedding? I'm telling you, my daughter will make a wonderful bride and lovely housewife one day. Just look at her mom. Can you imagine the beautiful babies they will make?"

I loved seeing Timothy turn tomato red. I also loved these impromptu visits. They helped me realize how similar we really were. Sure, their houses were decorated with a few traditional items they had brought from back home, like a traditional Moroccan table or small figures of the Pyramids and Egyptian Pharaohs, but they liked to watch sports, as the American people did. Their kids liked to play on gaming consoles, as American kids did. Their wives liked to shop online, as American wives did. In my opinion, Amazon should have been invented in Saudi Arabia, where women couldn't drive and make their way to Target so easily.

My mother was right when she said, "Can you imagine how boring the world would be if we were all alike?"

Pointing at the man's picture that hung on the wall, I asked Ali, "Is this your father?"

He laughed, but I was missing the joke. "Really, you don't know who this is?"

I was pretty sure it wasn't Mo Salah, whom I knew of thanks to my Egyptian students. "He's the Egyptian King," they said time and again. "He's the best player Liverpool has." I looked at Ali and shook my head, letting him know I was clueless.

"Now I'm going to have to be upset with you. This is Abdel Fattah el-Sisi."

"Oh! Why didn't you say so from the beginning? Of course, it is."

"You don't know who that is either. Do you?"

I shook my head.

"He's the Egyptian president. He's the future of our country. He's building hospitals and infrastructures. He's helping us get rid of the Muslim Brotherhood."

"I'll make sure to remember that next time." What I really wanted to say was, "Why would you hang the picture of your president on your living room wall? Or any wall in your house for that matter?" I didn't, though, because I didn't want to sound offensive. It must have been a political statement, the same way a Christian hung crosses in their house.

"So, whose picture do people hang if they support the Muslim Brotherhood?" asked Patrick.

"Mohammad Morsi. The biggest idiot in the world of idiots. You better hope you never walk into a house that has his picture on the wall."

"Hope" and "picture" were one of the harder ones to understand, because he pronounced them "hub" and "bik-shar." By the time I realized that, he'd gone deep into politics.

Ali was right. In this case, Morsi represented ultra-conservative people, who preferred to neighbor like-minded Egyptians, hence living in less liberal compounds, where dogs weren't allowed for religious reasons, where women wore burqinis, and parties were only for children.

"Man," said Batrick, "This is all so interesting to me. I read in an article once that people who live far away from home tend to build a stronger connection with their religious system. And when they feel like they're a minority that leads them to be even more opposed to the beliefs of the majority. Do you know what I mean?"

"What, then," said Ali.

"What does it say under the picture?" Timothy leaned closer to read it.

"Masr, my Egypt, the mother of the world," said a proud Yasmine.

Timothy was going to gain immeasurable cultural richness in the coming years as a consequence of living abroad, an opportunity I only got now as an adult.

"You're from America?" Yasmine said to Timothy. "My best friend, Fatima, is from America. We're going to go to college together in America one day."

"That's nice. What do you want to be when you grow up?"

"I want to make video games."

"Like Minecraft?"

"Yeah! Like Minecraft!" she said, full of excitement.

"That's so cool!"

It *was* cool that an eight-year-old girl from Egypt had such great ambition. Who knew what the future held for her, so long as her dad didn't sell her off for five camels or something. Sorry, I couldn't *helb* it.

People in our community treated each other like family, for, after all, we lived far away from our families. Every time we left Ali's house, he saluted us with the same sentence, "I have been here over 10 years. If you ever need anything, please let me know. As you know, our apartment number is 35. Please don't be shy." You'd never hear that in the US, so no matter how different Ali and I were, his cordiality told me we were the same.

Once Koala had a dump, we made our way to the recreation center. There was a group of men playing volleyball and a coach teaching kids to play tennis. Timothy ran to the play area, which had two trampolines. "The Single Section, and the Family Section," I joked.

Patrick and I made our way to the cafe that was next to the pool, where we found our friends, neighbors, and two other couples we had yet to meet. David and Laura, who were South African, introduced us to Jameel and Nur, who were from India and Indonesia, and Jackson and Cecilia from New York. I loved the diversity in our compound.

"Do you smoke?" David extended the cord of the hookah.

It's funny how I keep getting offered all kinds of things in Saudi —Ced, hash, hookah. Do I have a face that screams, "Give me the goods?"

"I don't." I reached for the hookah. "But I don't mind trying." It couldn't possibly be worse than the Afghani hash I had recently tried.

I was mentally preparing myself for a pleasant experience, where I looked so cool blowing the smoke out. I inhaled the first puff and coughed uncontrollably, making a fool of myself again. Before I knew it, I was the center of attention, and not the kind that I liked. I tried to stop, but I couldn't. I kept coughing and coughing. I expected Patrick to worry about me, or to bring me a glass of water at least. Instead, he got out his phone and took a video of me. "Haven't you learned by now to think twice before you accept everything that's handed to you?"

When I caught my breath—it was David, by the way, who brought me a bottle of water—Patrick said, "Check out your phone, I think you'll like what's in there."

He had already created a meme using my picture! It said, "Why did you leave your partner for his sister?" My picture was the answer. I hated that it was funny.

I was about to show the picture to our neighbor when I remembered that they didn't know we were a couple or that we were gay. I didn't know how Nur, who wore a veil, felt about gay people. I'd learned not to associate her with any stereotype, so maybe after a few more conversations, I'd know whether or not to trust her with my big secret.

My phone vibrated.

New notification: Email from Tom Knowles
Click

From: Tom Knowles <tknowles@adsj.com>
  To: John Callaway <jcallaway@adsj.com>,
  Cc: Patrick Mortensen <pmortensen@adsj.com>
  Subject: Urgent Meeting
  Date: 28th November

With surprise written all over my face—not the good kind of surprise—I looked at Patrick. He shook his head and furrowed his eyebrows, as if to ask what was going on. Before saying anything, I opened the email, which, it turned out, had also been sent to Patrick.

"Check your phone, I think you'll like what's in there." It sounded like payback, but really, it was just concern. We both dove into our screens.

Dear John and Patrick,
  Please come to my office first thing in the morning. I need to discuss an urgent matter. Please do not bring Timothy.
  Regards,
  Tom Knowles
  Principal"

Patrick looked up to me, his face full of confusion. He murmured, "Urgent matter?"

I was just as confused.

CHAPTER TWENTY

"Have you been tactile with your students?" I paced back and forth in our bedroom later that night, trying to figure out what the "urgent concern" was.

Patrick was a people pleaser, so my first guess was students felt he was behaving inappropriately. "Have you given anyone a pat on the shoulder for good behavior?" I thought out loud, my eyes focused on the tiled floor beneath my feet.

"Why did you automatically assume it was something *I* did, like it was a foregone conclusion?"

I didn't say anything, realizing that my words were arrows that I was aiming at Patrick. He stood with his arms crossed, as if they were his armor, but it wasn't impenetrable. His cheeks flushed, and he spoke fast, barely catching his breath between sentences. "I think it has something to do with your anonymous lover. You thought I didn't know about her, but Timothy told me. My bet is one of your "precious" students overheard your conversation and put it all over social media. Parents have probably found out and complained to Tom about *your* inappropriate behavior. And what were you thinking, telling Timothy this was a game you and I played? He asked me if it was an erotic game. And I'm quoting him on that."

I was flabbergasted because:

1. What if he was right.

2. I'd been asked out by the world's most beautiful woman, because she found me attractive, and I had to distract Patrick, before he noticed that talking about her made me blush.

"Oh, so we call him Tom now." I tried to redirect the attention back to him.

"What else am I supposed to call him?" said Patrick, who then went on and on about how reckless I was, and how I needed to learn to "measure my words before letting them out of my mouth." I lay on our bed and thought of what I was going to wear Friday, forgetting why Patrick and I were panicking in the first place.

Then, Timothy, who appeared out of nowhere, said something that triggered a lightbulb moment. "We're not through the first semester yet, and you are already being called into the principal's office. You're bad, bad teachers." He shook his head slowly, like a disapproving parent.

Patrick and I looked at each other in surprise, as if communicating, "Are you thinking what I'm thinking?"

Hopping off the bed, I leaned down on both knees before Timothy and tried to arrange my next few words so as not to come across as intimidating. "Timothy, do you think, maybe, you did something wrong?"

Patrick, however, was less gentle. "Ow! What are you doing to my hair?" screamed Timothy.

"I'm checking for lice," justified Patrick.

"I don't have lice!"

I tried again, "Have you been giving other kids the chance to answer the teacher's questions?"

"Yes, I have. It's not something I did! Why do you assume it was me? Why can't it be you? Did it ever occur to you that people might make fun of me because my dad has a male roommate?"

My son was being bullied, and yes, that was an urgent concern, one that kept me awake all night. So when Timothy called me in the middle of the night to change his bedsheets, I was prepared.

"What I am about to tell you is not representative of my personal opinion," said Tom the next day, his hands clasped and his elbows resting on his desk. "In the US, it would sound absurd, but we are in a different culture, so we play by different rules."

Come on, man, cut to the chase! Or as Elie would say, give me from the end, give me the butter!

"The solution I am going to propose was the best I could reach. Word got out that the two of you are a couple, and many parents have launched complaints, saying this was not the example they wished to set for their children."

Though the words went into my ears, and I knew what every individual one meant, I couldn't process them all put together. I didn't want to. Just when I had grown accustomed to the culture, this man was telling me that an avalanche was coming our way, making life here a tad harder—if there was still a life to be had here.

"After much negotiation, I got them to agree to the following: only one of you can stay and work for the school. Unfortunately, there is no one that can protect you, because I won't lie to you, this is not discrimination in the eyes of the law."

Patrick's eyes were wide open, and although Tom waited for one of us to speak, we were both at a loss for words. I pinched myself to check whether this was another nightmare.

"I know it's a tough decision, and there's a lot at stake. I will give you until the end of the week to make a final decision."

That's it? No apology? You're not going to give us a chance to explain ourselves? I guess even if we did, what is there to explain? We aren't called in because of something we did but because of who we are. What is this I'm feeling inside? Is it anger? Disappointment? Fear? Bewilderment? Rage? All of the above?

"What about our son?" Patrick slammed his right hand on Tom's desk, and it was the first time I'd witnessed him stand up for someone so passionately.

Before Tom could answer, the bell rang, and I forgot about the class I had to teach. Patrick grabbed my hand and helped me to my feet. We exited Tom's office, both looking at the floor, and waved at each other silently, before making our way to our classrooms.

This son of a bravo! He knew about our sexuality when he hired us, and somehow we are the ones given a foxtrot-ting ultimatum! What decision can we make? We can't stay in the country if one of us loses his job.

I wasn't in the mood to teach, so I gave my pupils equations to solve.

Which one of you little traitors is a homophobe? I bet it's you, Ahmed, with your perfect grades and long curly hair. You think you're better than everyone else. Well, let me tell you something, as a Muslim man, you shouldn't even have long hair. Or maybe it's you, Zeina. You think you're so funny, well, you can't make a joke out of me! Or maybe it was all of you, as a collective, playing innocent, making me believe I was your favorite teacher when all along, you were plotting against me.

I closed my eyes. *Breathe, John, breathe.*

It would've been easy to blame them for what had just happened in the principal's office, but they were sinless, and they were only the product of what society had taught them, a society that had told them time and time again that differences were bad, and that people should be punished for not conforming. Things weren't too different in the US.

Knowing that, I still couldn't help but feel culpable, even though I knew I wasn't blameworthy of anything.

It's my fault, I should've asked more before coming, I should've created a contract that protected me, I should've—no, wait, John—this isn't your fault.

Everyone was an enemy. Eyes burned into my skin, branded me a gay and judged me for it. With every step I took, from the classroom to the teacher's room, from the bathroom to the cafeteria, I wanted to shout, "I'm not a bad influence!"

Instead, those words turned into tears that choked me up, and it was a matter of time before I ended up drowning in all the insults, accusations, and unwanted attention. The school suddenly—and quickly—became a lonely place, and the worst part was that I was an adult. Not a child.

This kind of treatment wasn't new to me, and I knew very well that adults who belonged to "different" societal boxes had their own stigma to deal with. Baby mamas who had four kids with four baby daddies. Feminists who didn't shave their armpits. Black men marrying white women. Seriously, though, would they fire a qualified person simply because they found out they were married to someone of another race?

By the time we arrived home that night, Patrick and I had accumulated a thousand thoughts—all negative, clearly—and it was impossible for them to come out nicely.

"Your boyfriend is good for nothing," I said, not knowing how else to start the inevitable conversation.

"Well, maybe we can see if your girlfriend is good for something."

"What are you talking about?"

"You said you were going on a date with her Friday evening, right?"

I didn't say anything. Where was he going with this?

"Well, if you keep playing the part, maybe word will get out that the two of you are dating."

"And what? Suddenly, I'm not gay? Or suddenly, I left you for a female teacher? And what? Move in with her? Or do we all live here together? This isn't just some movie where we can play with people's lives without there being real consequences. We never should have come here. I can take the homophobia, but what I can't take is that my son is being bullied because of us."

My phone buzzed.

> THE GANG
>
> Joshua added Bas Kralingen to the group.

What kind of name was Bas Kralingen? Right after:

> THE GANG
>
> Joshua removed you from the group.

The message was clear, I was replaceable, I was unimportant. It was too much for me to handle. All the stress I carried that day, all the tears I held back, all the guilt caught up with me.

"You know what, Patrick? This was the most ridiculous decision we ever made. What were we thinking? You don't just throw fish in a tank with a crocodile and hope that it doesn't eat them. And I feel so stupid for listening to you and believing that this could somehow work. Sure, we were bored with our life in San Antonio, but it was temporary."

Bringing out the new profile picture of the group chat where Bas Kralingen stood in the middle, a smile spreading from ear to ear, I said, "Look. Look at what I just lost. Ten years of hard work, patience and dedication." That picture was a metaphor, of course, because I hadn't known the gang that long, but my old world as I'd known it was gone, and someone else was living it for me.

"All for what?" I continued, "to come here and teach elementary schoolers and be their clown? To be discriminated against and not have a voice? I can't believe it, I'm so, so, so—"

"Disappointed?" suggested Patrick, his hands on his heart.

"No."

"Mortified?"

"No, but you're getting closer."

"Abused?"

"What? No. I can't even figure out how I'm feeling. Whatever, let's settle on disgusted." With no energy left in me, I lost the strength to speak, so I whispered, "We did this to ourselves..." I broke down, unable to fight back the tears that flooded my cheeks.

"And now what?" I asked, words coming out between sobs. "If one of us loses his job, we can't stay here." Never in my life had I felt so helpless. This kind of problem didn't happen to people like me; I'm not from Cuba or Venezuela. I wasn't built to be tough like the people from those countries were. I wasn't someone who knew real struggle, who could predict an avalanche, and I hadn't been taught over generations how to persevere. Not me. I was fragile, and my world crumbled with the first snowflake.

I closed my eyes and went back to a time when I was a kid whose biggest worry was not having enough gel in my hair.

Patrick came closer and tried to hug me. "I need some space." I pushed him back. I didn't mean to, but my tense body preceded my brain.

Respecting my wishes, he left our bedroom and closed the door behind him. A feeling of loneliness crept over me. I wanted to play something on TV and escape reality, but I might as well "tile the ocean," as Elie so often said. I wanted the crying to stop, but I felt that I hadn't cried enough, as if my tears hadn't melted the avalanche.

If everything happens for a reason, what can possibly be the reason this is happening? I've never intentionally hurt someone. I've been good to my parents all my life. I'm an honest, hard-working man. Why is this happening to me? If there really is a God up there, why is He allowing all this to happen? What does He want me to learn out of all this? Why does it have to be this way for me to learn a particular lesson? How will all this end? What's on the other side of the mountain?

I desperately needed a distraction. I was tempted to text Elie and see if we could get high together, but he would see the state I was in and ask me what was wrong, and I was in no mood to explain. I grabbed the piece of paper with my anonymous date's name and texted her, unsure whether she'd received the news that I was gay.

JOHN

What could a single lady possibly be busy doing on a weeknight in Saudi Arabia?

She replied with a picture of a book she held in her hand, *Mindset*, by Carol Dweck. I noticed her pinky toe in the corner, and I zoomed in, like a creep. Why I was interested in knowing the exact tone of her red pedicure beats me to this day, but anything was better than having to think of the situation I was in.

JOHN

Nice, I'll leave you to it.

She replied with a thumbs-up emoji.

The chat died in a heartbeat, and as I threw my phone on my bed, a gentle knock on the door lit a small spark in my heart; *I am important.*

"Come in."

"Dad?" Timothy gently closed the door behind him. "Are you okay?"

Not knowing how to answer that question, I remained silent, and Timothy sat next to me, and although he didn't ask any further questions, or offer any advice, his presence brought solace. For the first time, I didn't want to hide how imperfect I was or give him the impression that grownups didn't break down. I wanted to show him my raw emotions, and I wanted him next to me. As sad as the events were that led to that particular moment, I'll cherish it forever.

"I think I'm ready to go out now," I said, realizing that Patrick had been alone this whole time.

"Hey," I whispered, as Timothy and I walked toward the kitchen counter, where Patrick sat on a barstool, his eyes on the laptop screen. There were six tabs open, one for each job site. Sales Associate, Marketing Coordinator, Project Administrator. These were all things he had no experience with.

"What are you doing?" I asked.

"Looking for a job."

"How's *that* going?"

"I'm trying, I'm looking. I couldn't find any positions for a male dance instructor, and I don't meet the requirements to be a personal trainer. So, here I am."

"Listen." He kept scrolling down his screen. "Can we talk?"

"I think you already said a lot."

"I know, I'm sorry. Can we try again? I didn't mean to take it all out on you."

He didn't say anything and opened more links.

"Can you please close the laptop, so we can have a talk?"

"Fine."

I grabbed his hand and led him to our living room couch.

"I'm sorry. There's no excuse for the things I said. You must be just as stressed out as I am."

"Don't you think I already feel guilty? Don't you think I'm aware that I corralled you into this situation with me? I know that, most of the time, you regret coming here, that you wish we could pack our bags and go back."

"Actually, I don't mean to interrupt you, but I just want to clarify that I actually like it here."

"You do?" he asked, leaning his back against the couch, as if relieved.

"I do. I was enjoying my job. I like living in this compound. And I think Timothy's enjoying being the cool American kid. It's just…" I paused, to plan my words, "I guess I'm weak, and when I feel stuck, I forget that all things in life are temporary, good or bad."

Although I was planning to let Patrick do all the talking, so he could let off some steam, but I went on and on, "I mean, if this happened in the US, it wouldn't matter as much, because we know the area so well. We know the law. We know how to find another job. But here, we're by ourselves, and I just don't see how we're going to get out of this one."

"Let me just understand one thing. You like living here, right?"

"Yes." My hands met Patrick's.

"So, it doesn't really matter if you work at the school or somewhere else, right?"

Right. Where are you going with this?

He continued, "Okay, great, because I was checking out some jobs, and they actually have a few openings at the US Consulate. And I think you'll be very interested in them. You won't have to be the class clown." He winked as he turned the laptop my way.

His face coming back to life, Patrick showed me a couple of jobs that perfectly described the things I wanted to do. The mere thought of working for the US government gave me goosebumps.

Patrick smiled, his fingers racing across the keyboard. I realized that mountains and avalanches were bound to come our way, wherever we were. Who knew, maybe if we'd stayed in San Antonio, my depression would've kept me home, causing me to lose contact with the gang. Or maybe I could've introduced Bas to the gang, and we all became Great And Not Good. What could have happened didn't matter. It didn't make my current life more right or less right.

As long as I had Patrick by my side, we would find a solution, and we lived the life we were supposed to live. I admired his attitude, his perseverance, and his commitment to consistently look beyond temporary hurdles.

"Do you mind if I take this?" I asked, referring to the laptop.

He pushed it my way before making his way to the bathroom. I applied for the jobs I was qualified for and looked on LinkedIn to see if I could find a job with a private company. If Elie was right, employers would be interested in hiring an American.

A couple of hours later, my brain was fried. My sad inbox was empty, and all I could do was be hopeful that the mailbox would be fuller in the morning.

God, I hope I get any kind of interview before the weekend. That way, I can shove that up Tom Knowles's alpha.

In the meantime, I needed to speak with Timothy, and for the first time, I was thankful for the dirty dishes in the sink.

"Timothy," I shouted from the kitchen. "Please come downstairs and help me clean up!"

As Timothy emptied the dishwasher and I wiped crumbs off the kitchen table, I sought words to break the ice. *I should've called Patrick down here for backup.*

"Son, do you want to go back to San Antonio?"

181

"I don't know," he said, "I don't know if it would help make things better."

That was Sunday. Monday came. Still no answer from any of the recruiters. Tuesday, same. As our deadline neared, Patrick and I applied for jobs, even if they didn't exactly fit our qualifications. In my case, that ranged from Electrical Engineer, to Procurement Manager, to Sales Engineer.

Wednesday afternoon, though, my inbox was still empty. Thursday too. Patrick didn't have any luck either. We would be meeting with the principal the next day, and we still hadn't come to a decision as to which one of us would keep his job at the school.

That week, a dark cloud hovered over me. I tried to keep a positive attitude, but deep inside, I was scared. I didn't look up when I walked. Instead, I stared at my shoes.

I need new shoes. Gosh, we're going to have to cut our budget. This is so freakin' depressing. I shouldn't have to worry about this sort of thing at this age.

I heard someone call my name. Running toward me was the most beautiful sight for sore eyes.

"John," she said, running out of breath, "you sure know how to make a girl run after you."

"I do?"

"Yeah, I've been calling for you. Didn't you hear me?"

"Oh, I didn't. I'm sorry." I was picturing our life if Patrick had stayed in Saudi while Timothy and I returned home.

"Too much Saudi champagne last night?"

A little laugh escaped me.

Why is she still interested in me? Hasn't she heard?

"Hey, are you okay?" She placed a hand on my arm.

"Yeah, yeah, sorry. I'm just running out of jokes to tell my students. They're a tough crowd, I tell you."

Maybe she's oblivious to my sexuality. Or maybe she's already turned a gay man straight before, so she's planning to do the same with me. I can see how a gay man would fall for her. Or, oh my goodness, does she think I'm bi? Maybe she doesn't categorize people. I'm overthinking this; she probably just wants a friendly date. After all, it can't possibly be so common to meet non-heterosexuals in Saudi Arabia, right? I should update my resume and title it, "Electrical Engineer Looking For Gay-Friendly Job." That's certainly click-bait.

"We're still on for this weekend?"

As tempted as I was to cancel, to say I was going through a rough patch, that I needed some time alone, I didn't want to disappoint her. How could I be the reason that beautiful face frowned?

"You know it."

"Okay, wonderful, I've got to run now."

"Sure, have a good one."

She was out of sight once I remembered to ask her name, and though she'd brightened up my day, it wasn't long before I sunk back into my mood.

Overwhelmed, we hadn't been to the recreation center all week, and without my friends' support, it was ten times harder. How I yearned to be discussing benign topics with the gang or to be having yet another boring Taco Tuesday.

As I waited for my students to enter my classroom, I stared at the blackboard, one question on repeat, *What am I doing here?*

I grabbed my phone one last time before students returned from recess, desperately hoping to receive an email from the Consulate. Nothing.

"Mr. Callaway?" said one of my students.

"Bilal, what's up, little guy?"

"I think you've been sad this week. I just want to say, you're an awesome teacher, and I like being your student a lot."

"Oh." I paused as I placed my hand on my heart. "That means a lot to me, Bilal. And I'm very happy to be your teacher too." Maybe not everyone at school knew about our "situation" after all.

I used to think I was born to be an engineer, but teaching those kids was much more rewarding; it developed my creativity and challenged me in pleasant ways, like having to cater to different learning styles. I adored getting to know my kids' personalities. Like Ashraf, who always related math equations to soccer. He was a bright one, he just didn't know it yet. Or Miriam, a shrinking violet who rarely spoke, and yet managed to be top of her class.

The diversity in my class was astonishing; I had students from Saudi Arabia, Algeria, India, Lebanon, Pakistan, Palestine, Sudan, Egypt, Jordan, Tunisia, Korea, Syria. I hadn't heard of the majority of those countries before moving to Saudi. I did know about Israel and Iran, but that was no use, since the people of those two countries were forbidden entry into Saudi.

I grabbed my phone again.

New notification: Email from Widad Rifai

From: Widad Rifai <widad.rifai@hotmail.com>
    To: John Callaway <jcallaway@adsj.com>
    Subject: Please read URGENTLY
    Date: December 3rd

Rifai, Rifai, the name's completely alien to me. Is Widad a woman's name or a man's name? Why does everyone keep using the term "urgent?" And more importantly, what do they have to tell me that's urgent? Are they one of the recruiters? Oh, God, let it be good news.

Dear Mr. Callaway,

I have heard of your unfortunate situation. I can help. Please contact me at your earliest convenience.

Sincerely,

Widad Rifai

050 001 1234

CHAPTER TWENTY-ONE

As I buttoned my favorite pair of denim pants, Patrick sat on our bed, staring at me and biting his fingernails, which he usually did when the Kardashians got in a big fight, but this time, he did it to keep his mouth shut. He'd asked me several times that day why I hadn't canceled the date, and in an attempt to refute his jealousy, I gave him silly answers like, "Because I want to check out the Family Section," or "So I can complain about you." If I'd given him a serious answer, it would be admitting that there was reason to worry about a potential affair.

I straightened my burgundy t-shirt, checking the mirror for wrinkles. Patrick pointed at the small logo on the bottom left corner of my shirt as he got off the bed and walked my way, a smile on his face. "Oh my God, John, I see what you're doing. You chose the shirt with the rainbow. You *want* her to know about your sexuality without having to say anything. Subtle move!"

Then, coming behind me, he hugged me so we were both in front of the mirror. "Let's hope she doesn't leave you when she gets the—"

His smile washed away quickly, he unwrapped his arms around me, like a silk ribbon, and after taking a few steps back, he looked at the floor. "What if she does find out and tells everyone that you're gay?"

Walking toward my shoe rack, I hoped my calm energy would soothe Patrick. "You're overreacting. Rainbows are for everyone. They're a reminder that, even when it's raining, there's a rainbow —a sign of hope."

Patrick rolled his eyes and left the room, only to return with a pint of Cookie Dough Häagen Dazs ice cream a minute later (yes, they have the good kind of ice cream in Saudi).

Hearing his cry of despair, I asked, "Why are you so nervous?"

"Are you serious right now? How would *you* feel if I was going out on a date with someone else? And she doesn't even know you're gay." He scooped up a big spoonful of ice cream and stuffed it into his mouth. I barely made out his words. "What if you like her?"

To think that this was a setup he'd created.

"Oh, honey." I sat next to him, my back straight so as not to wrinkle my carefully ironed shirt. "How can you possibly think I can like someone else? Especially when you're so attractive when eating ice cream? How about this? What if I tell her about you, about us, within the first five minutes of seeing her? And then she'll understand my intentions toward her are innocent."

"You would do that for me?" He put the spoon into the ice cream carton.

"Of course I would. I would scream from the rooftops of my love for you."

"Okay, well, in that case, I guess I can admit that you look gorgeous. She's going to be heartbroken."

"I don't know about that." I checked my outfit in the mirror one last time. "Anyway, my Uber is here. I'll see you gentlemen in a couple of hours."

My Uber hadn't arrived yet, but I needed a private space to call Widad Rifai. Hiding behind the bush outside our house, I copied the phone number at the bottom of the email and called it. At the sound of the first ring, I closed my eyes, my mind focused on the adjective Widad Rifai used in their email to describe my life: unfortunate. Who was this person, anyway, who had so much power to change my life? Were they going to stand up for me, for what was right? Were they going to help me start the school's first-ever movement? A march, perhaps? Oh—oh— maybe they were with the press!

"Hello?" came the calm voice of a woman.

"Yes, hello, is this Widad Rifai? It's John Callaway."

Sorry for butchering your name.

"Hi, John. Thank you for calling me back."

She was thanking me when I should have been thanking her.

"I heard about what happened to you, and let me just start by saying we don't all feel this way about…" She paused, as if trying to find an appropriate word.

Your people? Sodomites? Satanists?

"You and your partner."

It had been a long time since I'd heard those words in the same sentence. Ever since moving here, it was "You and Patrick," or my utter favorite, "You and your housemate". Thrilled, a sense of liberation ran through my blood, as if I'd been injected with a dose of adrenaline. I wanted to call every single person whom she claimed accepted us and hear them say those exact same words.

"When I asked Basma about her opinion of you," she contin- ued, "she had so many positive things to say. Now, although I cannot help you get your job back—"

Basma? Who's Basma? Does she mean Basma Saqqar, my

student? Also, what does she mean she can't help us get our job back? Then how is she going to help us?

"I can offer you another job. I would like you to tutor my three children, not just in math, but whichever other subjects they need support with. I can transfer your *residence permit* to one of my companies, and I can have one of my drivers pick you up and drop you off."

There was a brief pause while I processed the offer.

So, we aren't starting a movement? And I won't be in the press? Bummer. But hey, I can stay in the country. This is too easy, there has to be a catch. She's not going to ask me to convert to Islam, is she?

"Hello? John? Are you there?"

"Yes, I'm here. Are you Basma Saqqar's mother?" I came closer to our living room window, sneaking up on my own family.

"Yes, I am her mother. She told me about your situation and how sad it made her, because she likes you a lot."

Maybe she was a divorcée and Rifai was her maiden name. It didn't matter; her name could have been Ms. Potatoes for all I cared. An unprejudiced Saudi woman wanted me to tutor her children. Talk about an epiphany, talk about an oxymoron. I repeated it to myself to believe it. *An unprejudiced Saudi woman wants me to be face-to-face with her kids, five times a week, and she's not afraid I'll be a bad influence.*

Ms. Rifai got down to the nitty-gritty; her eldest would grad-uate that year, her second had three years to go, and her youngest was in my class. Every year, she'd take care of fees related to the transfer and renewal of my residence permit, or as the locals called it, *Iqama* (pronounced E-gahmah).

"Your son, is he under your sponsorship, or is he under Patrick's?" she asked.

I wasn't sure how to answer her question, but considering that he entered the country with me, I assumed he was under mine, which basically meant that we owed the Ministry of Interior almost $4,000 every year in dependent fees.

"Can't I transfer his sponsorship so he is under Patrick's?" I asked her, so the school would pay for Timothy's sponsorship fees.

"You cannot transfer the *Iqama* from one father to another. The option simply does not exist, you can guess why."

I choked on my own breath, which she must have heard because she comforted me. "Again, you don't have to worry about that. I am happy to take care of all the fees for you."

I could understand why a person wanted to be a Good Samaritan, but what I couldn't fathom yet was why this woman was willing to hire me as a private tutor when the other parents preferred I was nowhere near their children. Basma Saqqar was Saudi, so, if anything, I would've expected Ms. Rifai to be strongly opposed to my homosexuality. Aside from the job offer, I was curious to meet her, to know more about the side of the Saudi culture that was open to differences. I wanted to meet the person who accepted me for who I was when no one else did.

"Can I talk to Patrick before I give you a final answer?"

"Of course. Can I expect to hear from you by next weekend?"

"That's perfect. Thank you so much Ms. Rifai."

I put the phone in my pocket and got into the passenger seat of the Prius. The ride to Casper & Gambini's was silent. I didn't know if the driver, who wore the traditional Saudi dress, spoke English, and I didn't try to find out.

Less than fifteen minutes later, we had arrived. In that short span of time, we must have passed twenty five restaurants and cafes, because what other business can someone open when everything is illegal? Hospitals, of course, we passed a few of those, too, one of them called the Saudi German Hospital.

I extended my arm to open the glass door, but a Filipino waiter beat me to it. "Welcome, sir. Do you have a reservation?"

"I'm not sure, is there one under the name of—" *That's right, genius, you don't know her name.* "Erm, is there one under the name of John?"

He checked the list attached to his clipboard. "Yes, there is, please follow me."

I like the European look of this place. The simple, minimalistic decoration. The small, wooden tables. The leather couch. The open space. The fact that it's got one entrance, for both the single and family customers. So this is what it's like to be at a restaurant with women. I feel like a VIP.

"Here you are, sir."

"Thank you."

CHAPTER TWENTY-TWO

Anonymous Lady wore a turquoise abaya with floral sequins on the left side of her chest that matched the little bit of her shirt left uncovered. The gray belt around her waist accentuated her curves without revealing the details of the rest of her body.

She placed her phone in her purse and stood up. "John," the softness in her voice complemented her smooth hand, and I held on longer than usual.

A woman sitting at a table next to ours gave her a look I'd known too well, one of judgment. Unlike Anonymous Lady, this woman's loose, black abaya was zipped from top to bottom. Her niqab covered her neck and chest. Her eyes still focused on my date, she lifted the bottom part of her niqab just enough to fit her fork under the veil, without showing an ounce of skin. She took a bite, and her hands worked in synchrony, one to put the fork on her plate and the other to bring the niqab back down.

As I sat down, I browsed the crowd. The place owed its liveliness to the women who brought color to it (like, literally) with their abayas. It seemed like the way they chose to wear their abayas was a statement of how attached they were to traditions and rules. On the spectrum, some women matched a loose, uncolorful veil mid-scalp with an abaya in their favorite shade, intentionally ignoring the last buttons at the bottom, allowing them to show their pants. These women, I guessed, balanced tradition with aristocracy, graciously staying within the limits.

Somewhere else on the spectrum, women showed off a stylish hijab with designs that replaced the hairstyle they would've spent hours fixing in front of the mirror—think flowers and brand logos. They didn't always wear an abaya, as if their veil gave them the green light to wear loose blouses that reached their knees over baggy, yet fancy, pants. The true rule-breakers left their hair uncovered, naked. These ladies wore abayas like they were cocktail dresses, some of them preferring to leave them unbuttoned. What they wore underneath looked totally … American.

No one shone as much as my date. Moon fourteen, as Elie would say, a metaphor I loved, describing beauty as a full moon (on the fourteenth day of the lunar cycle).

"How are you?" she asked, and my heart raced at the sound of her voice.

"I'm well, how are you? Sorry if I kept you waiting." As if I'd been hit with an injection of dopamine, I was too excited to stay in my seat. I wanted to dance. I wanted to be funny. I wanted to sound smart. I wanted to be whoever she expected me to be.

"Not at all, you're right on time. Do you have Casper & Gambini's in the US?"

"Not that I know of."

She smiled, as if happy to be introducing me to a new place.

"Their burgers and pizzas look interesting," I said, focusing on the menu, trying to wait the adrenaline rush out.

"Of course they do, but don't you want to try something less —" She stopped mid-sentence, so I helped her finish it. "American?"

"Yes, sorry!" She blushed. "I don't mean to sound offensive, but this *is* an Italian restaurant, and they make homemade pasta. Here, how about I order for you? Any allergies I should know about?"

I'm allergic to beauty.

I shook my head. She called over our waiter, "*Kumusta ka, kuya?*"

"*Mabuti, ateh po.* You speak Tagalog, ma'am?"

"Not really, those are the only words I know. Can't really add Tagalog to my resume."

It was beautiful, witnessing her exchange greetings in a foreign language so graciously. She had a natural ability to make others smile, and I admired her for it.

After she placed our order—truffle sliders and Halloumi asparagus to share, a chicken roulade for herself, and fresh salmon on a bed of ink pasta for me, with cherry pomegranate mojitos—she came close to me, and grabbing her purse, she whispered, "Would you like extra rum with that?"

"I—I—I—"

She laughed. "I'm just kidding. You should've seen the look on your face." She looked at our waiter. "That will be all. *Salamat, kuya.*" She turned her face to me. "That's thank you, brother, in Tagalog. Take notes, you might learn a thing or two from me."

Her relaxed attitude, her independence, made me all the more nervous. She suited her confidence, and she carried it graciously, as if she knew that her beauty was a gift and not a threat that she could use against others. Or maybe she didn't know she was beautiful, which would explain why she was on a date with a guy like me.

"Do you miss eating pork?" she asked.

Perfect opportunity to mention Patrick.

"I do. Patrick's speciality is porn—" I closed my eyes, shook my head, and tried to correct myself. "I mean porn." I opened my eyes wide, shocked that I'd made the same mistake twice. I took a deep breath and slowly said, "I mean pork."

She laughed, but it was such an innocent reaction to my mistake that it didn't bother me. She was being herself, and I loved being there to witness it. Porn distracted me from the point I was trying to make—that I was in a relationship with a man named Patrick. Now, I had to figure out another way to mention his name.

Or not. You did keep your promise, you did tell her about him.

From there, the conversation flowed. She told me about her upbringing in Lebanon, how she missed life in her village, but she had to leave the country for a bigger salary so that she could cover her younger brother's medical bills. She never thought she would end up in Saudi Arabia, though there was a sizable Lebanese community here. "I went to the *Mamsha* once, do you know where that is?"

I shook my head.

"It's a new walkway in Tahlia that extends over two kilometers. It was built as an initiative to help fight diabetes, which is a big problem here. Anyway, the first time I went—actually, the only time I went—I was hit on left, right, and center. One guy said to me, 'Surely your mom is a bee to give birth to all this honey.' Can you imagine that?

"Some men were in their cars, trying to catch women's attention. Or, the best part, some men were too lazy to walk with their wives, but they didn't want them to be alone, so they drove next to the walkway, no faster than five kilometers per hour."

"Please excuse my ignorance, but would you say these kinds of things don't happen in Lebanon?"

She grabbed her drink from the waiter's hand. "Sure, women are hit on, but it's on a different level here. I don't want to spend the entire evening talking about myself. Tell me more about you."

I'm married to a man named Patrick. You can do it, John. You have to do it!

"What do you want to know?" I asked, playing with my straw.

"Erm—" The waiter interrupted her as he brought our appetizers, distracting her from potentially asking me questions I felt uncomfortable answering, not because they were inappropriate, but because it had been a long time since I'd been asked to introduce myself, and I was afraid to say too much, to scare her away.

"So, how often do you go back home?" I asked because:

(1) I wanted to know everything there was to know about her.

(2) I didn't want to tell her about Patrick just yet.

Just as she started telling me about her hometown, a village called Eden (which the Lebanese thought was the one and only Garden of Eden), I got excited, thinking she'd tell me about her childhood. Instead, she diverted the conversation back to me, and it was like we were playing pickleball, a game I disliked a lot, because I was lousy at it.

"Tell me about yourself. Were you a teacher before moving here?"

"Oh, no, not at all. I never thought I would be a teacher. I'm actually an electrical engineer."

"Is that so? Oh, my dad would love for me to marry one of those."

I choked on my food. *Alert! Alert! Read between the lines, John! Talk about Patrick, right now!*

"But I'm not thinking about any of that right now, I have to help my brother and make sure he is 100% healthy before I can even think about marriage."

Okay, we're safe. Abort mission.

I used a napkin to wipe the sweat off my forehead.

"Tell me about *your* hometown, I've never been to the US." It seemed she wanted to know everything about me too.

"Oh, well, I'm from San Antonio, Texas. Erm, we are known for saying 'y'all' a lot. Most of the city is in Bexar County, which is spelled B—e—x—a—r, even though it's pronounced 'bear.' What else? Oh, we've got the Alamo, the San Antonio Spurs, Six Flags and Sea World. And we love rodeos. And trucks."

The way she looked at me reminded me of my sixth-grade teacher who was disappointed by my presentation on the migration of whales, which was a collection of information I'd copied and pasted from Wikipedia.

"I'm sorry," I said, "I guess it's the first time someone has asked me about San Antonio. Here, let me try again. It's actually a very old city with lots of cultural heritage from the Spanish empire. So, we have lots of old churches and missions. A lot of people think that, because we're in Texas, we're in a desert or something, but we're close to a large river, the Guadalupe River, which is almost twice the length of the Lebanese coastline."

That's right, I did my share of research. Does it impress you?

"That's actually my favorite part of the city, the water. Every summer, we go canoeing, kayaking, and camping with our friends. Sometimes we'll even go fishing." I paused, to think of more things to say. "We're called Military City—"

Before I finished my sentence, she said, "And you're proud of that?"

"What do you mean?"

"It's no secret that Americans love war, in fact, every American city can be called Military City."

So much for sounding inoffensive.

She continued, "Look at what happened in Iraq, Afghanistan, Syria, Libya, should I keep going? You pride yourselves on spreading freedom, but at what cost? Blood. Lots of it. Even your land isn't your own, you took it by force. San Antonio, that doesn't exactly sound like Navajo."

Although I agreed with everything she'd said, I remained

silent, unable to justify our history that I'd been unwillingly associated with. I stabbed the last of appetizers with my fork, chewing slowly as my eyes searched the room for our waiter, who'd arrived just in time with our dinner.

Part of me loved her *franc-parler* and admired her for it, but another part of me felt attacked for acts that I had nothing to do with. She's not to blame for 9/11 just because she's Arab, and I'm not to blame for Iraq just because I'm American. Why couldn't she sit there, quietly and prettily?

Hoping to escape this heated discussion, I said, "You know what I just realized? I still don't know your name."

She made space on her plate and pointed at mine. "Do you mind if I try some?"

Although I wasn't much of a sharer, I smiled, pushed my plate closer to her. "Please, go ahead."

As she played with her food, taking her time to neatly wrap the pasta around her fork, I waited for her to look up and tell me her name. Whatever was going on inside that beautiful mind of hers that made it so hard to answer my simple question, I didn't want to be the reason she was brought back to bad memories, like being bullied because she had a funny name, or hearing an abuser repeat it to her. If she wasn't ready to share it with me, I wouldn't persist.

In such a scenario, Timothy would have made her laugh, telling her fun facts about spinach, like, "If you eat too much of it, it turns your poop green," but me, I relied on my goofiness, and before I knew it, as she separated the spinach from the other vegetables, I sang "Popeye The Sailor Man."

Anonymous Lady put her fork down, pushed her seat back and laughed. There she was, charming and down to earth again; I liked her better without her strong opinions. "Why do you want to know it?" she asked.

"What do you mean?"

"I don't understand why people make such a big deal about names."

"If it's not a big deal, then you can just say it."

She squinted, and in those few seconds of silence between us, I got a taste of what it's like to be questioning a spy, except I was asking for her name, not confidential information of which the future of the Earth depended on. Something told me this girl loved drama.

"It's Fairouz. There, happy now?"

She pulled her chair closer to the table, reinvesting herself in her dinner, as if I'd opened a can of worms, as if I'd asked her about her virginity. Someone had ruined her name for her, and I wanted to be the person who'd help her fall in love with it again. We'd have to suck the drama (and the strong opinions) out of her first though.

"Sorry, I just don't like my name. It's ancient. And my parents named me after Lebanon's most famous singer. Don't get me wrong, I love her, but after a while, it gets tiring hearing, 'Oh, just like Fairouz, the singer.'"

"It's not that bad, they could've named you Olive Oil."

What a rewarding feeling it was to make her laugh. Her voice calm, she said, "Batool. What a pretty name. But then people would have said, 'But aren't you Christian?'"

"Why, what does that name mean?"

"It's got nothing to do with what that name means. In our culture, we think of things from religious perspectives. Batool is typically a Muslim girl's name. You wouldn't hear a Muslim boy named Christian."

"Or a Christian boy named Mohammed."

"Right. Exactly. Are you going to finish that?"

"Oh, I'm full."

Being on a date with a woman wasn't much different than sitting across the table from a man. They finish your food, they do a delicate dance in which everything they tell you about themselves has a subliminal message, and they test your reaction to know if they can trust you with more of themselves. And with Fairouz, I wasn't sure if I'd signed up for Lindy Hop—fun, jolly and spontaneous, and, instead, I got Tango—dramatic, provocative and incisive.

Her cell phone rang, so she looked at the screen and said, "Oh, no, not him again. Please, John, will you do me this favor?"

"What is it?"

"Will you answer him and tell him you're my boyfriend and that if he ever calls here again, you'll kill him or something?"

Absolutely not!

"I guess."

Scaredy-cat.

We were like two dogs marking their territory. He wanted to know who I was and why I was with Fairouz, and I was supposed to threaten him with death, but I told him I'd call the police if he kept harassing her. He peed all over me when he laughed before hanging up.

"Sorry about that. My parents tried to arrange me with this guy—who's an electrical engineer, by the way—but he's a total creep. He won't leave me alone."

Something told me the drama would get worse as the evening progressed, so it was time to break her heart.

"Fairouz," I said, knowing that what came next would seem out of the blue, "do you know that I'm gay?"

She opened her eyes wide, her right one twitching a few times, which could have meant a million different things, and all I wanted to do was get up and run.

"John, do you know that *I'm* gay?"

CHAPTER TWENTY-THREE

W hen I got home later that night, Patrick had been
waiting for me, half asleep in the living room, the pint
of Häagen Dazs ice cream empty on the coffee table.

Sitting in my favorite armchair, I unlaced my left shoe.
"Before you ask me about my night, I have something I want to
share with you."

Patrick sat up straight and fixed his shirt so it covered his
belly. His smile grew larger with every word as I told him about
Ms. Rifai and the job offer she'd made me.

Like a six-year-old who'd been told he was going to meet the
real Santa, he jumped off the couch. "You're kidding! Please don't
be kidding!"

He held my shoulders and pulled me up, and my sock flew
out of my hand. "No, I'm not kidding!"

Patrick tried to lift up my forearms, so I could jump with
him, but I felt heavy as a stone as I realized what the realities of
the job implied.

"What's the matter?" he asked, coming back to earth.

"Well, think about it, tutoring means I'll have to work after school hours, which also means I won't be seeing you guys. She has three kids, so if I tutor each one for an hour every day, I won't be back home until after 8."

"Maybe you can ask her for some kind of arrangement where you only tutor when necessary. Maybe it won't be every day. And maybe not all the kids are equally behind. And Timothy won't have to spend a single second longer in the Saddest Place on Earth anymore, so you'll be his favorite parent.

Patrick was in a great mood. It was like he was trying to convince me that Santa was indeed real—unicorns were, too, for that matter. And he did.

"I've always been his favorite parent."

"You're mine too. Listen." He pulled my body close to his, so his mouth was by my ear. "Whatever the obstacles, we will figure it out. I think this is a great offer. Think of all the things you can accomplish during the day."

I had been a stay-at-home dad before, and it did not help me accomplish a single thing. On the contrary, it was lonely and demotivating, and that was at a time when I was surrounded with friends.

"Oh, yeah, I'm going to be the king of accomplishments," I said, without trying to hide the sarcasm in my tone of voice.

Patrick lay back down on the couch and opened his arms as a sign for me to join him. He delved back into the movie he'd been watching, a smile still on his face, forgetting to ask me about my date with Fairouz.

This was an absolute blessing that I should have been thankful for a thousand times over, but for some reason, I had a bad feeling (and it wasn't only because I was a dramatic guy). I locked my phone and threw it onto the other side of the couch before hugging Patrick and falling asleep in his arms.

. . .

"You will not move to a smaller house," I said to the person staring back at me in the mirror as I got ready mentally and physically for another experience behind the wheel. If I repeated it enough times, I might have believed it, killing in me the temptation to call Ms. Rifai and ask her to send me one of her drivers.

Now that I was driving, I'd seen it all; the drivers flickering their lights, gluing their car behind mine when I was driving within the speed limit on the far left lane. East Asian men in their traditional clothes, scaring me half to death as they crossed the highway on foot, as if their lives were as irrelevant as NPCs in video games. Motorcycles driving between cars. People littering, throwing their McDonald's drinks out their windows. Drivers honking at me if I didn't immediately drive when the traffic light turned green. Drivers honking for no apparent reason. Wrong-way drivers, who honked at me, even when they were in the wrong. People reversing into an emergency lane to get to an exit they had just missed.

My anxiety through the roof, I repeated the terms of road rage I'd learned from Elie, "Blindness in your eyes," "May God not give you success," and my favorite, "To my butt, I'm not moving." But once I got to the parking lot of Ms. Rifai's mansion, I let out a huge sigh of relief, the street's chaos behind me as I admired the large trees trimmed into an "S" shape that decorated the walls outside. There were security guards at multiple gates who checked over everyone, documenting my residence permit and keeping track of my entry and exit. Then there were the Indian laborers who maintained the colorful garden, which wasn't meant to survive in the Arabian desert. The dozen cars, the least luxurious of them a Maybach, collected dust.

The mansion was bigger than life, and yet, it seemed lifeless. Every time I knocked on the front door, I'd hoped one of the family members would be on the other side. Met with disappointment, I was greeted by one of the butlers, who walked me to Basma's study room. Along the way, we passed two kitchens, three living rooms, two elevators and one library, all there to be deceived that they'd never provide happy moments, because it seemed like no one actually lived there. *Silence.*

If it wasn't for the pictures on the walls, there was no way to tell that three kids lived in that mansion. No drawings on the walls. No toys or gadgets lying around. The white couches in one of the living rooms looked like they hadn't been touched ever. What good was a spotless house if it had lost its soul?

And maybe it was all in my head, but the pictures on the walls revealed everything to me: in every family portrait, the father stood on the left, the kids next to him from eldest to youngest, and to the right was Ms. Rifai. And in every picture, they had the same facial expressions, like it was a task they were performing, and the photographer gave them the same feedback every time, "Basma, pull your hair behind your ears so we can see your face. Okay, everyone, this is a family photo, so show me your smiles."

Smile, they did, but what about the times I had walked into Basma's study room, and she played with her Barbies, recreating the life she wished she had. Even though she pretended the dolls spoke in Arabic, I understood exactly what she was saying, "I love you, my baby. I love spending time with you." No matter how many decorations were meant to distract her from the loneliness she felt, whether it be the collection of Disney movies or the antique piano, there was no denying that what she'd yearned for was to hear those words.

Meanwhile, the servants sat in the kitchen, playing on their phones, uniforms on, but no one to serve. Like manicurists at a nail salon in the winter season.

Because Ms. Rifai couldn't have a family who spent time together, she drowned herself in work. And maybe she found love and satisfaction in her work, but who would fill up her children's cups? Who would make their sandwiches? Not her.

Or maybe that was just my interpretation, dramatizing everything.

It was a matter of time before I got one of the kids to tell me the truth about their family, but I hadn't decided which one yet.

Basma, the one who gave her mother positive feedback about me, dived into her books from the moment I walked into her study room until her nanny called, "Come on, Basma, it's time for your horse riding class," or "Basma, your mom's here to see you." She asked me a question here and there, when she didn't understand something, but other than that, she seldom talked. So, I let her study room do the talking.

One particular picture caught my attention. Basma was smiling, full teeth on display (which was unusual) as she jumped into a pool. And coincidentally (or should I say symbolically), in the background, were her brothers and mother only.

What had their father done that caused that kind of unsettling peace?

The corner shelving unit displayed the international culinary contests she'd won. She hadn't chosen basketball or another hobby that required her to work as part of a team, as if she wanted to decrease the risk of having her heart broken by more people she cared about.

As she focused on her math equations, I discreetly pulled my phone out of my pocket and searched her name. Twenty thousand followers on IG and over a million views on TikTok; I was sitting next to an influencer, a food blogger, one who had managed to never show her face on camera.

Her account hadn't been active in over a year, though, which raised another huge red flag. What happened last year that broke this family apart? And if it was irreparable, had I missed my chance to try her vegan peanut butter cookie bars or her turkey curried pot pie? If so, it was a tragedy, indeed, which meant Basma wouldn't open up to me, leaving me with Kamal and Sami.

Kamal, the eldest, was a hardcore activist, who wanted to "help change the future of Saudi Arabia." It was cute that he phrased it that way, because he wanted to change something that hadn't happened yet, the future.

"What kind of change?" I asked him one time, when I should've said, "I'm so curious to learn more, but let's focus on tomorrow's exam for now."

"Where do I begin?" His eyes came to life. "First of all, I want a better Saudi for my sister, one where she can choose to wear whatever she wants, whether that means she wears the abaya or not. I want her to have the freedom to decide whether or not she wants to get married. And you know what, since I'm dreaming, I might as well wish that one day, she can grant her children Saudi citizenship. If she chooses to have children in the first place"

His eyes searched the room, as if he was picturing everything he could change. If only he was as passionate about race in US history. "Or, or, like, why does she need a male legal guardian? Think about it, why does she need a man's permission to acquire a new passport? Why does she need their permission to work? Who are *we* to make such decisions for her?"

"Who can become a woman's legal guardian?"

"Her father, her brother, her partner, or her son. And she is passed from one to the other like a plate of hummus. Oh, oh, and get this, if a woman gets a scholarship to study abroad, can you guess what the requirement is?"

"That her legal guardian grant her permission?"

"Yes, and not just that. He needs to keep her company for the duration of her studies. Let's not forget my favorite of them all. A woman is to stay in jail until her legal guardian picks her up…"

He paused. "Even if he is the one who put her in jail in the first place!"

"That's admirable, that you want to change the world around you for your sister's sake."

Kamal looked down, and said softly, "My father taught me that," before zoning out.

It was the perfect opportunity to ask him about his father, so I did. "I never met your dad. Can you tell me more about him?"

Kamal ignored me, "You must be having a cultural shock. I'm sure you hate it over here, and you must feel like we live in a different era, like it was 1468. Actually, you're going to laugh at this. We're still in 1440, according to our Hijri calendar. It's like we're stuck in the past."

"Speaking of the past, let's focus on your history exam." *I'll ask Sami about your dad.*

The key to Sami's heart was soccer (if I didn't use the term "football," he gave a death stare). Soccer posters on the walls, soccer clothes, soccer games on his PlayStation. He even memorized which players had been bought by who and who had the best haircuts.

"Wait," I said to him one day when the alarm on his phone accidentally went off. "Is that you standing next to Messi?"

He nodded, so I tried to coax more information out of him.

"Who's that other guy? Is he a famous player I should know about?"

"No, that's my dad," which I knew of course, but I was getting somewhere with my questions.

"Wow," I said, like I used to say to Timothy when he tried to impress me by jumping off the bed. "Your dad is so cool for taking you to watch a game *and* take a picture with the world's greatest soccer—sorry, football—player ever!"

He didn't budge, so I pushed him a little further. "It's really cool that you were able to share such a special memory with your father."

"Yeah," he said, sighing. "It was the best time ever. It was the first time we flew together, just the two of us. We never did it again after that. After—" He exhaled.

My heart sank. *Stop it, John. This is too painful for them.*

"You know, me and my dad used to go hiking together, but now that we're in different parts of the world, we don't get to do that anymore. I really miss it. It gave us the chance to get to know each other better. And I loved going to him for advice," I said.

With puppy eyes, he asked, "So what do you do when you miss him so much?"

"Honestly, I like to look at old pictures of us together, and I try to remember conversations we had or funny things he said."

He nodded, as if agreeing that he did that, too, even though it proved to be as powerless as a magic 8 ball.

Even though their father was very much alive, Sami and Kamal spoke of their father as if he'd passed.

To cheer Sami up, I said, "There's an hour before the game ends. I bet you can finish your homework in fifteen, and then we can watch the last bit together. How does that sound?"

Here I was, volunteering to fill in for Sami's father in his most cherished activity. Meanwhile, what was his father doing? Maybe it was adultery, or maybe it was something benign; whatever it was, I vouched:

1. To keep my nose out of it, before I caused more damage.
2. To not get attached to these kids or feel sorry for them.
3. To call my dad more often.

CHAPTER TWENTY-FOUR

"Why don't we invite our friends over for *iftar*," said Patrick when I'd told him my dinner with Fairouz at Sakura (Saudis eat sushi too) was postponed for the tenth time.

"Well, it would be nice to have everyone over and break fast together. Although everyone we know isn't Muslim."

Since the beginning of Ramadan, we had attended at least ten iftars, not because we had that many friends, but because our neighbors celebrated the holy month together to compensate for the lack of family around. We ate with all the cliques; the Arabs and the East Asians. Although we stood out, they treated us like guests of honor, insisting that we fill our plates before them, as if we were the ones fasting, not them.

When the Americans organized iftars to pretend we were breaking fast, we respected all the rules. Except for the prayer part. And the part where the men and women sat at different tables. And the fasting part. So maybe we didn't respect many rules, but one thing was for sure; we shared huge admiration for Ramadan and the people who committed to it.

These iftars were held at the recreation center, and eating in the great outdoors reminded me of autumn in San Antonio; the soothing breeze, the pink skies at sunset, the trees that danced so gracefully.

Patrick was excited to bring his famous potato salad to these potlucks, so he bought fifteen pounds of potatoes. Except, he didn't realize he was missing the key ingredient that made it famous. Bacon. Whether he substituted it with eggplants or tofu, it didn't quite taste the same, but it didn't matter since it was more about being together than what we ate. In fact, some people broke their fast with a couple of dates and a cup of Arabian coffee (which was greenish rather than brown). That way, they could play volleyball or whatever sports they preferred, because apparently, Ramadan was a month when people gained weight.

Ali explained to me one time, "Even though we fast as a way of sympathizing with the poor, we eat as if there's no tomorrow. But we make up for it by paying *zakat*, which I believe in English is armsgiving, you know, like you're giving your arm to the people who need it."

"Do you mean almsgiving?"

"Yes, that's what I said. Anyway, during Ramadan, people and companies pay a portion of their yearly income, and it goes to the poor, the sick, Muslim converts who are struggling, organizations that fight human trafficking, soldiers in combat to protect the Muslim community—"

Before I had a chance to ask him just what exactly that last one entailed (the word "protect" was like a two-sided coin; was the money used to attack organizations like ISIS and preserve the Muslim community, or was it used to defend ISIS and preserve the Muslim community), one of his friends invited him to do the honors and cut the kunefe, which tasted nothing like the one we'd bought from Trader Joe's.

It was also about praying together. I didn't know that the first time we attended an iftar. When the adhan began (from three different directions), announcing the breaking of fast, the men simultaneously drank a glass of water and ate a date or two, which reminded me of the breaking of bread and drinking of wine. When I saw them make their way out of the recreation center, I almost lost it, thinking I had peeled those potatoes for nothing and that we'd have to eat leftovers for another week. But they came back, and there was only a small portion of Patrick's potato salad left.

After the feast, we rested. We stayed there, glued to our seats, at least Patrick and I did, until 9 o'clock that night. If anyone had to get up, it was to change the tobacco of their *shisha*, refill the coffee pot, or get a new board game. Then, those who worked in the service industry—mechanics, salesmen—went to work. Someone worked all night until it was time to fast again. They would be home by half 4 in the morning at the latest, just in time for a bite to eat before fasting again. For the month of Ramadan, everyone's routine changed.

On the days that we didn't eat with neighbors, we ate out. All restaurants were offering three course meals or open buffets at attractive prices. We tried everything; Turkish, Punjabi, Filipino, Syrian, Yemeni. The whole city was vibrant after iftar. There were lights everywhere, hanging in between buildings, lights in the shape of crescent moons, lanterns. It was like a fairy tale.

"There is one golden rule," instructed Elie, "as long as the sun is out, don't drink, eat, or even chew gum in public. No, really. If you do, you will go to jail. And it doesn't matter what country you come from. If you're driving before adhan, you'll notice volunteers standing at traffic lights, distributing kits with dates, water, and juice. Feel free to take one, but don't put anything in your mouth before you hear a sheikh on the speakerphone."

And so, when Patrick said, "We haven't had anyone over since we moved here," Ramadan seemed like a perfect time for our first dinner.

"Dad! You should try doing Ali's mom!"

"What did you just say?" I replied, hardly believing what I had just heard.

"You should try Ali's mom," Timothy repeated confidently.

"Timothy, that is beyond rude," said Patrick. "Since when do you talk like that?"

"Dad, it's the rice pudding we had at one of the iftars. It's called Ali's mom."

Before we discussed the menu, we had to agree who our "friends" were. Other than Elie and Fairouz, we didn't have any acquaintances, let alone friends, who knew about our situation.

Ramadan was part of the reason I'd postponed dinner with Fairouz so many times, but for the most part, I didn't know if I was ready to see her again. Fairouz was a beautiful woman, there was no doubt about that, but I wasn't into women, so there was only one way to explain my humiliating, brief crush on her. I wanted to believe that someone other than Patrick would find me attractive, and go so far as to ask me out on a real date. The likelihood that it would be a man was little, if not nil, so it had to be a woman.

The real question, though, was why. Why did I want external confirmation when my partner was caring and loving? The answer was that it wasn't about Patrick, but about me and my big confusion about who I turned out to be, and whether my life had any meaning at all. Two things that made me feel ugly as much on the inside as on the outside.

It was time to put this silly crush behind me and see where this new friendship could go. "Sure, how about next weekend?" I suggested, and when he nodded, I said to Timothy, "Want to invite Laura?"

"Laura? Who's Laura?" Patrick asked. Looking at me, then at Timothy, he said, "Oh, so that's how it's going to be. I see."

"There's no Laura, it's a long story. I don't want to talk about it. Let me know when dinner's ready," and off he went to his room. Something was definitely up, and curiosity burned inside of me, but I had to respect his boundaries, even though I may have helped prevent another bedwetting incident that night.

And just as I came up with a random excuse to escape the kitchen (before Patrick's interrogation on who Laura was began), Patrick called me by my name. But it was for something else; he'd given up on marketing his dance classes at school (my sweet, gullible Patrick thought rich kids cared about free snacks), since his turnout had been so low since the beginning of the year.

As I sat next to him, his eyes pierced right into my soul with an innocence and vulnerability I didn't recognize.

"You remember that argument we got into one time," he said, "and you said that sometimes it feels like I don't respect you anymore? I've been thinking a lot about that. I think it's not that I don't respect you. It's that I—"

After taking a deep breath, he said, like a confession that required courage, "I resent you. Sometimes. There I said it."

I didn't say anything, waiting for an explanation.

"Yes," he said, his lips moving quicker, "because you don't care what job you do, you do it well. Me? My one passion, I've banged my head against a wall trying to pursue it, and somehow, I always end up back at square one."

Although I usually begged all the gods to help me find the right words to say, this time, I was trying something different, something I'd learned from Timothy. I was offering my presence as a form of support.

"I have an idea," he said, and before hearing it, something told me it was another one he'd abandon before he started it. "I'm going to create an IG account where I post dances and aerobic moves. And in the background, I'll have pretty spots around Jeddah, a different location in every post."

That's actually a great idea.

213

A large smile on his face, he said, "That way I can show how impressive the city really is. Like no one does that. At least no American does that." Looking at the floor, Patrick hid his face, as if he was scared to see the disappointment in mine.

"That's right!" I jumped up off my seat. "No one in this house is moving to a smaller house."

When Patrick's eyebrows furrowed in confusion, I shrugged. "It's nothing, just a mantra I've been trying out. I'm so proud of you for turning a setback into an opportunity. The world is going to love you."

Patrick went into a whirlwind about the relief he felt that I wasn't disappointed or judgmental, as if persistence could ever be met with any of those things. Knowing Patrick, though, he sought external affirmation that this new project didn't mean defeat, that he wasn't giving up on his dream of becoming a dancer.

As he got up, I pulled his arm gently so that he was closer to me and whispered, "What you're doing is brave and original. People are going to love it, and one day, you'll understand why those doors were closed and this one opened. I'm so proud of you."

Blushing, Patrick said, "When did you learn to be so supportive?"

"I learn from the best," I said, winking. "I'll even become your very own personal chauffeur who drives you around town for this new project. Do I get 'Supportive Significant Other of the Year?'"

Patrick nodded. "And what do I get?"

"According to Elie, you should get 'Woman in the Relationship of the Year.'"

. . .

With the AC blasting, the sweat beaded across my forehead began to dry, but my breaths remained short, and my heart raced, until I changed the gear to "P," at the mall opposite to the iron fist roundabout, which was where Patrick would perform a choreography for his first ever Instagram post.

Patrick dedicated this performance to humanity, kindness, and unity, and to match his message that we were all one, even in our differences, he chose the song *One Love* by David Guetta and Estelle. He told the world (okay, maybe not the world yet, but his two followers) that it's understandable to believe the things your culture teaches you, as long as you made the decision to believe those things yourself.

Then, at home, we brainstormed future posts together, and Timothy edited the videos, while I monitored engagement—I waited and waited for a notification to pop up, hoping someone would comment. So when I heard a ping, I jumped onto my phone, but it was a message from Ms. Rifai, asking me to call her.

"Hello, John?"

"Yes, Ms. Rifai, how are you?"

"I'm well, thanks for asking. The kids have just given me their report cards. You've done a fantastic job."

"Oh, the credit goes to them, really."

"Please come by earlier than usual next week, I need to discuss something with you."

Oh, no. This is the end, she knows that I've been asking her kids personal questions. She's going to let me go. Foxtrot, foxtrot, foxtrot!

CHAPTER TWENTY-FIVE

From: Saudi Airlines

Subject: Reminder: Only 5 days until your trip to San Antonio

Hi, John Callaway,

We hope you are looking forward to your trip with us. We're writing to let you know about some of the services available onboard Saudi Airlines:

...

Forward to: Patrick

Email body: So excited!

And send.

"You've never fainted before. You're definitely not fine," said Patrick.

"I'm fine," I told him, for the nth time as I gently pushed his arm away to:

(1) Show him I could stand by myself.

(2) Recollect my memories and figure out what had led me to that moment in time.

"What's today?" I asked.

"Friday." Patrick tilted his head and furrowed his eyebrows.

It started after Ms. Rifai's phone call on Wednesday, which gave me pangs in my chest that grew bigger and bigger until I was fighting for air. Without thinking, I grabbed Koala's leash and went straight for the door without explaining to the guys where I was going.

"Alexander is making major changes at work, and it's not good news for you."

"I need to discuss an urgent concern with you."

"He explained why it made perfect sense to kill non-Muslims."

"Dad, I'm sorry, I wet the bed again."

I covered my ears with my hands to shut out the voices in my head, but they only got louder and louder. I would have preferred the loud adhans coming from different angles, but the sunset prayer had just finished. So much had happened in my life in such a short period of time, I wasn't ready to take another hit.

Every few yards, I stopped, closed my eyes, and took a deep breath. *I will not move to a smaller house. I will not—*

The leash escaped my hand as Koala ran toward one of the East Asian laborers, barking at them, as if she wasn't happy with their landscaping. I caught up with her, got down on my knees, and hid my face in Koala's fur, tears sliding down my cheeks.

"Sir," said the laborer in broken English. "Sir, it's okay, sir."

When I worked up the nerve to put Koala down, the traits of hard work on the laborer's face put my worries to shame, making me feel worse about myself, as if I hadn't earned the privilege of sadness. Real hard work, under the sun and under the moon, day in and day out, without his family by his side, because his pay grade didn't grant him that benefit. Tear up, Earth, and swallow me, as Elie would say.

The Good Samaritan extended his arm and helped me get back up. Walking away, I had no energy, but I wanted to run until I was exhausted; run, as if I could run away from my life. I opened my mouth, ready to scream at the top of my lungs, but I noticed Ali standing on his front porch, so again, because I was too embarrassed to express myself, I had to lock up my emotions.

"What's the matter with you today, Koala?" I asked a she tried to escape from her leash once more.

"She can tell I'm sad today," said Ali.

"Oh, is everything all right?" A single tear ran down his left cheek.

He blew his nose, took a deep breath, as if gathering the courage to speak without crying further. "The municipality passed by our workshop today, and when they saw our German Shepherd off his leash—" Ali placed his hands on the railing, squeezing it, as if for support or to ease the emotional pain. "They shot him. They thought Zeus was a menace."

After paying my condolences, to help take Ali's mind off Zeus, my selfish self brought the discussion back to me. As I sat on one of the lawn chairs, I said, "I started a new job."

"Good, good. Was it hard transferring the visa?"

"Not really, no," I said, as he sat next to me.

"Oh, that's good. You know, I know a lot of companies that bring their employees on a business visit visa, because it's cheaper than an employment visa or a residence permit. They're usually Indian or Pakistani or from that side of the world. These employees and their families have to exit and re-enter the country every 90 days. So, they'll go to Dubai for one night and come back. But you're American, so."

He stopped there. So, what? Why did everyone keep saying that, like it was supposed to make sense?

"What do you mean?" I asked.

"Well, the American passport is the strongest after the Saudi in this country. You get special treatment with everything. It's like positive racism."

"Hm, that's an interesting term."

I excused myself and resumed my walk. Once we are caught up with our own circumstances, we think that we're the center of the universe, that no one has it as bad as we do. Maybe we know that we have so much to be thankful for, but, still, we are unable to let go, sweeping under the rug that feeling that tells us everything will be alright.

I tried to get myself out of that negative mood, so I pulled my phone out to call Scott, but I was scared he wouldn't pick up. Lonely, I wanted to drink my misery away, but with Ced as my only option, I wasn't ready to experience death just yet.

My fingers led me to Fairouz's contact details. I pressed on the call button and hung up before the first ring. I was afraid I'd begin to sob, and she'd think I was a big crybaby, but I wanted her to be my friend.

Something told me that, as a gay Lebanese woman in her twenties, who hadn't come out to her parents, and moved to Saudi Arabia to save her brother's life, loneliness was a common friend.

"Hey, John, I'm so glad you're calling," she said after the first beep. "Spicy or ranch?"

"Huh?"

"I'm debating which bag of chips I should open. Never mind, I'll mix them both in a bowl. So, what's up?"

Looking for the right words to say, after a few seconds of silence, I remembered, "Are you free Friday night? You're invited to dinner at our place."

"As long as we're not having pizza and burgers," she said before laughing.

And just like that, we jumped from one topic to another. She told me about the guy who wanted to marry her, I told her about the traumatizing jokes Elie had made. We talked about music and movies, and about our favorite childhood memories. When I hung up, the screen showed we had been talking for "46:54," a mere few minutes, leaving me curious to learn more about her. And more importantly, I had something to look forward to now.

As I headed home, I smiled, because I wasn't alone on this planet. Although I hadn't even mentioned that something was bothering me, having someone to talk to helped me feel less empty on the inside. I fell in love with the idea that Fairouz was a phone call away. And it worked out well that she was in the same time zone.

"Honey," I shouted, as I opened our house door, unleashing a tired, yet happy, Koala. "I'm home! And I've got good—"

"Shhh," said Patrick, running down the stairs. "I just put him down again. He wet his bed."

It had been months since Timothy had had an accident. "Do you think it's an indicator of something?" Patrick emptied the bag of Doritos in a bowl (yes, they sell Doritos in Saudi Arabia) while I unloaded the dishwasher. "He never invites any of his friends over. Do you think maybe he hasn't made any friends, and he's been pretending to be the popular kid?"

Not to be egocentric, but maybe it indicated Timothy's frustration at our lack of quality time. Maybe the time spent working on Patrick's videos wasn't enough. Maybe my absence at home after school made him feel like he came second to my job. Maybe our home was the new "Saddest Place on Earth."

"Patrick—I—" although I didn't know where to start, my tongue wanted to spill everything, about Ms. Rifai's kids, about my poor parenting, about Scott's disappearance from my life. With a Tupperware dish in my hand, I stood silent. "Patrick—I —" I tried again, but his phone rang at the worst time. And I wasn't about to call Fairouz again, so maybe she wasn't a phone away after all.

CHAPTER TWENTY-SIX

On Friday, I texted Elie five times, reminding him to be on time, and though he replied to every text, he never mentioned:

1. He had a girlfriend (Tahani).

2. She was coming to dinner, which was great for him, but a bummer for me, because after a stressful week, I looked forward to Elie making a fool of himself by flirting with Fairouz.

After Elie and Fairouz discussed where in Lebanon they were from (Elie knew the intersection where *Zuzu's Barbershop* was located and had turned left there many times, unknowingly passing in front of Fairouz's house), we talked about the one thing we all had in common—living in Saudi Arabia. We told jokes, complained about our jobs, and shared embarrassing secrets from our adolescence.

Elie had reached a new record of cheesy jokes, when he looked at Tahani, a serious expression on his face, as if he was about to propose, and said "You know, if your parents don't want you to marry me, because I'm Christian, I'll convert."

Ecstatic, poor Tahani could hardly stay in her seat. "You'd do that for me?"

"Who said it was for you? I'm doing it for the seventy-two virgin wives I get when I go to heaven."

As he winked his girlfriend, who was now disappointed, she dropped the utensils out of her hands. "You're such an idiot sometimes. Only martyrs get the virgins. If I'm the only one on this earth who'll date you, what makes you think the virgins will want anything to do with you?"

"Yeah," said Patrick. "If they hear you're coming, Elie, they'll ask to be expelled to hell."

When Tahani laughed, we all followed along. Sitting at the head of the table, I appreciated the people surrounding me, as well as the ones I hadn't met yet, particularly the two people who'd fill up the two empty seats at the dining table one day. Maybe Fairouz's future girlfriend and a new friend of Timothy's?

Elie had been quiet that night, unlike his usual self, which only made sense once he finally spoke after dessert as if he'd been gathering the courage to ask for an uncommon favor. "I've been meaning to ask you guys something, but I guess I'm too embarrassed. We have a saying, if your friend is honey, don't lick them. I really don't want to lick you."

Then, he went ahead and asked anyway. "My sister is pregnant, and she wants to give birth in the US, but we don't know anybody there."

He swallowed and continued, "Do you think you can help us find out which hospital to go to, how much it's going to cost, and what steps she has to take afterward, you know, with the passport and everything?"

Why don't we deliver her baby while we're at it?

Before Patrick and I said anything, he added, "You know, Rima is married to a Syrian man. And the Lebanese woman can't pass her nationality to her children. And we all know that the

Syrian passport isn't worth much. The Lebanese, either, for that matter."

"Where does your sister live?" asked Patrick.

"Here."

"So, why doesn't she give birth here?"

"They don't grant birth right here either." When Patrick and I didn't say anything, Elie cleared his throat, and added, "It's totally cool if you guys think this is too much to ask for. I totally understand." Then, looking away from Patrick, Elie and I met eye to eye.

"You want to know what I think, Elie?" I asked. Elie nodded, looking hopeful. "I think I'm offended—"

Elie laughed, but I was serious.

"I don't know why you're laughing."

"John, dear—" said Patrick.

"Don't 'John, dear' me. He asked us, so why shouldn't I answer?"

Patrick tried to stop me again, but I wouldn't have it. "Everyone keeps saying how much value there is in being American, but my God, y'all are such hypocrites. You think being an American makes you more important than being Lebanese, or Syrian, or whatever. And instead of correcting that way of thinking, you reinforce it. Let me tell you why it's great being American. Newsflash: it has nothing to do with being better than others. Being American means that you're free to speak your mind, to fight for a better society for yourself, to be different. And so far, since moving here, I haven't had the chance to do either one of those things. So, what good is it, being American over here? You wouldn't do that favor for an Indian or an Ethiopian, why should we?"

If my passport was in my pocket, I would have thrown it onto our dining table like the worthless piece of paper it was. "Have at it," I would've told Elie.

Instead, I was panting, like I had just run a marathon. My heart squeezed, the pain more excruciating than before. I put my hand on my chest. "Ah!"

In an attempt to escape the scene (so much for Fight or Fart), I stood up, pushed my chair back, and when I took my first step, I found myself in a state of vertigo. Next thing I knew, I was on the floor.

Like an infant who'd been carried to their crib while they were asleep, I woke up in my bedroom.

"I'm fine, I'm fine, I'm fine," I repeated, trying to convince Patrick, but deep down, it was myself I was talking to. I pushed my knuckles against our bed, my arms failing to carry me. "Where is everyone, anyway?" I silently accepted defeat, extending my arm out for Patrick's support.

"They're waiting for news from you downstairs."

Up until that point, I'd forgotten that Fairouz and Elie's new girlfriend were there. *Gosh, I'm so embarrassed.*

"Do you mean to tell me that they stayed, even after how horrible I was?" When was the Earth going to swallow me?

"Yes. Yes." A full sentence made up of one word, and yet it meant so much.

As we neared the staircase, my arm interlaced with Patrick's, he whispered in my ear, "Listen, I don't know what that was all about, but that discussion can wait. For now, I have to take you to the hospital and make sure everything is okay physically, and we'll take care of what's going on inside your head when we're back home."

"Under one condition," I said.

"What's that?" He sighed, as if I was about to ask for something silly, like, "Can we have more dessert first?"

"I get to choose the hospital."

Patrick stood still, his eyebrows furrowed, so I explained,

"There's a hospital called *International Medical Center,* and I've been dying to go and see what it looks like on the inside."

"You've been dying to go to a hospital? I could punch you right now, and then you'll have the perfect reason."

"Believe me, this hospital looks like it's worth going to. Like, it's worth fainting for, even though all of this is caused by the evil eye."

Patrick shook his head. We reached the living room, and as I walked in, my arm still intwined with Patrick's for support, I couldn't make up the look in Fairouz and Elie's eyes. The room closed in on me; *what do they think of me?*

The pressure was more than I could take and the only thing I could do was look down. "Elie, about what I said, I'm—"

"Don't worry about it, bro, we've all been there. Let's just make sure you're okay."

"Where is Tahani?" I asked.

"I dropped her home and came back. Fairouz insisted on staying, just in case we need her help with anything."

Do I deserve such compassion? Why are you being so nice to me?

After a discussion on the logistics of our trip to the hospital (which took much longer than necessary), we decided Fairouz would accompany Elie and I to the hospital because:

1. Patrick had to stay home in case Timothy woke up.

2. We didn't want the doctor to get any funny ideas about why Elie and I were dining together, alone.

3. Since Fairouz hadn't yet applied for a Saudi driving license, Elie had to take us. She could pretend to be my wife, and that way, it made sense for Elie to come too as my pretend brother-in-law.

"Thank you, Fairouz," I said, unable to look at her for fear of seeing my reflection in her eyes. "It means so much that you're doing this." My head in a fog, her answer sounded like background noise.

I turned to Elie. "I thought men and women who weren't related or married couldn't be in the car together."

"Bro, you just fainted, and this is what you want to talk about? Fine, yes, that's the law, but we still do it. I've never been caught before. Can we go now?"

From the moment I met Elie, I'd been judgmental, taking his friendship for granted, and it was my belief that he'd never live up to my friends in the US. In that instant, I understood that I was sabotaging my friendship with Elie all along, fearful that I'd like him just as much as I liked the Gang, and if I moved on from my relationships with the guys, then how different was I from them? It was like I couldn't allow myself to form true friendships.

"You don't have to come," I said to Elie, and if he didn't persist, I'd be relieved that my meagerness could catch up with his generosity.

"Are you kidding? Of course I do!" As I read his lips, I wanted to cry and cry until I drowned in my own tears.

CHAPTER TWENTY-SEVEN

The IMC was prettier up close. As we neared the parking lot (I'd convinced Elie and Fairouz to go through the main entrance, instead of the ER), my spirits lifted at the sight of the colorful garden that surrounded a set of stairs, a fountain running through the middle of it, a symbol of life and eternity at a place that people associated with pain and death. Palm trees acted as pillars that held up the sky.

In front of the main door, a small desk was occupied by a man in a uniform, who walked closer to our car and opened the passenger door, where I was sitting.

"Sir, will you be needing a wheelchair?" asked the doorman, whose name tag indicated "Jameel."

Fairouz replied from the backseat, "Yes, please," but I spoke over her, "No, thank you. We will be fine."

"John, this isn't the Ritz Carlton you're checking into. I wish you would take this more seriously."

As Jameel led the way into the hospital, it was like walking into the Taj Mahal; everything was so grand, so majestic. I gained a sense of self-worth under the vaulted ceilings, almost as if they had been built for me. The balconies on the second floor were covered with natural plants, giving a patient like me a feeling of hope, even if we didn't know we were hopeless.

The chandeliers, oh, the chandeliers; they hung high, lighting up even the darkest corners of the mind. The bright white walls were decorated with Arabic on wooden boards.

Fairouz caught me by surprise when she held my hand. "I'm sorry. These Quranic verses get to me every single time I walk in here. There's something about them. A pacifying effect that makes you forget about all your worries for a second. Whether you're Muslim or not."

The way her small hand fit in mine took me back to the days when Isabelle and I were younger, and she held my hand whenever a scary scene came up as we watched our favorite horror movies.

I took a deep breath in, trying to recognize the odor that filled the room. Musk. I wanted to take the seed of that smell and plant it within my mind, so that if I smelled it again, even ten years from that moment, I would be brought back to the IMC, where I discovered how deep friendships could develop in very little time.

To think that the reason I ended up in this place was a bunch of scattered, exaggerated thoughts. The shame I felt quadrupled when I noticed that my reflection on the tiles shone brighter than any thoughts I'd had in the past few days. I didn't want to try my luck, but if I were to die in Saudi Arabia, this would be the place.

After we checked into the ER, we waited our turn in the Men's Section. Interestingly, in hospitals, there were no Family Sections, only gendered sections. Even through moments of pain, men and women couldn't socialize.

The television hanging on the wall played live footage of Mecca, even though it is only accessible to Muslims, it somehow consistently wins as one of the world's most visited places. When the patient sitting next to me asked me if I'd pray the *Salat Al Isha*

(Night prayer), I realized how potentially horrible a visit to Mecca could be for me, so it was better if I didn't infest it with my unholiness. A few times around The Castro District and I'd be closer to God.

In the background, a Quranic recitation filled the hospital, and patients who'd memorized their holy book whispered the words along, being calmed with every syllable. To those who stared at the television screens, it was like traveling back to their pilgrimage, remembering that, as long as their life was in Allah's hands, there was hope.

When my number popped up on the screen, we followed the nurse to Dr. Ahmed Abdulilah's office. The wall on the right was decorated with certificates and degrees he'd earned, all of which were from the US. They went back to the mid-seventies. On the left wall, he had various presents on a bookshelf that he had received from patients to show their gratitude. There were mugs and plaques with special messages, framed pictures of his patients, and my favorite, a bobblehead that looked like the doctor.

"I hope you didn't have to wait too long," he said. "My last patient came with his four wives, saying they're incapable of fasting. So he wanted to check their hearts, which was a good idea, but it's not a doctor they need. Anyway, how can I help you?"

Like a good wife, Fairouz explained to the doctor what had happened, adding a few details here and there that made me feel special to her, like, "He's been walking a lot lately, so isn't it weird that this happened?" and "He's had friends he can trust and confide in. Shouldn't that help?"

Hold my hand again, friend.

CHAPTER TWENTY-EIGHT

From: John Callaway <john_callaway@gmail.com>
    To: Widad Rifai <widad.rifai@hotmail.com>
    Date: June 9th
    Subject: Does my job include paid sick leave?

Dear Ms. Rifai,
    I hope this email finds you well.
    Due to health-related reasons, I am unable to attend work this week. Please find attached a doctor's note stating that I am to be on bed rest for five days.
    May you have a blessed Eid and a wonderful vacation.
    Sincerely,
    John Callaway

Stress, anxiety, emotional turmoil. Those were different words that shared the same meaning, and the doctor's voice rang clearly in my head the next few days. It was like he followed the protocol to humor me, because as soon as he put the stethoscope back in its place, he asked me about my mental wellbeing. "These things will suck the joy out of living, so you have to beat them and make sure you live out of joy. Not out of fear."

That's right, the only one who should be sucking is me.

I knew he was right (his ability to deduce what led to my fainting—that it was mental, not physical—was impressive, and honestly a breath of fresh air compared to American doctors who relied on the notorious Valium et al.), but I couldn't make out what needed changing in my life. I'd already come so far to become a better version of myself, I thought the work was almost over. For now, it was the perfect excuse to postpone my appointment with Ms. Rifai, who probably wanted to interrogate me on why I was discussing personal issues with her kids.

It turned out, however, that talking to her was exactly what I should have done, because the discussion we didn't have was all I could think of as I packed my bags, made breakfast, and drove to pick Timothy up from school. One minute, it was only a matter of overstepping boundaries, but the next, I was the reason Sami argued with his mom, adamant that he wanted to spend more time with his dad. And worst, the minute after that, I'd said something that encouraged Kamal to run away from their mansion, demanding that his parents get back together.

By the fifth day, I couldn't take the self-sabotage and decided to call Ms. Rifai. A little too late, she and her kids (and their servants and butlers) had already traveled to Switzerland for their Eid break.

Standing in front of the mirror in my bedroom, I appreciated the person staring back at me, but I also worried for him, that he would always need to grow. That the soul digging (and mining) would never end.

"Dad?" Timothy interrupted my train of thought. "Are you ready? Elie is outside. It's time to go to the airport!"

Life would be on hold for two weeks. As Patrick and I collected our suitcases from Elie's car, Timothy hugged Koala tightly, and then it was my turn. "We will be back for you, girl. Make sure Elie doesn't fall in love with you, alright? If he gives you a hard time, just pee everywhere."

Elie patted each one of us on the shoulder, his typical "manly" way of greeting, before getting in the driver's seat, rolling the window down for Koala and driving away.

"Ladies and gentlemen, welcome to Alamo City," said the flight attendant on the loudspeaker, but all I could hear was Ms. Rifai's voice in my ear. "Why? Why did you have to break my family further than it already is?"

"Local time is 11 o'clock, and the temperature is 84 degrees." We were back to the home of Fahrenheit, my home, the place I was free to be myself.

Before getting off the plane, I turned on my phone, with the Saudi SIM card still in it, but there were no notifications from Ms. Rifai. Zero. Niets. Nada. As Elie would say, "John has fasted, and he broke fast on an onion," or in other words, "John has put so much mental thought into this, and yet he learned—again— that he wasn't the center of the universe."

Yes, my problems were important, but only relatively, as in, they were important to me. It was time for a much needed break, where my productivity level was non-existent and my accomplishments were based on how many shows I could watch in a day or how many times I can order food in a 24 hour period.

For two weeks, there were no guilty pleasures—there were simply pleasures. I looked forward to sitting in a silent room and doing absolutely nothing, without comparing myself to this person or that person, who'd accomplished (and was still accomplishing) more than I did or ever would.

Last year, Scott would have picked us up from the airport, but now, I was afraid of being rejected. I was going to take it easy

233

with him, to try and put the ball in his court, but first, I had to know if he was down to play.

Considering that Carla seemed most upset about our departure almost a year ago, we asked her to pick us up from the airport (maybe it was a coincidence that she also happened to have the biggest car).

"Were you deported?" she asked upon seeing us, so unrecognizable when our eyes met. I kept searching for her around the terminal, thinking that that woman was a stranger. The Carla I knew didn't have blonde hair, she had at least thirty extra pounds and wrinkles that looked like rivers on a map.

When she hugged Patrick for less than two seconds, patting him on the shoulder like a coach did with his players after they've lost a game, I knew something was off. In the car, after the standard, "How was your trip?" and "Are you hungry?" she shifted from first gear to fourth. "Y'all must have a pretty busy life in Saudi. The only one who calls me is Timothy. But once you needed a ride, you don't hesitate. Huh, Patrick?"

Patrick took a deep breath in, as if preparing an answer, but Carla cut him off. "I booked you an AirBnb close to our house. Your room is now my warehouse where I store the products I sell on Amazon. Y'all get some rest, and I'll be back tomorrow afternoon once I've finished my orders." She looked at Timothy in the rear-view mirror. "If you need anything, you give me a call, okay? I can't believe how much you've grown."

The condo building sat opposite a Methodist church, and it wasn't until I moved to a country where there were no churches that I realized how many denominations we had. Diversity. I loved it. A drag queen walked past us, the train of her red dress sweeping the floor, her heels singing a song of pride and confidence.

"Don't forget your laptop bag," said Carla as she handed it to Patrick through the window. "I'll text you the owner's details so you can get in." Our eyes followed her car as she drove off, leaving us like abandoned puppies.

"I'll try to cancel the booking. I'm sure she's just playing with us to teach us a lesson." My eyes went back and forth between my screen and Patrick, who stood immobile, so devastated, he ignored the notifications on his phone, because they meant his mom wasn't coming back. Except this wasn't a silly joke.

As my mom's voicemail message played in the background, I checked the time. She was probably dreaming of Elvis Presley kissing her again.

We had no choice but to stay at that AirBnB (which Carla booked but didn't pay for), and something told me San Antonio was going to feel less and less like home, because who stays at an AirBnB when they're home?

Walking into that empty house, a familiar feeling swept over me, but I couldn't name it. Last time I had felt like that, it was our first night in Saudi Arabia. The only way I could describe it was, "What on earth am I doing here?" and worst, "I want to go home," only this time, I didn't know where home was.

After a few funky dreams—Patrick was stuck in Ryan Gosling's body, oh, no—I woke up to the sound of the doorbell, which was one of those famous symphonies. Patrick had ordered an all-haram breakfast with bottomless mimosas. He ate and ate and ate, and drank and drank and drank. Elie was right: what's forbidden is desired.

All that food combined with jetlag meant Patrick and Timothy passed out in no time. As I looked up the nearest car rental shop on the Uber app, I almost chose to walk, not believing how much more expensive it was in the US compared to Saudi. But it was too hot to walk, so I was determined to order it nonetheless, and as my finger hovered over the checkout button, I heard Timothy cry, which could only mean one thing.

Before he said anything, as he stood next to his bed, I hugged him. "I'll take care of it when I get back. It's okay, you're okay. Why don't you sleep next to your dad?"

Timothy nodded, his small body leaving mine, as he walked toward his suitcase. "I love you, son," I said in a proud parenting moment.

San Antonio was more crowded than I remembered. There was more construction, more bridges being built, and even though Texas was known for spacious roads, closed lanes caused traffic at all times of the day.

With no destination in mind, my mind went on autopilot, and I ended up outside my parents' house.

"Hey, Mom," I said into the little security gadget after ringing the doorbell.

"John? What are you doing outside my house?" asked my mom.

"Surprise! If you open up, I can tell you," but I'd forgotten that my mom could access her doorbell from anywhere in the world, and at that moment, she was talking to me from Lauro Villar.

"What part of town is that? I'll come to you." I really needed to see a familiar face.

"I'm not in San Antonio, honey. Your dad and I are in Mexico."

"Well," I said in the tone of a child who'd lost his parents at the summer fair, "when are you coming back?"

"The end of summer, honey."

"Okay, I guess I should go now," I said before walking back to my car.

My parents never went on vacation. We'd begged them to travel with us, so they could stay with Timothy while Patrick and I went out at night. But no, traveling was a hassle, in the past at least. My little family kept our bigger family grounded in the city, and without us around, the foundation was removed, like a band-aid, painfully and quickly.

The San Antonio I'd expected to return to was the city, the life, that I'd left behind. But I'd neglected to consider that perhaps the city had changed too.

Patrick and Timothy were still asleep (or they purposely ignored my fourteen calls), and I refused to return "home" and stare at the alien walls (although that was my initial plan), a constant reminder that I was being treated like a guest by my own family.

Next on my list of people to see was Scott, so in order to avoid another useless trip, I texted him, "Hey, are you free?" His profile picture popped up next to my text, which meant he'd read my message, but the three dots didn't appear. He ignored my message, and therefore, he wasn't even free for a phone call with me.

What does someone do when their former best friend ignores them? They give them space. Unless that someone is going through some desperate times, and well, as the saying goes…

As I parked in front of the tall building in downtown San Antonio, I received a call from Patrick. "Where on earth are you?"

The name of the office building was in front of me, and yet I couldn't repeat it out loud. Although I knew where I was physically, I was nowhere to be found mentally.

Patrick broke the brief moment of silence. "Why don't you come home?"

I'm trying to find home.

237

CHAPTER TWENTY-NINE

On the third day of our vacation, it became clear that I wasn't going to sit at home and do nothing all day. Maybe some people liked to spend time with themselves, but I wasn't one of them.

As I washed dishes, Timothy walked into the kitchen, and as he poured himself a bowl of cereal, I turned to him. "Son, I've been thinking … Since we're here—" His eyes lit up, as if he thought I was taking him to Six Flags. "Would you like to see a new doctor? You've been wetting the bed frequently, and what if there's something we've overlooked?"

Next thing I knew, Patrick popped out of nowhere. "Were you going to discuss this with me first?"

In the midst of our back and forth, I neglected Timothy's body language; in the moment, I interpreted it as a fear, worry, when in reality, it was something different, something more profound and alarming.

"John, I'm telling you this for the last time. We are not giving our son false hope that someone is going to find out the cause of his enuresis, only for them to put the blame on our gayness. End of discussion."

"You're right. I don't know what I was thinking. I have a better idea, anyone want to go to Six Flags?"

Maybe the universe will be on my side, and I'll run into Scott, Shay, and Shay's niece.

The universe wasn't on my side, of course, and as our holidays progressed, Patrick was becoming more irritated with me too. "All you talk about is Scott," he said more than once. "It's obvious you value your friendship more than he does. I actually don't know if you can call it a friendship anymore. Why don't you stop chasing after him?"

I would stop, but only after I got the closure I needed. I didn't say that out loud, naturally. I simply nodded.

Carla had finally decided we were worth her time. She rang the doorbell like a maniac or like someone had been chasing her. "What took you so long to open the door? I've got two hours before I have to go back to work. Where's my grandson?" She walked past me without even making eye contact, as if I was an ugly painting on the wall.

"Mom! It's so good to see you! Shall I make you your favorite coffee?"

"Sure. Do that, and bring it to me. I'll be with Timothy."

My eyes fixed on Patrick as I tried to make out how he felt about his new mom, but before I could make any conclusions, he raced into the kitchen. Everything in me told me to stay "home," because deep down, I knew Patrick was shocked by the new Carla, but I couldn't help but take advantage of the situation to try and see Scott.

"Hey, Patrick." I walked into the kitchen, but Patrick ignored me (or he was too caught up with his own thoughts). "I just ordered food. I'm going to pick it up. I'll be right back." He shooed me away, as if I was an annoying bug.

The right thing to do was to at least give him a hug before walking out, but I was running out of time, and I didn't know when I'd get a chance to go out by myself again.

Parked in the same spot outside the Alamo Business Center, it was like a good omen that I was there to finish what I'd started the prior day. But there was nothing to finish, because Scott's colleagues told me he didn't work there anymore, and after I practically begged them to tell me where his new job was, they pulled the confidentiality card, like?

I was known for giving up easily, but that day, I was a mule. Scott's house was only twelve minutes from his old office, and although I knew the likelihood that he'd be home was little, I drove there nonetheless. Besides, Patrick hadn't called to summon me back yet, so I was good on time.

Outside his house, there was only one car, and it was neither Scott's nor Shay's. Maybe one of them bought a new car, but I should've known better than to think they'd give up on their fuel-saving Priuses.

"I'm sorry," said the stranger who opened the door. "I don't know who Scott is, and I promise I can't help you find him." Of course I knew he couldn't help me, but I asked again and again. It was like trying to find a ghost.

There was one more place I could try to find Scott; his favorite nail salon. If I didn't find him there, I'd do something I couldn't do back in Saudi, get a pedicure (because that's not what men do). But that would have to wait for another day, maybe the next time Carla showed up—if she ever did again.

In the car, with the AC on blast, panic washed over me. I created an anonymous email account with the username, *Secret Invite*. I figured, since no one knew we were in town, I could plan a surprise dinner. If my plan worked, the curiosity to solve the mystery would push them all to cancel their plans and attend.

The location being an AirBnB, they wouldn't suspect we were the hosts.

I sent Scott, Shay, Leslie, Greg, Jackie, Albert, and Isabelle separate emails, inviting them to our *Very Exclusive Taco Tuesday* eight days from Monday, plenty of time for me to gather the strength and confess my plan to Patrick. More importantly, I had to prepare for his criticism.

I looked up the closest diner and made my way there—yes, I'd lied to Patrick about ordering food, but it was a white lie.

At every traffic light, I checked my phone for replies from my guests, refreshing the page to no avail. Every time my phone buzzed, it was either something from Patrick's IG account or an app requesting an update.

As I waited for our food, I deleted apps I didn't use (why did I have so many coupon apps) as a desperate attempt to prevent a heart attack. Even well after Carla had left our house and we'd gone to the community pool, I kept getting out of the water to check if I'd silenced my phone by accident, until finally, I stayed in my lounge chair, my phone under my thigh so that I'd feel if it buzzed. But the only thing that buzzed was my head after one glass of rosé and five shots of sunray, giving way for the jetlag to kick in, messing up my sleeping schedule.

Once I awoke—and I'd barely opened my eyes—I grabbed my phone from the bedside table and turned on the wi-fi. An email icon popped up on my screen, so I unlocked my phone. It was from Leslie. "Greg, please stop harassing me. I told you I don't want to see you again."

Why would Greg be harassing his wife? Something was wrong, and I had to find out what, because:

(1) I cared about Greg and Leslie.

(2) I wanted to hear that I wasn't the only one struggling with life.

(3) Leslie might lead me to Scott.

"Hello," said Leslie, her voice low, tearful.

"Leslie, how are you?" I asked, as cheerfully as I could.

"Who is this?"

Why had all my friends forgotten who I was?

"It's—it's John," I said, this time, my voice was more modest.

"John? John! I'm sorry, I changed my phone and lost all my contacts."

Leslie sent me her new address, and I raced there. *Selfish mode, activated. No, you can't think that way. You are going there to check on her first and foremost. That means you might not get anything out of this visit.*

Leslie no longer lived in her five-bedroom villa in that fancy part of town that had gated communities only. She moved into a one-bedroom condo closer to the South of San Antonio, or as she had called back in the day, "the ghetto." It wasn't the actual rundown section of the city, but it was as far as upper-middle-class people like Leslie made it. And now, her daughter, Agatha, was growing up there.

She made tea, but I requested something stronger, and as we sipped on our vodka cranberries, I confessed, "Leslie, the email about the mysterious Taco Tuesday..." She looked at me with surprise, as if questioning how I knew about it.

"That was me, it wasn't Greg, but I now realize it was a bad idea. I'll send another email to cancel it."

"I'd appreciate it if you did."

Sitting on the small loveseat in her tight living room, we threw questions at each other, both wanting the other one to talk, as if we wanted to suck on each other's misery to feel better about ourselves. I caved and told her about our life in Saudi, how much we loved the city, the culture, the food, but also the trouble we had gotten into.

And then, it was her turn.

"I don't know how much to tell you, because Greg is also your friend, and I don't want you to change how you see him because of me."

"Good people do bad things." Although I genuinely believed that, I was willing to say anything that might get her to talk. "Whatever happened between you is between you. It doesn't make Greg a bad friend to me."

She chugged her glass, closing her eyes shut, as if she had a brain freeze. Once she opened them back up, it was like the words overflowed after being bottled up for a long, long time. "When Agatha was born, he said he wasn't attracted to me anymore. I worked hard every day to shed the baby weight, but no matter how much I weighed, I heard those words in my head, over, and over, and over, especially during intimate moments. Then, I became obsessed with food. All I could think of when I opened the fridge was how it was going to make me fat. I became so mad, mad at Greg, yes, but mostly mad at myself for letting him play with my head like that. I just didn't see how I could ever be happy with him again. That anger grew into bitterness as I imagined him talking to our daughter like that one day. You want to know the worst part? He. Is. Fat. And did I ever say anything about it?"

She poured herself another glass and gulped it down. And then, the tears came. "Agatha," she said, one word that translated into an essay.

I tried to find words of comfort, but none felt right. "I'm sorry you had to go through this."

"Don't apologize. It's not your fault. Anyway, please, let's talk about something else."

Taking advantage of her presence to ask about Scott felt wrong after she'd made herself vulnerable in front of me, but my mind was blank. "Um. Have you heard from Scott? I've been trying to call him, but—"

"Honey." She placed her hand on mine. "You haven't heard?"

"Haven't heard what?" I was expecting her to tell me that he had died, and in a way, I wasn't wrong.

"Scott was captured by those conversion therapists." She examined my eyes before continuing, "John, it's like black magic what they did to him. I ran into him once at the mall, and it wasn't the Scott we once knew. He left Shay, can you believe it?"

It all made sense as to why he was ignoring me, and although this had nothing to do with me, I couldn't help but wonder if I could've stopped this if I hadn't moved to Saudi. If only I was there for him when he had questions and doubts.

First, Leslie's story, and now this? It seemed like everyone I knew was struggling just as much as I was, if not more (well, everyone but my parents), and although I expected to feel better about not sinking alone, it was the total opposite.

"I—I—I'm sorry. I just—I need time to process all of this." Leslie's gaze changed as she placed her glass on the coffee table. She opened her mouth to say something, but I couldn't risk hearing more bad news, so I stood up. "I want to see you again before we leave. We should still do Taco Tuesday. Just us. You, me, Patrick, and the kids. Are you free tomorrow? Just text me."

As I ran for the door, I thought of every person who had attended the dinner before we left for Saudi the first time.

This darn door, why is it stuck?

"Push the door first and then turn the knob."

Without turning back, I followed her instructions and slammed the door behind me. I rested my back against the wall; I thought I was the one with the biggest problems, and because of that, I believed people owed me their attention. Scott wasn't the bad friend, I was. Carla wasn't the bad mother, I was the bad son-in-law. Yes, I was the bad one; I never even thought of calling my sister, who'd have been over the moon at the chance to see Timothy.

There was only one way to try and make it up to them; I

drove a few blocks from Leslie's house, parked in the Costco lot, and called Isabelle, who had every right to be upset with me. My mother had told her about our surprise arrival, and because I hadn't called her, she didn't want to talk to me. I told her I was behind the mysterious dinner invite, but that was a lame argument, so I used the Timothy card, and the best-selling strategy, "This is a limited-time offer, because we leave in just over a week."

And then I had to talk to Scott. I opened my email, pressed the button to compose a new message, and let my fingers type, the words flowing out naturally. It was my turn to use "Urgent concern" as a subject headline.

My dear, dear Scott,

After months of wondering why you weren't returning my calls or answering my messages, I've discovered that you were on your own journey of self-discovery. I'm very happy for you, that you've found your identity and are able to be who you are, I just wish I didn't have to lose you. I'd still very much love to be your friend, I am in San Antonio for another six days and would love to see you before I leave.

If you're not ready to see me, I understand, I just wish you would answer this letter, to let me know you're doing well, even if with a simple thumbs up. I imagine that, in the midst of all the soul-searching, new aspects of your personality have come to the surface, and one thing I'm sure of is that you're still the strong, genuine Scott I've always known, loved, and respected.

I hope you know that you'll always have a special place in my heart, and that my arms will always be wide open for you, if you need your friend.

With so much love,
John.

As my finger pressed the send button, it was like sending the words off into the air, because for all I knew, Scott could have deleted the email without reading it first.

Next on my list was Shay, Scott's ex, who must have been devastated after Scott's "conversion." My finger hovered across his name as I tried to come up with an icebreaker, and hopefully, it was good enough that I could use it with Greg too. But then, Patrick called. "You need to come home ASAP. It's about Timothy."

CHAPTER THIRTY

Rushing through the door, I forgot to close it behind me, because:

1. That was a thing I did to keep Koala from running off.

2. I needed to see that Timothy was safe.

In the living room, Patrick gently rubbed Timothy's back.

"Dad's here now, you can tell us what's bothering you." As Patrick rubbed Timothy's back, Timothy kept hugging his knees, the sound of each cry tearing my heart into a million pieces.

"What is it?" My lips moved without making a sound. Patrick shrugged.

Sitting at Timothy's feet, I placed my hand on his left calf. "Son, would it help if you wrote it down on a piece of paper instead of saying it?"

Timothy sat up straight, wiped his snots with his forearm, and grabbed his phone out of his pocket. He clicked on a few buttons so fast, it was like he was pretending, and as showed us the screen, he closed his eyes.

"I've been keeping a huge secret from you guys, because I

don't want to get in trouble, and I think this made my enuresis worse. I'm really sorry."

Patrick and I looked at each other, both with the same expression on our faces as if we were trying to say, "Secret? What secret?"

Timothy gathered the strength to say, "Can we go for a walk?" And at that moment, I wished Koala was with us, so she could comfort us all the way only she knew how.

Timothy walked in front of Patrick and me, his stature familiar; slouching, looking at his shoes, slow paced. I was extremely worried. Timothy was never one to get into trouble.

Finally, some minutes later, he stopped walking, and said, "A boy from the compound kissed me on the lips, and I told him that I didn't like it, but he kept insisting. The rumors—" He burst into tears again.

Before I could process anything, I needed to calm my son down, or I'd be crying too. I held his hand gently and invited him to sit on the sidewalk next to me. Patrick and I didn't say anything. All I could think was, "How many times? Where was I when this happened? Could I have stopped it?"

And then, Timothy spoke again. "He told me it was okay. He said everybody did it, so I did it too. And—and—and if everybody did it, why were they making fun of me?" He shook his head, and I handed him a tissue so he didn't use his forearm again. "They think that because you guys are gay, I'm gay too. But what about him? Why don't they make fun of him? Why do they think he's a tough guy?"

Timothy was saying so many things, but at the same time, he wasn't saying enough. I wanted to ask him, but I was scared to learn about the things that had happened to him. I didn't have the strength to hear anymore from him, or to ask him to recite more of deep-seated trauma.

Not knowing how to react, I asked Timothy if I could hug

him, my eleven-year-old son, whose innocence was taken from him and could never be returned. This was going to be one of those things I'd be reminded of every time I saw Timothy, without the guts to ask him if he was doing better, because what if he was thinking of a video game or a history test and I brought the abuse back to his attention?

"I'm sorry," Timothy said, and this time, I knew what to say.

"My son. You have nothing to apologize for. You didn't do anything wrong. This isn't your fault."

If I repeated the same message enough times, maybe he'd understand and believe me.

"Laura wasn't supposed to tell anyone about me, or that my parents were gay. But she did, and somehow, the kids from her school told the kids from our school. And when the parents found out..." He paused, as if ashamed to say that his friend was the reason that I got fired from the school.

"Whoa, Timothy, if the secret got out, it's not your fault. It's not Laura's fault either. The other day, when you said you and Laura weren't friends anymore, was it because of this?" Patrick asked.

Timothy nodded. "And then Haya, my closest friend from school, found out that I was lying about my mom dying when I was born. And she's never spoken to me since."

Patrick fell to his knees in front of Timothy. "Baby," he said, his index underneath Timothy's chin. "Can you please look at me?"

Timothy pushed Patrick's hand away. Meanwhile, I felt like a paralyzed fly on the wall as more details were unveiled.

"Timothy, I hate to see you like this. Look at me, please," and when Timothy raised his head, Patrick took our son's hands in his. "John, can we switch places? What happened to you, son, is horrible, and I'm sorry you have to go through it. But you know what, I've experienced something similar."

"You?" I was taken back to the days when Timothy was a baby, and he'd learned to sing, "you" whenever we said, "I love." Oh, how I longed to go back to that moment.

"Yes, I have, and I can tell you, it's going to take a lot of work, but it's going to be alright. Dad and I will help you every step of the way. We love you so much. I'm so sorry, baby, I'm so sorry we forced you to lie, to cheat, to—to—to manipulate. I'm sorry that you've lost your friends, and I'm sorry that you've had to hide little Timothy away."

Our brief walk back to the condo was silent, overtaken by the songs of the cicada. Even though I wasn't the one who'd hurt Timothy, I couldn't help but feel somewhat responsible, at least for the reason he hadn't come to me the night the first time he'd been abused.

When he was a destructive toddler who showered me with "I love yous" after he'd broken a glass or spilled milk on the floor, I should have reciprocated instead of telling him to "just be quiet for a minute so I can clean up in peace." Maybe, just maybe, it was these small rejections that caused the voice in his head to whisper, "Don't tell your parents. Just be quiet, or you'll disturb their peace."

Or maybe he'd felt second to the kids I'd been tutoring, thinking that their homework was more important than his, or worse, that I no longer had time for our meaningful conversations.

If I hadn't encouraged him—nay, practically pushed him—to find new friends in the compound, just so I could get a break at home, these horrible things never would have happened.

What if the night he was abused was the night I pushed him to get off his mobile and get out of the house?

Abuse.

My son was abused.

My Timothy, the boy I'd vowed to teach independence, but

also to rely on my love, my arms, my time. Timothy, the one who taught me a new type of love, a type only he could give me—not my partner, not my parents, not my friends. I'd turned him down. I'd failed at my biggest job as a dad: to protect my child.

"Timothy, thank you for trusting us with your secret. You don't have to hide anything from us anymore, so if you don't want to go back to Saudi, you can tell us that." Patrick's voice echoed in my ear, causing my hand to shake as I tried to unlock the door.

I understood Patrick's despair, but that wasn't the solution, because what happened to Timothy could've happened anywhere. His abuser went to a different school, so the only place Timothy risked seeing him was at the compound. When I Googled, "compounds in jeddah," a dozen options popped up, and maybe the fact that none offered the same services as the Belleview Family Compound was a good thing. That way, if we needed to get a haircut, we'd have to go to an actual barber shop outside the compound. Or if something at the house required fixing and the compound didn't provide the service, we'd do it together, as a family unit. No more of Timothy being in the compound somewhere with God knows who, doing God knows what.

All I knew was, if we moved out of the country, it'd be the same as raising our hands in the air, teaching our son to run away from problems or finding a way around them, rather than dealing with them from within.

We tried to get Timothy to tell us what boy had kissed him, but he wouldn't let up. As much as I wanted the boy to be held accountable for what he'd done to my son, Timothy begged me to leave him out of it. The damage had already been done and confronting him would only make things worse.

I couldn't wait to come back to the US, and now, I couldn't wait to leave, so I contacted the AirBnB owner and claimed there was an emergency, but of course, they refused to only charge me for the days we'd stayed in their house. We decided to stay in San

Antonio and try to make the most out of it. Just the three of us—and Isabelle.

I just want to go home. I couldn't shake off that there was something wrong with that sentence as it replayed over and over in my mind.

Jeddah still wasn't home to me, but not because it didn't play by my rules. *Home isn't a place, it's the memories.* But San Antonio was the city where most of my memories resided, so why wasn't it home anymore?

Because, if home is made up of memories, then it's in my head; home is in me.

When I booked my ticket to San Antonio, my intention was to "go home," and in a way, I did, because I'd found myself. I was someone who let life happen to him, who lived by other people's expectations of what my life should look like, instead of asking myself what I wanted from my life.

It was time to turn the tables and take control over my life; it was up to me what memories I made after all.

Since home was in my head, the first change I needed to make was in that same place. When I look in the mirror, I wasn't going to judge myself anymore. No more unkind words. I wasn't confusing insecurities with flaws anymore, because regardless of what expectations I had of myself, I was flawless. I am me.

What does all of this matter, John? Just go to sleep.

No, I wasn't ready to go to sleep just yet, because this mattered. My insecurities pushed my decisions on a day-to-day basis. They got in the way of the good things that could happen to me. *The good things I could have done for myself, rather.*

I grabbed my phone from the bedside table and created a new note.

Title: Embrace the mess-takes

All my life, I thought being happy meant not making mistakes, so I shielded myself and avoided risks as much as possible. But then I found myself in a miserable state. I didn't know who I was anymore. Guess what? Turns out you can protect yourself as much as you can, and you'll still make mistakes. Why? Because that's life. It doesn't come with a handbook for a reason.

Alright, and if that's the case, then the solution is simple, fix every mistake when it happens, right? Well, not exactly because:

You can't always fix them,

It's so darn tiring,

Fixing them doesn't make my world perfect.

Success isn't the equivalent of no mistakes. If anything, it's the total opposite.

No more asking myself, "What if I'd told Tom Knowles he should be the one to lose his job, not us," "What if I'd told the doctor to do his job and find out why my son was wetting his bed instead of blaming it on his gay dads," or "What if I'm the reason Timothy was crying this night or that night."

From now on, mistakes serve one purpose and one purpose only: to learn how to get better at doing life. Embrace them and then let them go.

CHAPTER THIRTY-ONE

As we boarded the plane for our flight from JFK to Jeddah, I looked around, searching for Farah, the flight attendant, who'd served us on our first flight to Saudi. This time, I knew better than to judge her; she's probably not some conservative Saudi who isn't allowed to talk to men. The mere fact that she was working as a flight attendant was an act of bravery. And now, I wanted to learn more about her.

Although she wasn't there, I did get the chance to speak with twenty-five-year-old Bilal, our flight attendant, whose dream was to be the first Saudi man to compete at Wimbledon.

"See you on Netflix." I shook his hand as I got off the plane.

As we waited for our luggage to arrive, I found a quiet area far from Patrick and Timothy and called Ms. Rifai.

"Hello, Ms. Rifai."

"John. Welcome back. I hope you had a restful vacation." Her voice was calm as usual, neutral, which made me think of her as an Arab Meryl Streep.

"Yes, thank you." I should have reciprocated. I also wanted to ask her if it was a good time to talk, but gave her the butter, as

Elie would say. "I know it was wrong of me to ask your children about their personal lives, but there's a reason I did it, even though it still doesn't justify what I did. You see, when I started tutoring them, I'd promised myself not to get attached to them, but I'm a parent myself. Whenever I walked in Basma or Sami or Kamal's study, my mind told me to do what I was there to do, but my heart didn't let me. Ms. Rifai, I couldn't help but notice that something happened in your children's lives that impacted their psyche drastically. I know what you think, that it's none of my business, and you're probably right, but I had this small hope that maybe I could help them feel better, even if just for a few minutes. I don't know what I was thinking. Please don't fire me."

I didn't know if what I was saying made any sense, but I kept going. "I want to ask you for a second chance. Your kids are great kids and if we are able to discuss the boundaries that you wish for me to respect, I promise to never—"

"John. Take a deep breath." I realized everyone around me was staring at me, but not the good kind of staring.

"What are you talking about, firing you? What kinds of questions have you asked my kids that would make me want to fire you?"

I stuttered, looking for words.

"If you didn't want to fire me, then why did you ask me to come early to our last appointment?"

"I wanted to reward you. All three of them brought home record report cards, and they said they owed it all to you. I'm not going to lie to you, you're right about something happening in our life that has impacted my kids. And although I wasn't very fond of the idea of you talking to them about whatever it is you talk to them about, my kids seem to like it. They've grown attached to you, too, and I don't want to take that away from them. Basma is thinking of relaunching her Instagram account. You Americans are crazy about therapy, so I'm going to think of you as a tutor slash therapist. I've got myself a great deal, two for the price of one. Just promise me one thing. Two, actually."

"Anything for you."

"Don't ever let them think that I or my partner are the bad guys. And, please, whatever they tell you stays between you and them."

When I didn't say anything—because I was fighting back the tears—she asked if I was still on the phone.

"I feel like a big idiot," I admitted.

"Would a big idiot be rewarded for their hard work with a year's beach membership? The Red Sea Beach Resort, mind you. That place has a waiting list that never ends."

"No, they wouldn't. It's not too late for you to change your mind about rewarding me. In fact, you can un-reward me by sending *me* to therapy."

She chuckled. "John, everything will be alright." Although I couldn't see her face, picturing her genuine smile comforted my heart.

"As my close friend would say, your face is a blessing on me."

Talking to them wasn't a mistake. Night after night, I stayed awake in that comfortable AirBnB bed, thinking I'd lost control over my life, when in fact, I was learning to follow my gut. To care, even if it hurts. To be me, even if it scares me. All I needed to do was say yes to myself more often. And saying yes meant I wanted to help Elie's sister, and so, he became next on my list of people to call.

As I dialed his number, I walked closer to our belt and checked that our luggage still hadn't arrived. If it wasn't for these phone calls, I'd be just as annoyed as Patrick and Timothy were with having to wait. For once, I was thankful for their level of investment in their phones.

"Pick up." As "Rise Up" by Yves LaRock played, I knew there was one thing Elie could be doing, "fly over the rainbow so high".

I texted him, "I will be happy to help your sister with anything she needs to give birth in the US."

Judging by the rows of emojis in the message he sent back, I guessed he was ecstatic. "Wait until Rima hears the good news. She'll name her son after you."

I toyed with the idea of turning it into a business, which I'd called *Better Call John*. I'd take a modest commission per baby born in the US. Ten percent. The packages I'd offer would include *Baby From the Block*, the most cost-effective one with accommodation in the Bronx. The *Poor Bastard* would be for pregnant women traveling without their husbands and would include services like transportation to and from the hospital. The *Devil Wears Diapers* would serve bougie customers, and the pregnant woman would have a makeup crew awaiting her in the delivery room. Heck, why not add in a professional photographer to capture her newborn's first moments in our world, traumatic as that might be for the mom. And of course, there'd be offers for women pregnant with more than one baby. Pop one, get the second 10% off. Pop two, get the third 20% off.

Last but not least, there would be the *Anchored Forever*, for parents interested in applying for immigration and naturalization services when their American child becomes an adult.

On a serious note, though, I quickly looked up the cost of giving birth in San Antonio, which was approximately twenty thousand dollars, including flight tickets, hospital stay, accommodation, and other miscellaneous fees. A mind-boggling amount for the privilege of being an American citizen when their parents faced troubling behavior at most airports around the world.

As we waited for the bus to take us from the plane parking lot to the airport building, Patrick asked me to hold his phone and film him.

"I was going to do this at Al Balad, since it's a beautiful

UNESCO World Heritage Site, but the planes in the background will be just as symbolic."

As Patrick performed in front of the camera, I listened closely to the lyrics of the song, "The Final Speech" by Thomas Jack and Adrian Symes, which Timothy was playing through his phone. They were taken from Charlie Chaplin's speech, *The Great Dictator*.

The choreography was utterly dramatic, a dedication to humanity, kindness, and unity. Patrick poured his heart and soul into every movement, as if it was his last dance. It pushed me to question why I was wrong to feel offended by Elie when he made his request. It wasn't about whether his sister was abusing the system to her own advantage. It wasn't about the unfairness it represented to people of other nationalities who wanted to earn an "upgrade" in nationality. It was about humanity. It was about being there for a fellow human in their time of need. It was about the lengths that war pushed us to, that forced us to do things we would otherwise be humiliated to do. It was about a brother desperate to help his sister. She wouldn't do it if she didn't have to, if she didn't want to, secure a better future for her child.

"Timothy," I said, as the music stopped and Patrick caught his breath. "I love you, my son."

Yes, you don't need to be a good boy to hear these words from me.

CHAPTER THIRTY-TWO

With only a few days before school started, we had no time for jet lag. My mission was to find another compound we could move to "because of what happened to Timothy" (which was code for "so he doesn't have to see his abuser anymore," and "so healing can be less difficult"). I called Fairouz for help.

"John. How was your vacation? I bet you hated leaving home."

"Yeah, you have no idea." The sarcasm on my tongue tasted bitter. Again, I should have reciprocated, but the sense of urgency took over my manners. "I need you to help me decide on a new place to live."

"Okay. When are you thinking? End of summer?"

"Today."

"Oh, okay. Let me see what I can do. Is everything okay?"

"Yeah, yeah. Everything's fine. We just can't take it anymore. Five prayers a day coming from three mosques. After a while, it takes a toll on you, you know?"

"Yeah, it's like you're forced to do something you don't want to do. I get it." It was like this woman had a sixth sense.

She broke the silence as I drifted, Timothy's cries from that night piercing through my ears as if he was in front of me screaming in pain. "Hey, since you're on the phone with me, you free tonight? I want to take you guys somewhere."

As much as I wanted to reject her invitation, I needed to get out of the compound, before I went on a hunt to discover who ruined my son's adolescence, like an angry lioness protecting her cub.

"Boys! Get ready! Fairouz is taking us somewhere! I mean, we're taking her, but she's—you get the picture!"

Walking through an arts gallery was an agony, but nothing compared to having to face my demons at home, without the superpower of knowing what went inside my son's mind. Patrick loved it, however. As we strolled (and I pretended to be interested), Fairouz told me about the artists, and the fact that they were Saudi made our visit a tad more interesting. Okay, maybe more than a tad.

"It's only recently that they started opening galleries and exhibitions, because these kinds of events were prohibited. Come to think of it, you are experiencing history as we speak. Never before did you have couples from different religions, gays, female business owners, social media influencers under one roof. So if you will, it's not as much about the art itself as it is about how the art gathers people from several minority groups to come and celebrate progress. Without fear of getting raided. You see, we don't need to plan protests or sit-ins, we feel satisfied when we acknowledge our own existence together. This way, I don't need to tell this neighbor or that colleague to accept me, because I'm already part of something bigger."

Different from the US, indeed; back home, artists were broke, sacrificing a decent living for the sake of expressing what's inside of them. In Saudi, though, artists were somehow both young and rich.

We stood in front of a table that displayed miniature versions of everyday items made of clay, like plates, forks, and chairs. I certainly didn't get it, but that didn't matter as much as what Fairouz whispered next. "The artist behind this is gay."

To make sure she wasn't bluffing, I examined her. "Is he here with us tonight? Can you introduce us?"

She browsed the room. "I don't see him. If you hadn't gone to the US to have a blast without me, you could've met him last time I came."

Yeah, a real blast.

"How did you meet him? Wait, do you have some sort of gay-guy-magnet I should know about? You could make it on Ellen!" Seriously, though, how did gay people—or people in general—socialize in this city, if not through work or if they weren't neighbors?

She looked around to make sure no one was paying attention to our discussion, came closer to me, and whispered, "Through this gathering I've been attending. It's—" She looked around again and said, "It's gay-friendly, if you know what I mean."

"Oh my God, isn't that totally against the law?" My voice came out louder than intended.

Fairouz motioned with her arm, indicating that I should lower my voice. "It is, but they're very careful about who they bring in and where they meet. They never meet at the same place twice."

My mind is telling me no, but my body is telling me yes!

"Can I attend this mysterious gathering one day?"

"I don't know…" She took a sip of her ice tea.

"Come on, I'm dying to see what a gay Arab looks like. A gay Saudi. It'd be like hitting the jackpot."

"You're so American!" She rolled her eyes. "You should be careful not to use the term 'dying,' you don't want to tempt fate."

"It's going to make me feel way less anxious, or like I'm constantly under threat if I saw with my own eyes that people from our community can lead a happy, safe life here."

"Fine, I'm like 90% sure you're gay, so I don't fear that you're undercover, or that you'll call the cops."

I rushed to catch up with her as she moved on to the next "masterpiece."

As Fairouz whispered the rules to me, I tried to keep mental notes:

1. This group strictly comprised members of the LGBT+ community, so unless a person fit in that category, they didn't need to know about it.

2. The only way to join the group was through a trusted member of it.

3. Even if a person identified with the LGBT+ community, I had to seek Fairouz's advice first before telling them about the group. After all, she had that flawless gaydar.

4. Don't ever, under any circumstance, mention the group over the phone or via text, not even with members of the group. Throw your phone out the window before you think of talking about the group.

5. Timothy can't know about the group.

That last one stung a little at first, but then I quickly remembered "what happened to Timothy." She was right.

Unable to go for a drink or two at a nearby bar, we had no choice but to go home.

"I'll see you tomorrow."

As she opened the door to leave our car, I looked back to see her. "Why? What's happening tomorrow?"

She tilted her head and pursed her lips, as if to say, "The secret gathering we were talking about earlier that we're never supposed to talk about ever again."

"Oh, yeah. Tomorrow."

A smile on her face, she gently closed the door behind her.

Patrick, who usually played his music out loud and sang like no one was listening, was invested in his screen, a serious look on his face.

"What are you doing?" My eyes focused on the road, I couldn't make out the words under the big logo.

"I'm on the US embassy website."

"I don't think you'll find info on how to get a bottle of wine there."

I glanced at him, expecting a smile, but instead, he looked at me from the corner of his eye, and then back at his screen. He read out loud, "We cannot get US citizens out of jail overseas, provide legal advice, or represent US citizens in court overseas—"

"Wait, who's in jail?" I asked, wondering what episode of *Keeping Up With Patrick* I had missed.

"No one yet. But *you* might be as of tomorrow."

Why would I be in jail tomorrow? Oh, because of the gathering, you mean.

"Relax. Fairouz wouldn't invite me if there was a risk of the cops showing up. Besides, we're American. We're untouchable. You should know that by now."

"She didn't invite you. You invited yourself."

Although Patrick was right, I had to defend myself. "I'm tired of letting life happen to me instead of me taking charge of my life. I don't want to feel like there's always an excuse as to why things aren't going my way anymore."

There was more on my mind that I wanted to say, but when Patrick shook his head and looked out the window, I refrained. I had a feeling I was going to be getting the silent treatment, and I was right. He didn't talk to me until the next day, just as I was about to walk out the door, but there was no changing my mind. I had had so many worries since we'd arrived in Saudi, and every time, I'd learned that I had more to lose by *not* attempting to make a mistake.

"Remember what you told me about this city when you were trying to convince me to move here?"

"What?"

"People call Jeddah a gay heaven," and it was time to get out of hell.

CHAPTER THIRTY-THREE

A large sculpture in the shape of a camel—which resembled a malnourished diplodocus—marked our entrance to Obhur, a coastline in Northern Jeddah. It looked like Jeddah's original architects and engineers sat down for a meeting with one purpose, and one purpose only. "If we could build Jeddah all over again, what would we do differently?"

It seemed like the answer was to build taller, thicker gates, which made turning a blind eye easier, giving locals and expats alike a huge window to taste a more lenient set of rules. As I drove past gate after gate, it became clear that the Red Sea kept the secrets of what happens when all good things are forbidden.

In the beach houses owned by Saudi elites, parents threw their children big sweet sixteen parties, a local adaptation of the ones I used to watch on MTV. Their friends from the American school or whatever international school they went to, were invited to indulge in what should have been just another party. A sense of normalcy that only those with big numbers in their bank accounts had the privilege to experience.

For the rest of us, they built beach resorts, which, past the gates, took us on a trip to paradise, even if just for the weekend. Sand in our feet. Tattoos. Food by the beach. The smell of booze. Jet skiing. Chalets. For expats, these places were a breather. For locals, I imagined, these resorts were their favorite meetup locations, which could have been the big medical college, if there weren't two different campuses separating men from women.

Everyone broke the rules, which helped me feel better about having a female passenger to my right. Apparently, in that part of the world, taking risks was the status quo, and I was going to learn to drive around with a woman who wasn't family, without getting caught.

The further we got from the ocean, the smaller the properties. Smaller, but still modern, reminding me of the time we studied Zaha Hadid in my first year of university, and I couldn't help but wonder if Saudi women were on the team of engineers or architects who had built these homes.

We parked in front of the villa where the gathering was taking place. It wasn't as neat or modern as the other ones, but it had a pool, a guest house, and a small football (I mean soccer) court. Villas like this, a dream house for me, were rentals—probably owned by the same elites who lived in the mysterious properties right on the beach.

Outside the entrance of the villa, two hosts stood on either side of the door, each one holding a large tray, where we were asked to place our phones. I wanted to send a text to Patrick that I was unreachable, but I didn't want to seem suspicious either. Besides, if he called, it would come through on my Apple watch.

We must have been the last ones to arrive, and before I could browse the faces in the crowd, the lights were turned off, the speaker took to the stage (or rather, dais) a spotlight following his every move, attracting everyone's attention.

"Welcome everyone," said the speaker. He looked familiar, but I couldn't place his face. He wasn't the guy who worked at the

SIM card shop. He wasn't the guy who sold us his car. He wasn't the security guy who almost didn't let us inside the mall. Who was he? And when I had met him, was he wearing casual clothes like he was on the night, or did he wear a thobe? More importantly, how could I have met a gay man and not noticed that he was gay?

"We're so happy to be able to organize one of these again. Thank you all for coming, I hope you have a good time. Before I let you mingle, I have a few reminders that I hope you'll receive in good faith. Please, please, please, whenever you plan to attend one of these meetings, don't mention anything that might catch someone's attention on WhatsApp or on phone calls. You know, like 'gay' or 'gathering.' Or anything like that. Erm, what else? Oh, yeah. If you're willing to open your house for our next meeting, please let me or anyone on the team know. We're always looking for new locations, because as you know, the gay bars are always packed."

For a split second, I thought he was serious, until the audience laughed in unison.

With the lights back on, I finally had the chance to check out the crowd. They, much like the kids I taught at the American school, were from all sorts of nationalities. Egyptian, a couple of Saudis, Filipino, Indian, and Lebanese. More Lebanese than any other nationality. I wondered what their stories were, when they figured out they were gay, and if they came out to their families. If they were anything like my students, their parents would never accept them—they'd probably blame the gay teacher for being a bad influence. I wondered if they were as terrified as I was to be living in Saudi, and if they had to learn, like I did, that that fear was irrational.

"Are there any newcomers with us today?" asked the speaker, much like they did at the Protestant church my parents attended. Fairouz hit her elbow against mine, and, looking at me, she tilted her head toward the speaker, indicating that I should introduce myself. I waited for other newcomers to lead the way.

"Hi, I'm Tristan."

And I am addicted to alcohol.

In harmony, everyone said, "Hi, Tristan."

The speaker, still on stage, invited Tristan to join him. "Everyone knows your name, but no one knows what you look like."

Tristan's hair gel shined bright, overtaking his shy smile. "I'm from the Philippines. I moved here thirteen years ago. Thank you for welcoming me into your group."

As he stepped down, another newbie ran up the stage, holding onto the speaker as she tripped. "Hi, I'm Lara."

Again, everyone in harmony said, "Hi, Lara."

"That was just an act to get you to laugh. I'm gay, not clumsy." As Lara stirred up the crowd, I thought of all the possible underground groups that might be meeting up at the same time we did; comedy clubs, churches, book clubs, and my personal favorite, mixed sports leagues. "I'm Lebanese, but I grew up here in Jeddah. I recently came out to my family. They're pretty traditional and don't know much about gay people. They're freaking out, but they're trying to understand what it means for one woman to love another woman. A lot of people ask me why I came out to my parents, because I kinda risked giving them both a heart attack. My answer is simple: I want them to quit trying to marry me off to some doctor or engineer. Or whatever man at this point."

With smiles on their faces, everyone nodded, like her statement summed up their realities too.

They didn't have an organization name. No fancy titles. So far, no pitiful stories. And sadly, no booze either. The anonymity made it feel safer, like it didn't exist, or like it was just a group of friends getting together.

"Hi, I'm John." Being among misfits like myself, the connection with the audience was undeniable, because we didn't just share an identity, we also shared a sense of strength in our unity that made the rules conquerable. Although we didn't know each other, we were partners in crime. Undefeatable.

"Hi, John."

"I'm from the US. I moved here less than a year ago. I'm in a relationship with my boyfriend, Patrick, and we have an eleven-year-old named Timothy. I'm happy to be here with you today."

It felt so good making those statements in front of such a large number of people. Finally, I'd found a place where I wouldn't be judged. With time, I might even let my guard down and be my awkward self.

As the speaker wrapped up, everyone dispersed into smaller groups. I followed Fairouz. "Hey guy," she said, "I want to introduce you to John."

"Hey, John, I'm Eliana. This is Roger (which she pronounced ro-geh) and this extremely silent person is Zeinab. And together, we're Roger's angels."

"More like my nightmare..." Roger rolled his eyes. "No, you know what? You're God's nightmare, because you keep calling yourself an angel, but there's nothing angelic about you."

As the girls laughed, Roger turned his body to me. "I'm glad to have another man on the team. What do you think about this —" he paused, swirling his finger in a circle to gesture toward the room "—thing? Personally, it reminds of the church attended while I was growing up. It's the same concept. It's underground, and it's for a minority group."

"You grew up in Jeddah?" I asked.

"Yes," he said, before giving a speech about what it was like to grow up in this city, but the more he spoke, the less sense he made. My mind drifted, curious to talk to the people who walked past us, and Roger must have noticed. "Have you decided about this weekend?" he asked, his eyes on Fairouz.

"I think I'll pass," she said.

Roger looked at me again and said, "Your friend over here would rather spend Friday night at home instead of going to an exclusive party thrown by a Saudi prince. And did I mention there'll be an open bar and free cocaine?"

Wait, an open bar? Cocaine? Saudi prince? Do we live in the same city?

"Yeah, and the reason being that I'm not into that stuff. So thank you very much, but I'd rather spend the day at the beach."

"I can't believe you still have the guts to go, I haven't set foot at the Red Sea Beach Resort ever since the Mutawas raided it last year," said Eliana.

"Sorry for not wanting to mess with the Islamic police." Fairouz was the same person around her friends as she was with me; perceptive, mature, and charming.

"Just dye your hair, they'll think you're European, and you won't get arrested. Or ask John to go with you. You'll be untouchable."

Yeah, yeah, I'm American, so ... I get it.

Out of nowhere, as Eliana's lips moved in slow motion, someone bumped into her, pushing her onto me, and her cup of orange juice across the room. As I tried to get myself off the floor, I couldn't hear anyone or the low volume music playing in the background. My body was immobile, and yet everyone around me ran in different directions, fear on their faces, as if cats had been released among mice. In the midst of the panic, I had no clue what was happening.

Fairouz grabbed my hand, bringing me back to reality. "John! Come on!"

"What's happening?" My eyes focused on her hands. *Why is she pulling me?*

"We just received a notification that the cops are coming to arrest us. We have to move very fast!"

But I thought we were in gay heaven.

"John!" she said, her voice more distinct than the others, "Move! Now!"

I tried, but my legs failed me, like the time Timothy almost fell off a cliff, and for the life of me, I couldn't move. Or the time when Ben, my boyfriend in eighth grade, and I were alone at his house, and his parents came home earlier than expected and almost caught us fooling around.

The cops were only minutes away and all I had to do was run. The hosts ran in different directions, trying to get rid of any kind of evidence that might help the authorities prove the nature of our gathering, that we were a bunch of queers, spreading our "disease" among each other. They were trying to protect everyone, even though they didn't have to, because we came at our own risk. Despite their efforts, I couldn't protect myself.

A loud bang came from another room and a dozen men in uniform ran into our room. It happened fast. I stood there, expecting police women to arrive, but they never did, and I remembered that there were no police women in Saudi.

As one officer handcuffed Fairouz, anger washed over me; wasn't it against this man's tradition to touch a woman? Unable to think straight, my mind focused on the wrong ideas. I needed to come back to the present, to my surroundings, but how could I remain zen in the middle of chaos?

Fairouz's lips moved, but I couldn't make sense of what she said. I had lost my senses; what good were my eyes if they hid the truth from me?

"John!" The sound coming from Fairouz's mouth was distorted. "Run, John! Before they get you, too! Please, John! Now! Go!"

But I'm untouchable.

A cop held onto my arms, so I gathered the courage to whisper, "Amreeki, Amreeki." He put my arms behind my back and grabbed his handcuffs. I repeated, a little louder this time, "Amreeki! Amreeki!"

He replied in Arabic, so I couldn't make out what he was saying, and although he handcuffed me, it wasn't myself I was worried about. *I'm sorry, Fairouz. I'm so sorry. I wish you had gone without me. I can't believe I'm the reason a face so beautiful is crying. I don't deserve your friendship. Please stop crying. This can't be the last image of you I have in my head.*

More cops emerged from the other rooms, each one leading a pack of two or three of us "criminals," like shepherds collecting their herd.

"*Yallah, yallah,*" said the officer who arrested me, pushing me to join the dozens of others who were paying the price for wanting to fit in.

My old shoes, ripped on the side, were weary, and so was I, and when I took the first step, I couldn't stop my body from shaking. I wanted to hit my thighs like I did when they felt sore after a workout. I pulled my hands, forgetting that they were restrained, and when that fact hit me, I couldn't stop the tears.

I wanted to be elsewhere, at the House of Donuts we'd passed by on our way here, the same one Elie took me to once when he noted that the guy in the logo looked like he was smoking a joint because he made the "okay" sign with his hand to communicate "delicious." High as kites, we laughed without a care in the world. Their donuts weren't even that good, but I'd much rather be there (or anywhere) than in that villa. I wiped my nose against my shoulder and accepted the humiliation.

Every step hurt more than the prior. I walked a total of twelve steps, the longest I'd ever walked. I stood next to the other men who had been arrested, closed my eyes, and cried until my tears ran dry.

To everyone who told me Americans were untouchable, that we were gods in this land, look at me now and take note.

After searching all the rooms and making sure they had arrested everyone, one of the policemen ordered us to follow him. We marched in a queue, all of us different in every possible way, but also united in one common way. I was the last one; if I turned around and ran, where would I go? What if I stopped walking and stood still, would anyone notice?

But there was no way out. Walking past the villa gates, a plane flew in the clear navy blue sky.

The moon was nowhere in sight; it might have been hiding somewhere, not wanting us to see it in tears. I needed to see it, though, before I forgot what it looked like, if it was white or silver, days, months, or years from that day. *Patrick. Timothy.*

Or maybe the moon was trying to tell me something; to stop looking at the sky, and to observe my surroundings instead. The main speaker stood on the side between two policemen, his arms crossed against his chest. I couldn't decipher the nasty look on his face; was it anger or was it disgust? More importantly, though, I didn't understand why he wasn't in handcuffs.

There was only one reasonable explanation; he was an undercover cop. He was the one who ratted us out, the same guy who'd advised us on how NOT to get caught less than an hour ago. It was disgust then.

If I ever get the chance, I'm going to kill you with my own bare hands. You're the reason Fairouz and I lost our freedom.

As I walked past him, I stared him in the eye, because I wanted to get as good a look as I could, so I didn't forget. I mirrored his facial expression to let him know *he* was the disgusting one. I hoped he would take a step back or change something about his posture, but it was like trying to communicate with a wall.

The headful of dark curly hair, the brushed beard sprinkled

with white hairs, the mole next to his right eye. It was the same man in Sami's phone, the one they took with that professional soccer player, whatever his name was. His father. Of all people, he was the last person I expected to find at the gathering.

In disbelief, I stopped walking, but the police officer standing opposite to Sami's father signed with his hand, speaking Arabic, probably telling me there was nothing for me there, that I should follow the others.

Ms. Rifai's husband is an undercover cop who busts gay people? Does he know that his wife hired a gay man to tutor his kids? Is his job the reason his kids are psychologically scarred? Does Kamal know that his father is actually anti-human rights and freedom? I can't believe this is happening. Foxtrot, foxtrot, foxtrot!

CHAPTER THIRTY-FOUR

As the police officer stripped me of my belongings, my phone and smartwatch vibrated in synchrony, and even though I couldn't see who it was, there was no doubt it was Patrick. It was going to be the first of many calls. I regretted the anxiety I was about to cause him, and I was thankful he'd chosen to stay home.

Fairouz's face was inexplicable as a male police officer searched her. If Mr. Saqqar, Ms. Rafai's (ex?-) husband cared even an ounce about women, he should've hired and trained female officers. Or did he think only men were gay? I didn't know for certain if the guards at the women's police station would be men, but the thought of it broke my heart. Maybe those guards thought that to teach these women a lesson, they must do unspeakable things. As if these women brought it on themselves. *Allah, God, whoever is up there, please don't let them get raped.*

The police officer pushed Fairouz into the back of the seatless van where all the women in the group were before slamming the door behind her. The tires turned but the van didn't move, as if the driver had pressed the pedal too hard. Like he urgently (and excitedly) wanted to take the sheep to the slaughterhouse. Leaving behind them a small cloud of rock and sands, a metaphor to what might happen to them within the next twenty four hours, there was nothing I could do to protect Fairouz.

Who's going to pay zakat for these women and save their lives?

Then it was the men's turn to jump into a dark vehicle that would take us to our sentence.

I put my right foot in, and it took everything in me to pull my left foot up, and since I was the last man, the police officer, a large smile on his face (what kind of man smiles at the sight of other people's devastation), shut the back door before I had the chance to sit. Motioning in circles with my foot, I found an empty spot and pulled my body down as gracefully as possible, so as not to hit anyone with my behind.

The abandoned villa behind us, with the cups of juice that would never be drunk and the soccer ball that wouldn't be kicked, was supposed to be a place of belonging. Instead, the colorful flowers that pretended to give us life were actually a Venus flytrap, showing no mercy even to a titan beetle like me. The same place that we had gone to to let our guard down and be ourselves was the one that punished us for wanting to do so.

"Why would I want to move to a country where people like us are treated like criminals and pay the price with their own lives?" I laughed at the irony that this was a question I'd posed to Patrick less than a year ago, never in my mind believing it would actually happen to me. And here I was, possibly on my way to my death sentence. So maybe I did deserve the punishment, for after all, I knew the consequences and committed the crime regardless.

I jolted forward with every speed bump and pothole, my bum landing back onto the floor with a thud. With our hands cuffed behind our backs, the pain was ten times worse. It felt intentional. We were pushed against each other every time the driver hit the brakes, and yet no one apologized, partly because we were physically and psychologically drained, but also, what would we be sorry for?

I tried to recall the sequence of events from the moment Fairouz grabbed my hand, begging me to move, up until I got into the van, to try and understand why I didn't run away, to wish I could take it all back and decide to stay at home with my family instead of attending the gathering. Even though it had just occurred, the loopholes in my memory were unretrievable. "You never listen to me," Patrick often told me, and for the first time, I agreed with him.

Oh, my God! Patrick! Timothy! What's going to happen to them? How are they going to find out what's happened?

My face was drenched, both with tears and sweat. I begged my heart to calm, but with no knowledge of how the next few hours or days would play out, it got stuck in a beat that matched the speed of an AK-47.

My silent cry in the dark, in harmony with that of the men around me, was nothing short of a play for the deaf and the blind, who've also been stripped of a privilege and can feel our pain. If only Elie was with me, he'd teach me how to "man up."

All I wanted was to take charge of my own life, to make things happen for myself, to figure out who I was and what I wanted in life. In the meantime, I was scared to make the wrong decisions, like moving to Saudi Arabia. Except, not everything is either right or wrong; it takes courage to explore myself and see if I can live in a certain environment. It's true, there were parts of me that I never could have discovered if I hadn't gone to Saudi Arabia, but where was the limit to risk-taking?

But some decisions were wrong, like going to that reunion that day, a mistake that pushed me to question whether or not I wanted to stay in Saudi Arabia—if I made it out alive.

The van stopped suddenly, so I held my hand out to break my fall but landed on what felt to be someone's stomach. Again, despite the stampede, no one said a word. As I sat up straight, nervous to see where we were, a police officer forced the backdoor open, an ugly smile on his face.

I jumped down, trying to land as far away from the officer as possible, exigent that our bodies shouldn't meet. North Obhur Police Station resembled a residential building that had been turned into a transitional locale for quick arrests, until they figured out what to do with us.

I guess that's good news. It's not a prison. There is hope. Maybe.

CHAPTER THIRTY-FIVE

The first ones to walk into the cell made themselves comfortable on the bench, then the less lucky ones—including me—sat on the floor, and the most cursed of us stood. In the midst of all the confusion, I found myself unable to panic any further, no longer a victim of the claustrophobia that usually tormented me.

Meanwhile, Mr. Saqqar went back to his comfortable little life and slept in his palace, a city within a city.

If only I'd known that the money he'd purchased that territory with was dirty; it would have changed my perspective. I'd lost all respect for them, and worst of all, it was with that money that they'd hired people like me. If I made it out alive, I had to make it known to his wife and kids who the head of household really is.

With no guards around us, my body fell lifeless, hopeless that they might give us any piece of information on our fate. In a fraction of a second, I fell asleep, taken over by a wave of weird dreams, all of which I'd forgotten, except one that woke me right back up; a parody of Kesha's Tik Tok that Patrick sang, facing his phone's camera:

Wake up in the mornin' feelin' like pee and poop
Grab my phone, I'm on the seat, I'm gonna text my group
Before I leave, wash my butt with a handheld bidet
'Cause that's the only poop I'm having today"

Before he posted it for the whole world to watch, he wrote the caption, "Saudi Arabia, your bidets will be missed." What if this was a sign that Ms. Rifai's husband had captured Patrick and Timothy and was deporting them? Or worse, what if they were leaving without me voluntarily?

A few hours and a thousand scattered thoughts later, two policemen appeared. One of them held a clipboard. I could hardly understand him when he called out my name.

Wait, why am I the first guy they're calling? Is it a good thing or a bad thing? Can't I be second?

The policeman opened the gate as I tiptoed over the heads of my cellmates, their eyes weighing heavy on me, causing me to lose balance a few times. Without saying a word, the guard signed for me to follow his colleague, who led me through a maze, before stopping in front of a payphone.

"One minute," he said, pointing at my lifeline.

My fingers shivered as I dialed Patrick's number, trying my best to press the right numbers. One ring. Two rings. Three rings. *Please pick up.*

"Hello? John?" Patrick's voice sounded the same as the night when he called me to inform me that Joao, his best friend, had passed away after a long battle with cancer.

Tears.

I didn't know what to say. "You're still here."

"John, where are you? I've been worried sick."

I took a deep breath. "I'm at a detention center. I mean a police station. I don't know what's going to happen." And then, out of nowhere, I said, "Call Ms. Rifai and ask her to help us. She has to help us. Please, get me out of here."

I could hear Patrick cry on the other line.

"I'm so sorry, I'm so sorry. Please forgive me. I love you and Timothy so much." I sobbed at the possibility of never seeing my family again.

"I'll do everything in my power to get you out of there. Do you know which station you're at?"

"Yes, North Obhur Police Station. I love you. I'm so sorry. I should've listened to you."

"Be strong—"

Our minute was up, and the call cut automatically.

"Can I use the restroom, please?" I asked the policeman, unsure he would understand me, so I pointed at my crotch.

Back in the cell, I found a small spot and sat down. The man sitting next to me said, "Did you get your phone call?"

I nodded.

"I don't think I'll get one," he said, the gap between his front teeth catching my attention.

"What do you mean?" I turned toward him.

"It's because I'm Syrian." It was the first time I'd seen a Syrian man in person, and he looked a lot like me—ash brown hair, really light skin, thin eyebrows—I wondered:

1. Why the refugees we'd gotten used to seeing on the TV looked terribly different (dark hair, dark skin, and thick eyebrows).

2. If he was a refugee or an expat. *Are there Syrian refugees in Saudi Arabia?*

"Did you know that they put the Egyptian guys in other cells with real criminals? And they tell them, 'These guys are gay, do whatever you want with them.'" His accent was melodious (I'd later learned from Elie that Syrians stretched out words like in a song), and yet his voice was low and beaten.

"How do you know that?" I asked.

"I don't see any of my Egyptian friends here, but I saw them come out of the van with us. One of them is more than a friend," he whispered that last sentence as he aggressively bit off a fingernail, ignoring the blood that came out.

"Maybe they put them in another cell because there's no space in this one." I was unsure as to why I was playing devil's advocate, maybe to comfort this stranger.

"No. For sure they did not." His voice was bitter. "At least he and I are not Muslim. The worst we will face is jail, abuse and maybe—" With his palm facing down, he raised his hand in the air like a plane taking off, as if he'd grown tired of speaking.

I thought all Syrians were Muslim…

I didn't want to ask what would happen to the Muslim gays. I didn't want to hear it.

"Do you know when we will get to speak to a lawyer?" I asked, as much to this stranger as to anyone else in the cell who might have useful information.

The man hissed, but I couldn't interpret his message, so I stared at him, hoping he'd answer with words. "They won't let you see a lawyer."

As my mind repeated the word "won't," I tried to pay attention to the rest of his speech. "There is no law. The judge will decide your fate."

Then, from behind me, another cellmate said (he never told me his name, so I chose Mohammed), "Just pray that his favorite wife will hug him or something before he leaves his house the day of your … what's it called, when you have to go to court? Anyway, you sound American. You're American, right?"

I nodded, not knowing whether he looked back as he spoke to me.

"You should thank God a hundred times. You can defend yourself. For us, the Muslims, we can get lashed until bye-bye."

"Oh, so they're going to release you?" Feeling an ounce of happiness for Mohammed, I turned around to meet him eye to eye and share a moment of hope. The light died quickly when I was met with a smirk and no words.

Silence took over the cell once more, as I, and my cell mates probably as well, contemplated our fate, with the occasional screams of one guy, who sat in the corner, shaking his head every few minutes and hitting his temples with the palm of his hands.

With no windows to tell if it was night or day, there was no way to keep track of time; all we could do was sleep and hope that the loud, awaking sound of a key turning in a lock meant we were free. Only, when it was followed by the shouting of a new man being brought into the station, I stopped opening my eyes and moved on to the next ugly dream, and at times, it was like Patrick was right there, almost tangible.

"Hey," I said to the skinny Syrian man sitting next to me, "I never got your name." I needed a conversation of any kind, even if it meant dragging the words out of his mouth, or I was going to lose my mind. How could it be that a cell so overcrowded felt so lonely?

"Emad." There was no way I'd successfully repeat his name, the Arabic sounds seemed more difficult than usual.

"I'm John. Do you happen to know if we're allowed to receive any visitors?"

"I don't know. Not on a Friday."

And of course, that day was Friday, and the noon prayer had just finished, which I knew because a group of sheikhs had left the mosque and entered the station. One of them stood at our gate and preached to us in Arabic.

His messy beard was spotted orange, black, and gray. The shemagh (red and white head scarf) reminded me of the way my sister wore a towel on her head after a shower. His glasses were smudged with fingerprints. His above-ankle thobe, a yellowed white, matched his crooked teeth. Clearly this man was not a leader, nor a respectable authority, nor someone approached for comfort. The sight of him scared me.

With every dull, monotonous word he spoke, it became clear he was harmless. As I'd learned later from Elie, he was probably a convict who'd been brainwashed and radicalized in prison, before he was released back into the world, like a sheep, whose mission was to find more sheep to join the herd.

As soon as the man turned his back, I asked Emad to translate, like a bug he couldn't get rid of. "We will burn in hell unless we change our life and follow the almighty."

As he spoke, my mind raced with offensive, Islamophobic jokes, ones I'd take with me to the grave. And I forced myself to differentiate that my problem was not with Islam; it was with abusers of human rights.

Mohammed spoke again, pushing Emad to sigh a few times. "You can say the *shehada*, I witness that there is no other God but Allah, and Mohammed is the prophet of Allah. You can go to Mecca to do Hajj, and your sins will go away. Then you can go to heaven. Personally, I'm not interested in virgin wives, or mermaids as they call them, so unless I can get man-mermaids, I won't do it. Someone like what's his name, Jason Mamoa in that movie, you know? For him, I will do like everyone and cut my hair to zero after I do the Hajj."

Sudden repetitive screams from around the corner made my ears bleed, and although they came from another room, they echoed in our cell. I hunched my back, covered my ears, closed my eyes, and traveled back to the day Isabelle gave birth to Timothy. *Delivery room. Isabelle. Baby. Man screaming. Blood. Whose blood?*

And when it was finally over, I, like many of my cellmates, were in tears because:

1. I sympathized with that man.

2. I feared I was next.

Emad shouted in Arabic, his hands covering his ears. Maybe he feared those were his boyfriend's screams.

The four walls around me told me stories, the red spots decorating them a constant reminder of our possible fate. How many men had been lashed and beaten up before us? Did they endure that kind of humiliation in front of their cellmates?

I need to get out.

Tired, hungry, and scared, the room was eventually shrinking around me, and with no fresh air coming in or out, it became harder to breathe with every passing second, until my chest got used to the tightness. The walls screamed. The screaming stopped but horror was still in the air; how could they clean that away?

"What were they doing to him?" I hated myself for forcing Emad to reiterate what had just happened, but I needed to know.

He whispered something inaudibly, and as if he could barely hear his own words, he cleared his throat. "They were lashing him." Then, he embraced his knees to sit in a tight fetal position. Either it was a coping mechanism, as if his body was shutting down, or it was a shelter he was building to protect himself from the storm that was our conversation.

"Do you think he's one of us?" I needed to prepare myself mentally, in case my turn was coming.

He didn't answer, which could have meant yes, no, or he had no idea. Mohammed took the liberty to educate me. "It must be the Pakistani guy. They come here illegally, what do they expect?"

"No," Emad said bluntly, like it was personal, like *this* discussion was worth the effort. "Don't say it if you're not really sure. They don't lash you if you're here illegally. They lash or beat if you bring drugs or alcohol, or—or—" His cheeks turned red.

Another man shouted something in Arabic, interrupting our conversation for a few seconds. Mohanmmed translated, "He said to stop talking about this issue like we're talking about potatoes and not death. The Pakistani guy could be innocent, like us, he could have a family who will never know what happened to him."

I've got to see my son; he can't think I'm a criminal. Oh, God, if you're really up there, whatever your name may be, whether it's Allah, Jehovah, or Buddha, please help me out here. If not for me, please do it for my son; he doesn't deserve to grow up with such trauma. Please.

It was the first time I'd prayed in my life, not believing in the power of the words I whispered to myself, so when the guard called me again, "John Calla`way, visitor," I thought I was hallucinating. My system shut down, but the guard repeated himself, and a voice in my head told me, *Patrick's here! Patrick's here! Wake up!*

CHAPTER THIRTY-SIX

When Patrick's best friend, Joao, passed away, he'd spent countless sleepless nights trying to accept his departure. Bags hung beneath his droopy eyes, swollen and puffy, as if he had been in a fight. The only thing he'd eat for a long time were black eyed peas, in memory of the times they gathered around a plate of Baião de Dois, Joao's favorite dish. Try as he did to stuff his heart with peas to heal the pain, all he was left with were horrible stomach aches, that kind of suffering more bearable than the other.

This time, Patrick had to face the heartache I'd caused him, for nothing reminded Patrick of me more than Tequila (Saudi Champagne wouldn't do the job this time). The puffy bags mushroomed under his eyes, catching my attention before anything else as I walked into the lieutenant's office where Patrick sat.

I'd have to live with the memory of having caused such agony to the person I loved the most, worse than any hangover I'd ever experienced for sure.

The lieutenant watched my every move as I sat in the chair next to Patrick's. His hands glued onto the armrest, Patrick turned his head slowly, as if hesitant to look at me. I told myself it was because there was no way to "unsee" me in my dirty clothes, my hair thick as a broom, my skin greasy, and my fingernails brown, and not because he was so angry with me, which was probably closer to the truth.

All I wanted was to wrap his arms around me and cry on his shoulder, but even if we had the room to ourselves, I would have kept my distance, giving Patrick the time and space until he felt ready to show me love again. Maybe he didn't have sympathy to share, needing someone's shoulder to cry on as well.

We stayed silent, both of us focused on the lieutenant, who showed two fingers. "Two minutes."

Even after he left his office, leaving the door open behind him, we didn't know how to start the conversation.

I'm scared, Patrick. I'm petrified. He could have said the same to me. It was a good thirty seconds before he finally looked my way again, and when he met me with void eyes that said, "What am I doing here? What happened to my partner?" All I could say was, "Patrick, I'm sorry."

There was so much more I wanted to say, to apologize a million and one times for putting him and Timothy through this horrible—probably traumatic—experience, but putting the words out there would only make the pain all the more tangible.

"Patrick, please say something."

He stuttered, as if he'd been trying to pick out a word or two among his messy thoughts. He closed his eyes and shook his head. Once he began speaking, he didn't stop. "I tried contacting the embassy, but they're closed, because it's the weekend. I'm using Instagram to tell people about what happened to you. I know I don't have many followers, but all it takes is the right person to see the post and help us do something."

Though I hadn't expected Patrick to get down to the nitty

gritty so quickly, I understood why, so I met him where he was. "What about Ms. Rifai? What did she say?"

He ignored my questions, as if sticking to the speech he practiced in the car. "I contacted Tom Knowles to see if he's got any contacts who can help us," which meant he neglected my plea to reach out to the only person who could help us. Checking the room for hidden cameras, I whispered, "Ms. Rifai's husband was the main speaker at the gathering. Or he might be her ex-husband, I'm not sure. Anyway, he's an undercover cop. He's the one who ratted us out. So if he can get us in here, I'm sure he can get me out."

"If he put you in jail, why would he get you out? Besides, if this guy puts gay people behind bars for a living, how happy do you think he'll be when he finds out his wife hired a gay man to be with their three children five days a week?"

Realizing he was right, I changed the subject. "Hey, um, before you have to go, if you and Timothy feel safer going back to San Antonio until this has been sorted out, I totally understand."

Patrick picked a plastic bag up off the floor, leaving my statement in the air the same way I left his question hanging. Before he moved on to something else, I tried once more to show him support. "At least ask Tom to give you the coming week off. You look like you haven't slept in days."

Ignoring me again, he opened the bag. "I didn't know what they'd allow me to bring and how much, so I brought you these."

I took a peek. There were two sets of clean clothes, two large bottles of water, and some fruit. His gesture, though small, comforted me more than words.

"I'm sure these are harmless. Do you have a picture of Timothy, by any chance?"

"Maybe I can bring him with me next time."

Next time? How long do you think I'm staying here? What if they've killed me by then?

We both smirked, and in a brief moment, we could have laughed at how ridiculous the scenario was, which we would have done had this whole thing taken place in the US. After a short night, he'd pick me up, and on our way to In-N-Out (to celebrate my quick in and out trip to jail), I would tell him about my favorite moments teasing the security guards. In return, he would come up with absurd ways I'd have to pay him back for the bail money, like flying him out to San Francisco to watch his favorite ballet dancer perform.

What would I be arrested for, though? The closest equivalent to the crime I'd committed in Saudi would probably be some kind of illegal protesting for LGBTQ rights. Or hosting a house party to celebrate a new law benefiting the LGBTQ community and violating the noise ordinance. Except my life wouldn't be at risk in these scenarios. Community service, at worst.

When the lieutenant walked back into his office, he brought with him such dread that pushed us both to sit straight in our chairs. The little boy in me who'd been summoned to the principal's office for kissing another boy in class many years ago wanted to cry.

Two minutes with Patrick reminded me that whatever I went through in life, I didn't experience it alone. Fortunately, but also unfortunately.

The guard took me to a new cell, a man with a messy afro and ripped jeans (not as a fashion preference, unless the stains came with the pants) my only mate, and if I was just a little lucky, he'd speak enough English to help me figure out:

1. Why they'd moved me.
2. Why that particular cell.

At least he had the ghost of a friendly smile on his face (one that would pass for a passport picture), the first one I'd seen since Roger's demeanor brightened up as he tried to convince Fairouz to go to that underground party.

I sat on the bench next to him—what else could I do? "Man, the things I'd do to know how to smile right now." I'd thrown that sentence out there as bait.

"I am here for one, four, two days. I cry, it doesn't help. I smile." Like a dolphin, his voice matched his face, and it was time to turn the reel of the fishing rod.

"How do you know how long you've been here?"

He shrugged. "I say any number. Tomorrow, another number."

Did they put me with this guy because they want me to stay here for a long time?

Redouan, my inmate, was arrested for cheating on his wife. Like me, he might be facing execution.

His smile disappeared, but his wrinkles remained rooted, more as a sign of brokenness than old age. "Advice from me, marrying a Saudi woman is no good. She has my passport, so I can't go home. I am her slave. Her brother hit me. I am Moroccan, so the police will not help me. I want to marry a Moroccan woman who loves me."

Yes, what he'd experienced was unfair, but to me, it sounded like he was down on his luck; after all, not all Saudi women were the same. Ms. Rifai wouldn't do something like that.

One of the guards shouted something in Arabic and hit the bars of our cell to intimidate us, and it worked, sending us into piercing silence.

I had to face the status quo: *are they going to throw me from one cell to another until they decide what to do with me? Will I, like Redouan, meet men who've been arrested for apostasy? Or for having alcohol in their homes? Or for sorcery and witchcraft?*

CHAPTER THIRTY-SEVEN

"John Callaway." The guard butchered my name, pronouncing it Jun Calahwee—a dryness in his voice like he'd been reading out a list of ingredients.

Oblivious of where he was taking me, I followed him past the visitor's room, and then, to my surprise, out of the police station.

Why won't they bring a translator who can explain things to me? Has Patrick found a lawyer who can get me out of this, someone who'll risk his career for this lost case?

My hands were still behind my back, but my ankles were free, so we went down the stairs, a total of twelve steps. When the guard opened the main entrance door, there he was, Ms. Rifai's (ex-?) husband, his bright, wide smile nearly contagious if I hadn't been a victim of injustice because he thought he was a better person than me.

"Mr. Callaway." Mr. Saqqar had a brief conversation with the guard, who went back into the building.

"What's happening? Where are you taking me?"

Insha'allah, Allah willing, he was taking me to see Ms. Rifai, my guardian angel, who must have sent the same email to Patrick as she did to me a few months before. "I have heard of your unfortunate situation. I can help. Please contact me at your earliest convenience." Or in more authentic words, *I might not be married to him anymore, but I know him inside out. I'll help you convince him to release John.*

"Home." For a crook, he had a soft voice and shiny eyes, probably the reason he was chosen to be a deceiving speaker at these events. He was so good, I couldn't tell if there was sarcasm in his answer; was prison my new home?

"I'm so happy for you." A sudden innocence emerged in the way he pronounced his words. The more he spoke, the stronger his English accent became.

"What?"

"I know the past few days have been rough on you, but don't worry, you won't have to come back here ever again."

Wait, when you said home, did you mean hell? Are you killing me today? Is this some sick, sadistic game?

A police officer parked his car in front of the building, and as he walked in our direction, he and Mr. Saqqar conversed in Arabic. When he reached the sidewalk where we were standing, they greeted each other the traditional way, reminding me of the time Tom taught this tradition to Patrick. At that moment, like never before, I really wished I'd learned the language.

When they laughed, I focused on each word they said to see if my name was mentioned, if they said something like, "His name's John. Watch this, I'm going to have him think we're here to save him, then I'm going to cut his throat."

Mr. Saqqar held my arm. "Turn around, please." He wasn't a typical bad guy, if there ever was such a thing. I couldn't eliminate the possibility that this was a trap. For all I knew, he was about to lash me right there, for any passers-by to see.

"But—" I tried to find an argument based on what my friends in Saudi had told me. "I'm not Muslim. I'm American. Please."

"Turn around," repeated Mr. Saqqar, his voice steady. To avoid gathering a crowd, I did.

Closing my eyes tight, I prepared for excruciating pain at the back of my knees, but all I felt was a slight tugging on my wrists. And then the police officer pulled my hands out of the handcuffs.

"What? What's happening? I thought—"

"Follow me, John." Mr. Saqqar placed his hand gently on my back to guide me toward his car, kind of like I did with Timothy to keep him from tripping.

"*Salam.*" Mr. Saqqar waved his hand in the air and the police officer walked toward the police station. Peace, indeed.

Something didn't feel right though. I stopped. "What about Emad? What about Redouan? You have to save them!"

"John." With the same hand on my back, Mr. Saqqar gave me a little push.

"No! No! You have to save them." The injustice was more than I could bear, forcing me to freeze, still on the path. "You said 'salam.' How can I have peace knowing their pain? Do you know what's going to happen to them?"

In a calm voice, Mr. Saqqar tried to assuage me, the same way Ms. Rifai did when I panicked about her firing me. His words hung like a fog in the air. I couldn't stop my heart from racing. *Those men.* Just behind those doors. Right there. Whatever their fate, I couldn't help them, and unless I pretended they were dead, right then and there, I would carry their weight wherever I went.

What about Fairouz? If she dies, I don't think I can ever recover from that. The world as I know it will be over. There will be no hope.

Just then, the voice of the muadhan in the staticky loudspeaker filled my heart with inexplicable stillness, a spiritual feeling I hadn't experienced before. I somehow knew then that Fairouz was going to be okay.

Using one hand to wipe my tears, I used the other to look for tissues in my pocket.

"Come on. I have tissues in the car."

Mr. Saqqar turned on the engine and the AC, and before driving off, he placed his back against his window. His eyes were kind and honest. "John, I don't know what you think of me, so I must introduce myself properly before I drop you to your house."

He looked at the steering wheel before focusing on me again. He took a deep breath, like he was about to make a confession. "It's never easy saying this. My brother Ahmed was gay. Erm, and he committed suicide five years and six days ago."

The words sounded heavy on his tongue, like they were pieces of glass stuck in his mouth. "As you can imagine, he wasn't accepted by anyone. Not my parents. Not his friends. And … before he came out, he was my best friend. I didn't know how I felt about gay people back then, but when he died, my dad said it was a good thing he took his own life, or our family would suffer from shame. At his funeral, we told people a bacterium attacked his brain, causing a fatal episode. I never forgave my dad, and I use that fury to make sure other people like Ahmed have a community where they feel loved. I made him a promise that I would find a way to make a difference in other people's lives. Gay people."

Not knowing how to react or what to say, I sat still, my eyes wide open.

"I know you're wondering why I wasn't sent to jail. Let's just say I have a very strong *wasta*. What's the word in English? Erm, clout, I think."

Clearing his throat, he paused to wipe his eyes and his nose. "And it's thanks to that wasta that I was able to bring you out."

"Thank you. And I'm so sorry for your loss."

He blew his nose once more.

"I'm so glad Patrick called y'all for help and I got to know the truth. I really thought you were an undercover cop."

"Patrick? I take it he's your partner." He folded a pile of tissues in one tissue and put them to the side.

I nodded, daring to share a small smile.

"It wasn't him who called me. It was a very special friend of yours. Fairouz Makhoul. She and I go way back. I met her shortly after Ahmed died, and we started this whole movement together. She never told you that?"

Poor Patrick.

I shook my head. "Does that mean you got her out too?"

He briefly closed his eyes for a split second, his face brightening up with a small smile. "This morning. She's a real special person, that one. We like to fantasize about what Ahmed's life would have been like if he'd married another man. It was his dream, you know? Or what his life would have been like if my parents forced him to marry one of our cousins, which was *their* dream."

He took another deep breath as he opened the center console, where he kept my belongings. "I'm drifting away, I'm sorry. Before I hand these back to you, I need you to promise me two things. Number one: that you won't tell anyone about what happened. It might just be better for you to pretend like you never met those men inside, because talking about them won't change anything anyway. If word gets out about them, they might get killed, because they'll be accused of bringing shame to our country. And then the whole community will pay the price because stricter rules will be imposed on us, taking us many steps back in our battle. Number two: that you don't come back to our gatherings. I know you Americans are all about human rights, but this isn't your battle to fight. You're here for a short couple of years before you move onto the next phase of your life. Us, we are aware of how much time this will take, and we'll wait as long as need be to see change. Do we have a deal?"

You mean the white man can't save you?

I grabbed the items out of his hand, and before putting on my uncharged watch, I extended my arm. "Deal. Although, I must say, I'm surprised y'all are going to keep gathering." And with that sentence, our conversation ended.

As he drove off, I stared at him; the bravest person I knew was someone I'd hated just ten minutes prior. What he did for his brother was beyond admirable. I wanted to do the equivalent for Timothy, by starting a blog with him, to raise awareness on the social issues boys his age may face. *And maybe, along the way, we will heal too.*

"I'm Yousef Saqqar, by the way." He extended his left hand over his right arm to shake mine.

We shook hands clumsily as we both kept our eyes on the road. "Very, very nice to meet you Yousef. Now, I see where Kamal gets his passion for human rights from." Using his son's name strategically, I was testing out whether he knew I was his children's tutor.

"Kamal? Who's Kamal?"

"Kamal, your son."

"How do you know about my son?"

"From your ex-wife, Ms. Rifai. She hired me to tutor your kids."

"My ex-wife? I don't have an ex-wife."

After a long discussion on how small the world was (and how women in that region kept their maiden name after marriage), I sank into my chair, trying to recollect the series of events from the moment I last left my house.

I will not move to a smaller house. This was the mantra I tried to live by, breaking several important rules along the way—and almost getting myself killed.

What I failed to realize earlier was that, by extracting a life lesson from my mother's journey, I rushed my own. There was a time when my own country had similar laws as Saudi Arabia did, and just because there was progress in the US, I couldn't expect the world to "catch up." The problem wasn't the house *per se*; the problem was me.

I wanted to believe that my presence in Saudi proved something, like, "Hey, I'm here, and I'm queer, what are you going to do about it?"

As wrong as it felt to pretend like the past week of my life hadn't happened, and to do absolutely nothing to save these men, I owed it to this country that had offered me so much to trust it to grow at its own pace. My role? Well, I didn't have one.

Was moving to Saudi Arabia a mistake then? Absolutely not, because it helped me grow in ways I never imagined possible.

CHAPTER THIRTY-EIGHT

"Welcome home." The rainbow-colored banner occupied the biggest wall in the entryway of our house. Koala came running to me as I opened the door, her claws scratching my knees.

As Patrick, Timothy, Elie, and Fairouz shouted, "Surprise," they threw their hands in the air like they were cheering for their favorite football team.

God, Allah, whoever is up there, I can't help but think of Emad, Redouan, and all the other men from the cell. Please don't let their death be painful.

Our furniture still in place, I was secretly disappointed that Patrick hadn't packed up our stuff and booked our flight to our next destination, wherever that may be. Wherever they had an American international school and same-sex marriage was legal.

As the four of them walked closer and closer to me, their arms wide open, I could hardly fight back the tears, which were a mixture of joy, because I was with my family again, and extreme sadness, because this chapter in my life was coming to an end. If people didn't make a home, I shouldn't care that I wouldn't see Fairouz and Elie again. But I did.

"John. You're out! It's really you!" Patrick embraced my stinky body, and I rested my head against his shoulder, crying my eyes out.

When I lifted my head up, the tape that held the word "home" had fallen off. I couldn't see a way for me to keep living in Saudi Arabia without carrying the weight of my cellmates wherever I went. They were now trapped within me, and I couldn't wash off the guilt of having made it out alive.

"Oh, Dad," Timothy whispered softly before wrapping his arms around my waist, his sob louder than mine. Timothy didn't need to speak. I knew precisely what he was trying to say, "Oh, Dad, I thought I was never going to see you again. Oh, Dad, I'm so happy I'm touching you again. Oh, Dad, I'm sorry for everything wrong I've ever done to you. You're back, Dad, and now I know what it means that you don't know what you've got until it's gone."

How could I keep walking through this hallway with the memory of this painful moment?

Because of my reckless behavior, I forbade myself of good memories. I stole my own future, replacing it with ghosts of the past.

I breathed in Fairouz's perfume, barely paying attention to what she had to say. "You should be glad Patrick's hugging you. The whole time you were in there, he talked about how he was going to kill you if you ever made it out. Piece of advice? Listen to him from now on."

"What makes you think I changed my mind?" Patrick's tears settled in the dimples of his cheeks as he smiled once again.

Although I was surrounded by love, one question occupied my mind. *Do Patrick and Timothy also want to leave Saudi Arabia?*

And so, right after lunch (Patrick had made lasagna for the

special occasion), I cut to the chase as the three of us sat down on the living room couch.

"I don't know if I can ever say sorry enough. What I did was stupid and unfair to you. I hope you can find it in your heart to forgive me, and I will make it my life mission to help you heal from this traumatic experience, starting by leaving this country."

I paused to examine their reactions. Patrick squeezed his eyes shut, his palms against his temples. Timothy stared at me, an unrecognizable look in his eyes, as if he'd grown years in a few moments.

"It's like I ate a whole platter of shellfish knowing that I'm fatally allergic to shellfish. Maybe it's a dumb analogy, but the point I'm trying to make is there is so much more to enjoy than shellfish. I want to live a life where mistakes are allowed. There's so much to see in this world, and I want us to see it all, but it has to be a place where same-sex marriage is legal."

Patrick shook his head. The room was still, Koala's quick breaths the only sign of life.

"Patrick, do you want to stay here?" Unable to tolerate another second of silence, I pinched Patrick's arm, which made him open his eyes.

"I don't, but I don't know where else to go. We don't have a home in the US anymore. This is all my fault. We never should have left in the first place. I'm scared. I don't know what to do, what if we make another mistake?"

I took a deep breath as I calculated my next words to explain to Patrick that it was our move to Saudi Arabia that helped us grow exponentially.

"Patrick, I wish you could see yourself from where I'm standing. You used to chase after your dreams with fear behind the steering wheel. In the passenger seat were lies that made you believe you were going to crash. Over time, you lost focus and became a reckless driver."

"You never failed, Dad. You opened a studio, and that's huge."

Patrick caressed Timothy's face with his thumb.

I turned off the TV to stop the background noise from disturbing my train of thoughts. "You know what's huger? Is that even a word? Doesn't matter. The point I'm trying to make is this: you've learned from these experiences to find new ways to express yourself, like your IG account. And people love you. I don't know who's behind that steering wheel today, but it sure ain't fear."

In a shy voice, Patrick said, "You're right. The past week, so many of my followers have sent me messages of support, and it helped me get through this nightmare."

Because I wasn't there to support you. No, John, this isn't about you. It's about Patrick.

Patrick lifted his shoulders and smiled. "I'm not gonna lie, I've loved trying something new. It's like I give the world my all, and I watch silently as they react to that, which is scary, but also so worth it."

"Dad, don't you see it? Your wildest dream was to dance for tens of people, now you're dancing for the whole world. Now, the world loves you. They're begging to see more of you."

"And I'll be darned if I get in my own way."

"I'm so proud of you, and I'm happy for you that you've found a community you connect with. But I have to ask you to delete any posts related to what happened. We must never speak of this 'event' ever again."

Patrick looked at me from the side of his eye, his famous, "We will talk about this later" expression. "Okay, so now that we agree that moving here wasn't a mistake, what are we deciding for the future? Timothy, what do *you* want to do, son?"

"I think we should leave. Every time I want to go out for fresh air, I can't, because I'm scared I will run into him. It makes me so angry to feel trapped. Not to mention the anxiety I get whenever someone looks at me, it's like they know my biggest shame and they think I'm to blame for it. I miss my old friends, who'd never do anything to hurt me. If something like this happens again, will I protect myself, or will I be a victim again? Can we go somewhere that teaches martial arts as part of the curriculum?"

Patrick extended his arms, his palm facing upward, and Timothy responded unhesitatingly, his hands resting in his father's like a perfect match. "Son, I'm sorry I haven't been emotionally present this past week. I haven't been present at all. Thank you for letting us in on your fears and weaknesses. You are not alone. We *will* get through this together."

My son, my perfect son, I'm sorry I've been parenting you the way my dad parented me.

Old John would have panicked in the face of the paralysis that kept him from speaking from his heart right there and then, but new John trusted that good moments couldn't—nay, shouldn't—be rushed. Old John learned that good moments came in the mundane, and so no longer did he rush breakfasts, walks from school, or bedtime talks.

I was a changed man. Better yet, I was a *changing* man.

In the two months before the end of the school year, Patrick applied to teaching jobs at American schools around the world, so long as same-sex marriage was legal there. As for me, as much as I enjoyed working with kids, I missed solving complex problems that didn't involve cracking the brains of children (which honestly required more work than an engineer could ever muster).

"So what *do* you want to do?" Timothy threw that question out there one night over dinner, as if the answer was as easy as ABC.

"I know what I *don't* want to do. I don't want to look for the best-paying job. I don't want to be a manager. OMG! I can't believe I said this out loud! Hah, it all makes sense now! The depression. My old job. I don't want to move up. I want to move sideways and try out different engineering jobs, manufacturing, communications, automobiles—"

"We got the picture, Dad. I'm really excited for you."

"Let's get married!"

Patrick gasped, the same way he did when Caitlin Jenner introduced herself to the world.

"I'm serious. Let's do it! Since we can't do that here, we can get married wherever we choose to live next. It'll be kind of like a rebound after breaking up with Saudi Arabia, a way for us to recognize each other as one another's homes."

"You mean we're going to have a destination wedding? Yes. Yes. Yes!"

When the time came to vote on our preferred destinations, Patrick chose Milan (so we could get married in Venice, the city of romance), Timothy wanted Copenhagen, because Denmark had the world's happiest kids, and I picked Johannesburg for its weather (but also to create a pattern; from San Antonio, to Saudi Arabia, to South Africa).

Before we went anywhere, though, I wanted proper closure with the people I'd grown attached to; that way, if Fairouz had a major identity crisis the way Scott did, she knew she had a listening ear, and if Elie's sister was serious about having an American baby, I was ready to recommend Isabelle a new tenant.

I was sad that our days with Elie, Fairouz, and Ms. Rifai's family were coming to an end, but I'd also learned that the friends we made served a purpose for a period of time in our lives. And we did the same for them.

In that sense, I wasn't leaving them behind; I was shaking their hand, and telling them, "Thank you for helping me grow, for allowing me to see myself in you in lots of ways. I now entrust you to the new friends you'll make, and all I can say is lucky them!"

As for Ms. Rifai, although she wasn't a friend *per se*, she'd been there for me at a time of need, and although there was no way to repay the favor, I invited her family for dinner. It meant more than simply gathering them around a table for one night. With a chance to talk about their favorite family moments, to share a few laughs, they could be reminded that being that family again wasn't a dream, but a challenge they could face together.

If I was really lucky, Ms. Rifai and Mr. Saqqar would see what has been in front of their eyes the whole time, that their children didn't need a tutor. What they needed was their parents.

Having served my purpose in all my new friends' lives, I began to prepare for my departure alongside Patrick and Timothy. I took from Jeddah all it had taught me about myself in a way only this city could. At the end of the day, it wasn't about whether or not homosexuality was allowed. It was about me and my family, and our journey through life, exploring our limitations and boundaries, discovering our passions, and understanding the importance of honesty and genuineness.

This was a great John, a John I loved to be. I wasn't perfect, and I didn't long to be perfect. Living a messy life excited me. Making mistakes meant I was growing. I didn't even care so much about (not) knowing who I was, because when I thought I did, I stopped challenging myself. It was only when I tried something that made me uncomfortable that I understood, taking risks pushed me to discover what I was capable of: being my own home.

John of the future, I can't wait to meet you. Gosh, I love being my own home.

ABOUT THE AUTHOR

Nadia Sakkal grew up in Saudi Arabia, where her parents' interreligious marriage had to stay secret. When she pretended to be Christian in Ramadan and Muslim in Lent to avoid fasting, her classmates discovered her secret, and their innocent questions only made her more confused about who she was. Nadia is still on a journey of self-discovery and has written this book for anyone who's ever had to keep their identity hidden and to celebrate friends and family who've accepted them the way they are. Make sure to show her some love on Instagram and TikTok (@ifyouwannabemywriter).

Printed in Great Britain
by Amazon

23414419R00182